Love Under the Stars

The Lilac Lake Inn Series
Book 3

Judith Keim

BOOKS BY JUDITH KEIM

THE HARTWELL WOMEN SERIES:
- The Talking Tree – 1
- Sweet Talk – 2
- Straight Talk – 3
- Baby Talk – 4
- The Hartwell Women – Boxed Set

THE BEACH HOUSE HOTEL SERIES:
- Breakfast at The Beach House Hotel – 1
- Lunch at The Beach House Hotel – 2
- Dinner at The Beach House Hotel – 3
- Christmas at The Beach House Hotel – 4
- Margaritas at The Beach House Hotel – 5
- Dessert at The Beach House Hotel – 6
- Coffee at The Beach House Hotel – 7
- High Tea at The Beach House Hotel – 8
- Nightcaps at The Beach House Hotel – 9
- Bubbles at The Beach House Hotel – 10 (2025)

THE FAT FRIDAYS GROUP:
- Fat Fridays – 1
- Sassy Saturdays – 2
- Secret Sundays – 3

THE SALTY KEY INN SERIES:
- Finding Me – 1
- Finding My Way – 2
- Finding Love – 3
- Finding Family – 4
- The Salty Key Inn Series – Boxed Set

SEASHELL COTTAGE BOOKS:

A Christmas Star
Change of Heart
A Summer of Surprises
A Road Trip to Remember
The Beach Babes

THE CHANDLER HILL INN SERIES:
    Going Home – 1
    Coming Home – 2
    Home at Last – 3
    The Chandler Hill Inn Series – Boxed Set

THE DESERT SAGE INN SERIES:
    The Desert Flowers – Rose – 1
    The Desert Flowers – Lily – 2
    The Desert Flowers – Willow – 3
    The Desert Flowers – Mistletoe & Holly – 4

SOUL SISTERS AT CEDAR MOUNTAIN LODGE:
    Christmas Sisters – Anthology
    Christmas Kisses
    Christmas Castles
    Christmas Stories – Soul Sisters Anthology
    Christmas Joy
    The Christmas Joy Boxed Set

THE SANDERLING COVE INN SERIES:
    Waves of Hope – 1
    Sandy Wishes – 2
    Salty Kisses – 3

THE LILAC LAKE INN SERIES
- Love by Design – 1
- Love Between the Lines – 2
- Love Under the Stars – 3

LILAC LAKE BOOKS
- Love's Cure – (2024)
- Love's Home Run – (2025)
- Love's Bloom – (2025)
- Love's Harvest – (2025)
- Love's Match – (2025)

OTHER BOOKS:
- The ABC's of Living With a Dachshund
- Winning BIG – a little love story for all ages
- Holiday Hopes
- The Winning Tickets

For more information: **www.judithkeim.com**

PRAISE FOR JUDITH KEIM'S NOVELS

THE BEACH HOUSE HOTEL SERIES – Books 1 – 10: "*Love the characters in this series. This series was my first introduction to Judith Keim. She is now one of my favorites. Looking forward to reading more of her books.*"

BREAKFAST AT THE BEACH HOUSE HOTEL – "*An easy, delightful read that offers romance, family relationships, and strong women learning to be stronger. Real life situations filter through the pages. Enjoy!*"

LUNCH AT THE BEACH HOUSE HOTEL – "*This series is such a joy to read. You feel you are actually living with them. Can't wait to read the latest one.*"

DINNER AT THE BEACH HOUSE HOTEL – "*A Terrific Read! As usual, Judith Keim did it again. Enjoyed immensely. Continue writing such pleasantly reading books for all of us readers.*"

CHRISTMAS AT THE BEACH HOUSE HOTEL – "*Not Just Another Christmas Novel. This is book number four in the series and my introduction to Judith Keim's writing. I wasn't disappointed. The characters are dimensional and engaging. The plot is well crafted and advances at a pleasing pace.*"

MARGARITAS AT THE BEACH HOUSE HOTEL – "*Overall, Margaritas at the Beach House Hotel is another wonderful addition to the series. Judith Keim takes the reader on a journey told through the voices of these amazing characters we have all come to love through the years!*"

DESSERT AT THE BEACH HOUSE HOTEL – "*It is a heartwarming and beautiful women's fiction as only Judith Keim can do with her wonderful characters, amazing location. and family and friends whose daily lives circle around Ann and Rhonda and The Beach House Hotel.*"

<u>COFFEE AT THE BEACH HOUSE HOTEL</u> – "Great story and characters! A hard to put down book. Lots of things happening, including a kidnapping of a young boy. The beach house hotel is a wonderful hotel run by two women who are best friends. Highly recommend this book.

<u>HIGH TEA AT THE BEACH HOUSE HOTEL</u> – "What a lovely story! The Beach House Hotel series is a always a great read. Each book in the series brings a new aspect to the saga of Ann and Rhonda."

THE HARTWELL WOMEN SERIES – Books 1 – 4:
"This was an EXCELLENT series. When I discovered Judith Keim, I read all of her books back to back. I thoroughly enjoyed the women Keim has written about. They are believable and you want to just jump into their lives and be their friends! I can't wait for any upcoming books!"

"I fell into Judith Keim's Hartwell Women series and have read & enjoyed all of her books in every series. Each centers around a strong & interesting woman character and their family interaction. Good reads that leave you wanting more."

THE FAT FRIDAYS GROUP – Books 1 – 3:
"Excellent story line for each character, and an insightful representation of situations which deal with some of the contemporary issues women are faced with today."

THE SALTY KEY INN SERIES – Books 1 – 4:
<u>FINDING ME</u> – "The characters are endearing with the same struggles we all encounter. The setting makes me feel like I am a guest at The Salty Key Inn...relaxed, happy & light-hearted! The men are yummy and the women strong. You can't get better than that! Happy Reading!"

<u>FINDING MY WAY</u>- "Loved the family dynamics as well

as uncertain emotions of dating and falling in love. Appreciated the morals and strength of parenting throughout. Just couldn't put this book down."

FINDING LOVE – "Judith Keim always puts substance into her books. This book was no different, I learned about PTSD, accepting oneself, there are always going to be problems but stick it out and make it work.

FINDING FAMILY – "Completing this series is like eating the last chip. Love Judith's writing and her female characters are always smart, strong, vulnerable to life and love experiences."

"This was a refreshing book. Bringing the heart and soul of the family to us."

THE CHANDLER HILL INN SERIES – Books 1 – 3:

GOING HOME – "I was completely immersed in this book, with the beautiful descriptive writing, and the author's way of bringing her characters to life. I felt like I was right inside her story."

COMING HOME – "Coming Home was such a wonderful story. The author has such a gift for getting the reader right to the heart of things."

HOME AT LAST – "In this wonderful conclusion, to a heartfelt and emotional trilogy set in Oregon's stunning wine country, Judith Keim has tied up the Chandler Hill series with the perfect bow."

SEASHELL COTTAGE BOOKS:

A CHRISTMAS STAR – "Love, laughter, sadness, great food, and hope for the future, all in one book. It doesn't get any better than this stunning read." CHANGE OF HEART – "CHANGE OF HEART is the summer read we've all been waiting for. Judith Keim is a master at creating fascinating characters that are simply irresistible. Her stories leave you

with a big smile on your face and a heart bursting with love."
~Kellie Coates Gilbert, author of the popular Sun Valley Series

A SUMMER OF SURPRISES – "Ms. Keim uses this book as an amazing platform to show that with hard emotional work, belief in yourself, and love, the scars of abuse can be conquered. It in no way preaches, it's a lovely story with a happy ending."

A ROAD TRIP TO REMEMBER – "The characters are so real that they jump off the page. Such a fun, HAPPY book at the perfect time. It will lift your spirits and even remind you of your own grandmother. Spirited and hopeful Aggie gets a second chance at love and she takes the steering wheel and drives straight for it."

THE BEACH BABES – "Another winner at the pen of Judith Keim. I love the characters and the book just flows. It feels as though you are at the beach with them and are a part of you.

THE DESERT SAGE INN SERIES – Books 1 – 4:

THE DESERT FLOWERS – ROSE – "The Desert Flowers - Rose, "In this first of a series, we see each woman come into her own and view new beginnings even as they must take this tearful journey as they slowly lose a dear friend.

THE DESERT FLOWERS – LILY – "The second book in the Desert Flowers series is just as wonderful as the first. Judith Keim is a brilliant storyteller. Her characters are truly lovely and people that you want to be friends with as soon as you start reading. Judith Keim is not afraid to weave real-life conflict and loss into her stories.

THE DESERT FLOWERS – WILLOW – "The feelings of love, joy, happiness, friendship, family, and the pain of loss are deeply felt by Willow Sanchez and her two cohorts Rose and Lily. The Desert Flowers met because of their deep feelings for Alec Thurston, a man who touched their lives in different ways."

MISTLETOE AND HOLLY – "As always, the author never ceases to amaze me. She's able to take characters and bring them to life in such a way that you think you're actually among family. It's a great holiday read. You won't be disappointed."

THE SANDERLING COVE INN SERIES – Books 1 – 3:

WAVES OF HOPE – "Such a wonderful story about several families in a beautiful location in Florida. A grandmother requests her three granddaughters to help her by running the family's inn for the summer. Other grandmothers in the area played a part in this plan to find happiness for their grandsons and granddaughters."

SANDY WISHES – "Three cousins needing a change and a few of the neighborhood boys from when they were young are back visiting their grandmothers. It is an adventure, a summer of discoveries, and embracing the person they are becoming."

SALTY KISSES – "I love this story, as well as the entire series because it's about family, friendship, and love. The meddling grandmothers have only the best intentions and want to see their grandchildren find love and happiness. What grandparent wouldn't want that?"

THE LILAC LAKE INN SERIES – Books 1 – 3:

LOVE BY DESIGN –"Genie Wittner is planning on selling her beloved Lilac Inn B&B, and keeping a cottage for her three granddaughters, Whitney, the movie star, Dani an architect, and Taylor a writer. A little mystery, a possible ghost, and romance all make this a great read and the start of a new series."

LOVE BETWEEN THE LINES – "Taylor is one of 3 sisters who have inherited a cottage in Lilac Lake from their grandmother. She is an accomplished author who is having some issues getting inspired for her next book. Things only get worse when she receives an email from her new editor with a harsh critique of her last book. She's still fuming when Cooper shows up in town, determined to work together on getting the book ready."

LOVE UNDER THE STARS – out June 2024.

Love Under the Stars

The Lilac Lake Inn Series
Book 3

Judith Keim

Wild Quail Publishing

Love Under the Stars is a work of fiction. Names, characters, places, public or private institutions, corporations, towns, and incidents are the product of the author's imagination or are used fictitiously. Any resemblance to actual events, locales, or persons, living or dead, is coincidental.

No part of *Love Under the Stars* may be reproduced or transmitted in any form or by any electronic or mechanical means, including information storage and retrieval systems, without permission in writing from the author, except by a reviewer who may quote brief passages in a review. This book may not be resold or uploaded for distribution to others. For permissions contact the author directly via electronic mail:

wildquail.pub@gmail.com
www.judithkeim.com

Wild Quail Publishing
PO Box 171332
Boise, ID 83717-1332

ISBN 978-1-959529-36-1
Copyright ©2024 Judith Keim
All rights reserved

Dedication

For my writing friends who always encourage me at our Wednesday morning coffees.
Thank you so much for your friendship and encouragement. You know how much I love you!

CHAPTER ONE
WHITNEY

On a bright August day, Whitney Gilford sat on the sunning rock she and her two sisters had used since they were kids spending time at Lilac Lake in the Lakes Region of New Hampshire. It was the best place she knew to gather her thoughts.

Too upset to sit still, she jumped to her feet, picked up a nearby stone, and threw it as hard as she could into the water, observing the spray of water it created with little satisfaction.

"Dammit, Zane! Why wouldn't you let me help you? Or help yourself? You could've had such a wonderful life." Her voice carried across the lake in angry waves, scaring several birds from their perches in trees sprinkled along the coastline.

Breathing hard, Whitney unclenched her fists and sank back onto the rock, letting tears of frustration and sorrow escape onto her cheeks. Then, angry again, she swiped them off. It was time to get to work, time to try to clean up his mess and make things right.

She knew on an intellectual level she wasn't to blame for Zane's death, but she'd gone into an emotional tailspin after hearing about it. And then, when she found out he'd left her his house, his money, and everything he owned, she'd filled with remorse for not succeeding in getting him into rehab. Now, she was dealing with anger at his decision to end his life like that.

Almost a month ago, she'd received the shattering call

telling her Zane Blanchard, her co-star on the television series, *The Hopefuls*, had died of a drug overdose. She and Zane had fallen in love soon after the series began four years ago, but it hadn't lasted long. Even when drugs changed the nice guy Whitney loved into someone she detested, they'd tried for the sake of the series to pretend they were still together. But after repeated failures to get Zane into a rehabilitation center and the cruel changes in his behavior toward her, Whitney ended the relationship.

At one time, back when she and Zane were dating, they'd discussed different ways they could use some of their earnings for charity. Whitney knew exactly what to do with the inheritance Zane had given her. She'd set up a foundation to help children with mental health issues. Heaven knew, there were plenty of kids of all ages needing that kind of assistance.

She gazed out over the lake and listened to the water gently lapping at the edges of the rock, smothering it with soft kisses. She watched as ducks glided in the water nearby, and smelled the aroma of the evergreen trees that dotted the shoreline helping to soothe her soul.

Here at Lilac Lake, Whitney often relaxed on the patio of her rental house at night, sitting under the stars, staring at their glittering beauty, finding solace in the continuity of life.

"Hey, Whitney. I thought I might find you here," said her sister, Dani, walking toward her across the front lawn of the cottage the three sisters owned and were renovating. At thirty, Dani was the middle sister and a talented architect. She had agreed to marry Brad Collister, one of the two brothers who owned a local company, Collister Construction, which the new owners of the Lilac Lake Inn had hired to do a complete renovation.

Whitney waved, and Dani joined her on top of the rock. "Now that the interior of the cottage is complete, minus furnishings, we'd better talk about attacking the attic. We've put it off until now, but we need to decide whether to leave it or take advantage of the workmen available to us to turn that into a unique living space."

Genie Wittner, their grandmother, whom they lovingly called GG, had sold the Lilac Lake Inn to new owners, who'd agreed to leave the family cottage and three acres of the property out of the deal as long as the three sisters renovated and then used the cottage for at least six months of the year. If that didn't happen, the new owners of the inn had an option to buy the cottage at a fair market price.

GG had done her best to keep the entire property in the family, but with her age and financial issues, this was the best solution for her to honor her father's wishes. Now it was up to Whitney, Dani, and their younger sister, Taylor, to keep that promise.

The cottage they'd inherited had been left in poor condition. With her architectural expertise, Dani had agreed to supervise its renovation. Even with the attractive work already done on the house, there remained a major problem—the belief that the house was haunted.

Taylor, especially, was bothered by the presence of a spirit. Neither Whitney nor Dani could deny feeling something amiss inside the house. They, along with Taylor, had agreed to follow through on investigating what facts they could find about the ghost, whom townspeople thought was Mrs. Maynard, a woman who'd lived there twenty years ago.

"Let's keep the attic as it is for the time being," said Whitney, "but I'll try to investigate and resolve the issue. We know only a little bit about Addie Maynard and her husband, but we know nothing about the box that held a wedding dress along with baby clothes. I believe it's connected in some way to the mystery of the ghost."

"Yes, and the envelope holding birth and death certificates for a baby named Isaac Thomas might play a part, too," said Dani.

"What are you two up to?" asked Taylor, joining them. The youngest at twenty-five, Taylor was a successful author who'd recently become engaged to her editor. With her dark hair and brown eyes, she was physically different from Whitney and Dani's blonde looks, but she had the same Wittner family spirit, as GG liked to say.

"We were talking about the need to finish the attic," said Dani.

Taylor held up her hand to stop her. "We have to take care of Mrs. Maynard first. But that's not why I'm here. I heard something disturbing that I think you should know about, Whitney. Some fans on Instagram are blaming you for Zane's death. One of them threatened to confront you and make you confess to ruining his life."

"I don't like the sound of that," said Dani, frowning.

Whitney held up her hand. "It's just talk. Don't let it concern you." She didn't want to go there because she still blamed herself for not preventing his tragic death.

"Yes, but with Dani spending time with Brad and me going back and forth to New York City, I'd feel better if we asked Nick to keep an eye on you." Nick Woodruff was the police chief of Lilac Lake, and though people admired him for his dedication, there wasn't a female under 80 who didn't also admire his sexy looks. He'd been one of the summer gang of kids back when Whitney, Dani, and Taylor spent summers visiting GG. After an amicable divorce from Crystal, Nick showed no signs of being interested in anyone.

"I don't think we have to go that far. People say hurtful and nasty things like that on social media all the time, but it's only bravado," said Whitney. "Zane's drug habits are well-known."

"Taylor may be right, though," said Dani. "We'd feel better if Nick was aware of the situation."

"Look, I don't want him checking on me unless the situation escalates. I've tried to keep a low profile in Lilac Lake," said Whitney. "After dealing with the details of Zane's death, I'm finding my footing and don't want people hovering over me."

"I understand," said Dani. "But at the first sign of trouble, I'm going to ask Nick for help."

"Deal," said Whitney. "In the meantime, I'll do some investigation into our ghost. Dani, you said Addie Maynard married Milton in 1958 after his first wife died a year or so before. After Milton died in 1997, Addie took up GG's offer to live at the cottage. That was almost twenty years ago."

"Yes, she died in 2002," said Dani.

"The house was empty for that time?" said Taylor. "Why would GG let the house go empty for so long?"

"I'm not sure she did," said Dani. "Let's ask her. I'll call and see if we can join her for tea." Their grandmother was now living at a nearby assisted living facility called The Woodlands, which Brad and Aaron Collister's construction company had built with GG's backing.

The women stretched out on the rock, basking in the sun, as they used to do when they were younger. Then as now, it was a soothing place to be.

Dani popped up. "Okay, I can't stay any longer, but it was great to catch up with the two of you."

Taylor got to her feet. "I'm taking a short break, but I need to get back to work. Being here gave me a new thought for a plot twist."

Whitney waved to her sisters and lay back against the granite rock allowing her thoughts to drift. The last two years of growing conflict with Zane had taken a toll on her. She needed quiet time to heal.

That afternoon, Whitney joined her sisters in a visit to GG. Their grandmother had always been a huge emotional support to the three of them. Their mother, a valuable supporter of causes in Atlanta, Georgia, where she lived, wasn't the warm person GG was. Maybe because her first marriage was to an alcoholic who died in an accident while driving drunk, and though their union had produced both Whitney and Dani, it had also been filled with a lot of heartache and self-doubt. Her second marriage was, thankfully, a happy one and had created Taylor.

As Whitney exited the car and headed inside to GG's apartment at The Woodlands, her heart beat a little faster in anticipation of seeing her grandmother. GG had a way of always making things seem better, and Whitney needed that now.

When they entered GG's apartment, they found her sitting in her favorite chair reading a book. She noticed them, and a wide smile softened the wrinkles on her face.

"There they are. My lovely girls," she said, holding out her arms to them.

Whitney lined up to give her grandmother a hug and a kiss on the cheek.

"What are you reading?" asked Taylor.

"Something you might like. *Breakfast at The Beach House Hotel*," said GG. She set the book down. "Now, let's enjoy one another. After Dani's call, I had lemonade and cookies delivered to the room. But first, tell me why you're here. Dani mentioned my giving you some information."

"Yes," said Whitney. "I'm starting to do some investigation into the mysterious box we found in the garage at the cottage."

"We're trying to get to the bottom of the rumor about a

ghost living at the cottage," said Dani. "We know that Addie Maynard died outside the cottage in December 2002. Has the cottage remained empty ever since? We know you'd moved to the inn by then."

"When we were here in the summers, it was unoccupied," said Taylor.

"After Addie used the cottage, I allowed people in the community to house refugees there on a temporary basis, along with other people, mostly women in need of a safe space. But I was saving the cottage for you girls, so I never rented it out to a family on a permanent basis." GG shook her head. "Then when taxes and other expenses of running the inn began to become unwieldy, I simply tried to keep things going while I decided what to do. After being caught in that financial scandal in Boston, I had no choice but to sell the inn, keeping the cottage for you girls to enjoy with your families in the years to come. Sadly, it was the best I could do to keep my father's promise to hold onto the land."

"We're going to honor your wishes and keep the cottage in use," said Whitney, taking hold of her grandmother's hand and squeezing it.

"I know you will," said GG. "That makes me very happy. I remember summer days when you girls visited. It was always such a pleasure, something I looked forward to all year."

"What do you know about Addie's daughter, Carolyn?" said Dani.

"I remember her as a pretty girl, a bit on the shy side," said GG staring into space. "I don't know what happened, but there was a painful rift between Carolyn and her mother, and she left town in the early fall of 2001. I never heard anything more about her, but others may have more knowledge than I."

Taylor was busy writing down notes, but she looked up at GG and said, "There's got to be a story behind it. We want to know what it is before we decide to work on the attic."

"How is the cottage coming along?" asked GG.

"We're getting ready to put the last few finishing touches on it. The outside needs to be painted," said Dani. "Once that's done, we'll complete the landscaping around it. For the time being, we're holding onto the funds we have before making any other decisions."

"We can't wait for you to see it. We're having a celebration when it's all done," said Taylor.

"There are going to be some nice surprises for you," said Whitney. She was in charge of decorating the house and was using some of the family portraits and photographs they'd recovered from the inn to decorate walls inside the cottage.

"How are things going for you here? Has JoEllen Daniels come into your room uninvited recently?" Dani's nostrils flared with anger. "Brad's trying to stay away from her, but she too frequently calls him to come fix this and that at the cabin she's renting."

"That woman is such bad news. When you think about her believing Brad would marry her to fulfill his dead wife's wishes, it's ludicrous," grumped Taylor.

"It's really a twisted belief," said Whitney. "But she's desperate to marry someone."

"And in the meantime, she's annoying," said Dani. "I try not to say much about it to Brad because he gets so frustrated with her that I don't want to add to it."

Just then, there was a knock on the door. A tall, thin, blonde stuck her head inside. "Good afternoon, Ms. Wittner. I'm checking to make sure you're all right. Is there anything I can do for you?" She looked everywhere but at GG.

"No, thank you, JoEllen," said GG in a tone of dismissal no one could ignore.

"Okay, then, I'll be on my way. I knew you had company

and wanted to make sure." JoEllen smiled at Dani.

After JoEllen left and closed the door behind her, Dani seethed. "JoEllen told Brad she'd be here in town to check up on him, and now she's doing that to me too. It makes me furious."

"It's best to ignore her," said GG. "You and Brad will be living out at The Meadows someday, and that will make it easier."

Dani's frown disappeared. "It *will* be nice, but it won't happen for some time. Customers take precedence over us." Dani and Brad had decided to build a house for themselves at the development.

"And how are you doing, Whitney?" GG asked, giving her a penetrating look.

"Better," Whitney said. "But it's going to take a long time to get over the anger and sadness I feel. I'm starting to work on structure and ideas for the foundation I'm setting up in Zane's name. That helps."

"Yes, keeping busy is wise," said GG smiling at her.

Whitney's heart filled with love for her grandmother. GG had been a comfort to four-year-old Whitney after her father died and before that when fighting was a constant in her parents' home. Luckily, a couple of years later, her mother met a good man, married him, and gave birth to Taylor.

"You're going to be fine," GG said to Whitney, squeezing her hand.

Whitney gave her a weak smile. She wouldn't worry GG by telling her about the crazy social media talk that she, herself, was the cause behind Zane's death.

CHAPTER TWO
DANI

That evening, as they snuggled on the couch, Dani told Brad about seeing JoEllen at the Woodlands. "It makes me furious to think she's keeping tabs on us."

With his arms still around her, Brad looked down at her, his blue eyes troubled. "We can't let her interfere with our lives. Most people who've met JoEllen feel there's something off about her. Best to stay away as much as possible. I've told her I'll no longer be available to help her with the cabin, that if there's a problem, she'll have to talk to their rental office."

"I think it's sweet that you've tried hard to be kind, but you're right; we have to go on about our business and stay away from her." She nestled against his broad chest. She was so lucky to have made such a quick, solid connection with him. Better yet, her work as an architect was helping his construction company and had allowed her to leave her old firm in Boston where her talent was never appreciated.

Pirate, her black lab, impatient to get her attention, pressed his head against her hand. Chuckling, she turned to him and gave him a pat. "Okay, I see you, Pirate."

She and Brad pulled apart. "How about we give ourselves a treat and head to Jake's for dinner? I'm ready for one of their big burgers."

"Sounds like fun," said Dani. "Saves me from putting together a meal."

Jake's was a local bar on Lilac Lake's Main Street, popular with both residents and visitors to the resort area.

"We can walk from here," said Dani. "Are you willing to do it? I know you've worked hard all day."

"It'll be good for me," said Brad. He was in excellent shape, but he'd told her he liked to eat and didn't want to get heavy As they headed out, leaving Pirate behind, they could feel the heat of the summer day easing a bit. Compatible, they walked hand in hand, easily keeping in step.

Brad's house was only a few blocks away from the town center. His white Cape Cod house wasn't the only one with a white picket fence in front of it or proudly flying an American flag. Roses clung to the fences, their blossoms peeking through the pickets, adding color to both sides. Walking along the street, Dani thought of Hallmark movies. This setting was perfect for one.

Storefronts and restaurants lined the six commercial blocks on Main Street. Each time Dani saw it, she filled with a sense of pride that her family had been a presence in town for many years. Lilac Lake had changed dramatically from a cute little town to a stunning resort area with the renovation of storefronts into picture-perfect places with colorful awnings and potted flowers by the brightly painted front doors. Trees lined the street providing protective shade, And in areas away from the street, lilac bushes thrived, preparing to put on a magnificent show in the spring of next year, when the town filled with their distinctive aroma.

They arrived at Jake's and went inside.

At this time of day, televisions strategically placed for viewing had their volume turned down for dinner hour. Later, they'd blast the sports news, competing for attention from people conversing in groups or simply relaxing by themselves.

Dani waved to Quinn McPherson sitting at the bar with his partner Liam Richards. Quinn, his sister, Rachael, and Ross Roberts, retired baseball star, were the new owners of the

Lilac Lake Inn. Liam would manage the inn upon the completion of its renovation.

Quinn and Ross were the ones taking on bigger roles working with Collister Construction on the renovation of the inn. After Brad had rejected her overtures, Rachael had more or less disappeared. When asked about it, Quinn explained that Rachael was involved in another hotel project, which suited all of them.

Dani turned and saw Nick at a table with Garth and Beth Beckman. She and Brad headed over to them.

"Hi! Have room for a couple more?" Brad asked. "Pretty crowded tonight."

"Sure, sit down," said Beth, as Garth pulled up another chair. Garth's family owned Beckman Lumber, and Collister Construction worked with them on all their local projects.

Dani sat beside Nick. "Just the man I want to talk to. I know it's your day off, but I'm worried about Whitney."

Nick straightened and gave her a look of concern. "What do you mean?" Whitney and Nick had gone on a few dates years ago but seeing his reaction now, Dani wondered if he still had feelings for her sister.

Dani filled him in on the conversation she'd had with her sisters earlier that day. "I told Whitney I wouldn't tell you unless I had cause. I've been thinking about it ever since and feel you should know. Whitney doesn't want to feel like anyone is watching over her, but both Taylor and I are hoping you'll keep an eye on her. I'm not staying at the house I've rented with them because I've moved next door to Brad's house. Taylor is going to be spending time in New York City, leaving Whitney alone in the house from time to time."

"I understand," said Nick. "I agree with Whitney it probably isn't anything to be too concerned about. But the moment the situation escalates, you're to let me know. Okay?"

"Yes. People can get away with saying things on social media that they would never say face-to-face," said Dani, "But you never know what trouble it might produce."

"I agree. So, let's keep Whitney as safe as possible." His mood lightened. "Any more news about the ghost at the cottage? Taylor told me she doesn't want to move into the house until you know for sure all strange happenings have ended."

Dani couldn't help returning his smile. It seemed silly to talk of ghosts, but she and her sisters were committed to finding out all she could about the Maynard family. Then the cottage would truly be theirs.

CHAPTER THREE
WHITNEY

The next day, Whitney carefully lifted down the small suitcase in which she'd stored the items from the box of things she and her sisters had discovered hidden away in the garage at the cottage. As Taylor said, they held a story. She had no idea if they were connected in any way to the ghost of Mrs. Maynard or if it was foolish to even try to find out the mystery behind them. She didn't believe in ghosts. And while she hadn't seen or felt anything uncomfortable in the house, both of her sisters had.

She opened the case and carefully lifted out the simple white dress. Made of a fabric with a satiny finish, the dress was sleeveless and fell to the floor. Whitney went over to the mirror and held up the dress in front of her. Its simplicity was appealing, something she'd consider if the time ever came when she married.

Still holding the dress in her arms, Whitney sank down onto the bed. At one time, she'd thought she'd be married to Zane. When their relationship began to disintegrate three years ago, she'd dismissed any thoughts of marriage. Now, though, with both of her sisters engaged, Whitney wanted a man to look at her with love, like Brad did for Dani and Cooper for Taylor.

The dress held a special memory for someone. Who was it? And why had it ended up hidden away in the garage?

Whitney laid the dress on the bed and stood to look at the other items in the suitcase.

Love Under the Stars

Baby clothes, including hand-knit items in blue, looked unused, which tugged at Whitney's heart. What had happened to that baby? Was the baby Isaac Thomas as the certificates GG had kept for someone indicated? Someday, they hoped to find out. Carefully replacing the items in the suitcase, Whitney emitted a long sigh. Life was so uncertain.

Whitney picked up the briefcase she was using to keep all materials associated with the foundation she was creating and headed downstairs.

She'd just walked into the kitchen when the doorbell rang. She glanced out the window. A police car sat in the driveway. She opened the front door, surprised to see Nick Woodruff. A smile quickly replaced her frown.

"Hi, Nick. Nice to see you. What's up?"

"Hi, Whitney. Mind if I come in?"

"Not at all," she said. Her heart warmed at the sight of him. She stepped aside to allow him to enter. "What brings you here?"

"I saw Dani at Jake's, and she told me that she and Taylor are worried about you."

Whitney placed her hands on her hips. "I told them not to bother you unless the situation called for it."

He held up a hand to stop her protest. "I was concerned enough to do a little investigating. The person making this claim on Instagram is a braggart who loves to make controversial statements. At the moment, I don't think there's anything to worry about. But, Whitney, at the first sign of trouble, I want you to feel free to call me."

"Okay, I promise." she said, pleased by his concern. "Do you have time for a cup of coffee? I have some made."

Nick checked his watch. "Sure. 'Can't stay long, but one cup of coffee won't hurt. One of the guys is handling the office."

Whitney went into the kitchen and poured them each a cup

15

of coffee. "Black, right?"

He grinned. "You remembered."

"When we were together at the café, I noticed," said Whitney, handing him his cup. "Let's sit outside. It's a beautiful day, even with all the clouds."

The minute Nick sat down in one of the Adirondack chairs outside, Mindy, Whitney's adopted dachshund, went to him for an ear rub. Smiling, he obliged her and then lifted his cup in a salute. "Here's to welcoming you back to Lilac Lake. I'm very sorry to hear about all you've been through. And though I don't think you're in imminent danger, if you should ever feel that way, I want you to contact me day or night."

Touched, Whitney said, "Thanks for that. I remember the summer you and I dated. It seems such a long time ago. But even then, you wanted to help others."

He smiled, sending a sparkle into his light-blue eyes. "That summer was very special. But I knew you were meant for bigger things than staying in Lilac Lake even when you were eighteen. I was glad to see you have such success."

"Thanks. That's so typical of you. When I learned you married Crystal, I thought it was a good match. What happened?"

"She and I both agree it's much better to be friends than to be married. We still love each other as the friends we were always meant to be."

"No other women in your life?" Whitney asked.

"No," said Nick with a bluntness that indicated he wasn't interested in any. "When the time is right and the woman is the right choice, I'll be ready. But I've learned not to rush into anything."

"That sounds like smart advice. I'll have to remember that," said Whitney. She liked that he was so open.

"I heard you're going to try to do something with a theater

program for children in the area," he said. "That sounds like fun."

"I was trying to set it up, but it'll have to wait. I'm busy working on forming a foundation in Zane's name. Something to help children with mental health issues. Sometime, I'd like to talk to you about needs in this area and how it might complement kids in trouble with the law."

"I'm willing to help anytime. Just let me know." He stood. "Guess I'd better get back on the job. Thanks for the coffee."

"It was nice to see you," said Whitney. "Stop by anytime. Nothing like being with an old friend after the craziness of L.A.."

He met her smile with one of his own.

She walked him to the door and watched as he climbed into the chief's car. Nick had always been a nice guy watching out for others. When they were all young and treating summer days as if they owned them, she'd always felt safe with him. And that summer they dated was still a tender memory.

He gave one last wave before pulling away.

After Nick left, Whitney thought about the theater program for children. She'd told Nick she didn't have time to do that this summer, but it didn't seem fair to some of the girls at the dance school in town to pull back after mentioning it.

Feeling good about her decision to do something, Whitney called Linda Forrest at her dance school. They talked about giving some of her students a chance at participating in a short play to put on at the community center as part of the Labor Day Celebrations in town.

"I found something short and easy, and it would be an introduction to doing bigger productions," said Whitney becoming enthusiastic about it. "If you think enough children want to be involved, I'll call Angelica Hammond at the community center to see if we can work something out for that long weekend."

Linda laughed. "Believe me, there are enough girls and a couple of boys who'd love to do something like that. They're all about being on stage. I love that so many of my younger students feel free to be themselves. When they hit teen years, a lot of that is gone."

"Can I make a presentation to your classes today?" asked Whitney.

"Of course. This will be exciting for them. I'll send out a notice to all the classes to meet up at the studio today. What time shall I say?" Linda said.

"Let's do 4 o'clock," said Whitney. "In the meantime, I'll make a couple of calls. I already have the play script booklets for a production about a mouse who loses her squeak. Your kids could put it on for younger ones."

"That sounds delightful. I try to talk to some of my students about doing things for others whenever I can. We've even put on a little show at The Woodlands," said Linda. "The kids had a good time, and the older people loved it."

"Perfect. I'll see you at four," said Whitney, ending the call with a rush of satisfaction. She'd been so buried with details regarding Zane's estate that she was pleased to be doing something on a happier note.

She put in a call to the community center, and after she and Angelica talked it over, they agreed to set aside space at the community center on Labor Day to coincide with the annual tradition of neighborhood picnics throughout town.

"Mid-afternoon is perfect. The little ones will already have had naps, and most of the parties won't be underway yet," said Angelica. "Who knows? This might become an annual event."

"That would be wonderful," said Whitney. "I'll get back to you after meeting the kids this afternoon."

As she clicked off the call, Dani entered the kitchen. "From next door, I saw Nick's police car in the driveway. What's going on? Are you alright?"

"I'm fine. He was checking up on me after a certain sister told him she was worried about me," Whitney said, settling her gaze on Dani.

A sheepish grin crossed Dani's face. "I'm sorry if I acted too quickly, but it was the perfect opportunity to tell him. He was very concerned. He's always had a thing for you, and he really cares. It's very charming to see."

"He and I are friends," admitted Whitney. She refused to think beyond that. "On a brighter note, let me tell you about the project I'm starting. Something not related to Zane. I feel better already."

Dani listened to Whitney outline her project and then spontaneously hugged her. "You're sounding more like the sister I know and love. Maybe small-town living will ease some of the pain you're experiencing."

Whitney smiled. "I hope so."

Whitney was still hopeful when she gazed down at the faces staring up at her with interest. Ten girls and two boys had showed up for the meeting. A cast of eight left room for four others who could be put to work on production.

She handed out the play scripts to the twelve kids and explained that after they each read different parts, she and their dance teacher would select the cast. "Remember, though, the cast isn't the only valuable component of a play. The production team behind it is sometimes even more important. If any of you want to be part of that team, you don't have to read for a part. Anyone prefer that?"

One boy and a girl raised their hands.

"Excellent," said Whitney. She handed out the scripts to

the other ten kids and after giving directions to them, sat with Linda to listen to them speak.

Elissa Sawyer, whose head was covered in corn rows, was the perfect choice for the mouse, bringing a chuckle to Whitney as Elissa pretended to lose her voice. Another little girl, Tessa Knight, with shiny black hair and sparkling green eyes, clawed the air as she spoke the part of the cat, making her the right choice for the role. The other, smaller parts were distributed among the remaining students.

"This is going to be so much fun," Linda said to Whitney. "I'm glad Jamie Thompkins and Susy Sandler will be on the production team. They're hard workers. And for Jamie, it will be a safe place."

"What do you mean?" asked Whitney alarmed.

"Just that Jamie has to hide the fact that he's one of my students. His father is a truck driver who's gone a lot of the time, and he wouldn't be pleased to know his son, at ten, is a dancer. His father is 'old school' about things like that. It's a shame because Jamie has a natural ability to dance."

"What if his father finds out about Jamie working on the play?" asked Whitney.

"I believe Jamie's production work shouldn't bother him," Linda said. "But dancing? Oh, no."

"Okay, we'll keep Jamie busy behind the scenes," said Whitney, studying the red-haired boy with broad shoulders who stood a little taller than the rest of the kids. In truth, he looked more like a young football player than a dancer.

With everyone satisfied with their assigned parts, Linda discussed a time when they could come to the studio to practice. Though Whitney had thought of using space at the Beckman Lumber Company, the studio would work better.

"Okay, take your booklets home with you and study them," said Whitney. "We'll meet tomorrow to go over them. We have only three weeks to prepare so it's important to learn your lines, and when you speak your part. I'll go over them with you." She turned to Jamie, Susy, and the two other girls on the production team. "I need you to come up with suggestions about decorating the stage for the play. Any thoughts will be appreciated."

With the twelve children chatting happily among themselves, Whitney hugged Linda. "Thanks for everything. I really appreciate it."

Of medium height, thin and wiry, with brown hair that she wore in a ponytail, Linda wasn't beautiful, but had a style of her own that made her attractive. In talking to her earlier, Whitney learned that Linda was from a small town in New York and had moved to New Hampshire following a divorce a few years ago.

"Putting on this play is going to be good for the kids. There are many outdoor activities for them here but not many programs for the arts. I'm hoping to change that," said Linda. "To have a television star like you help to make that dream come true means more to me than I can say."

"I'm happy to help," said Whitney sincerely. "My family always encouraged me to sing and dance. That made it rewarding for me. I can't imagine what someone like Jamie must put up with. It's such a shame."

"It is, but I keep encouraging him," said Linda. "The fact that his father is gone so much of the time helps.

Whitney left the dance studio filled with fresh excitement. Taylor had given her the idea of doing something like this for kids in the area, and their enthusiasm was the best medicine she could hope for to help her achieve a happier balance in her life.

Later, telling Taylor about the program and the different

kids, Whitney thought about Jamie Thompkins and the fact that he had to hide his love of dancing and the theater. "This kid has so much talent naturally that it's a shame his father is so adamant about Jamie not doing anything theatrical," Whitney complained.

"I get it, but you're going to have to be careful," said Taylor. "It's a small town and talk goes around. The father is bound to find out."

"I know, but if you saw how happy he is to be helping with the play, you'd think it was worth the effort to allow him to be part of it," said Whitney.

"I'm glad to see you so excited about something," Taylor said. "I know these past few weeks have been difficult for you."

"The sadness of Zane's death will never completely go away, but I have to remind myself it wasn't my job to keep Zane on the straight and narrow."

"Exactly," said Taylor. "You can't blame yourself. I'm hungry. What do you say we go to Jake's for a quick dinner? I'm trying to be productive while Cooper is in New York, but I've almost forgotten what it's like to be out of the house and with real, live people."

Whitney laughed. "Okay, let's do it. Dani's with Brad as usual, but it'll be nice for the two of us to spend time together."

Whitney gated Mindy into the kitchen and joined Taylor outside to walk to town. Though she wasn't as careful as she'd been when shooting the television series, she still watched her weight and made sure she exercised every day.

As they walked, Taylor discussed the new book she was working on. "I'm not showing it to Cooper until it's complete. We decided it's best to work that way."

Remembering Taylor's fury and hurt over Cooper's first editorial email to her, Whitney couldn't help smiling. Taylor and Cooper had learned to work together, but Whitney understood Taylor's need to be free to create on her own.

As she thought of the latest offer her agent, Barbara Griffith had presented to her, a sigh escaped Whitney. As much as she loved acting, she wasn't going to use Zane's death as a means to gain a role. And with the work of overseeing the formation of a new foundation, she was busy enough not to worry about securing an acting job.

"I wonder if Nick will be at Jake's?" Taylor said. "It's his day off, and he usually likes to mingle with old friends there."

"Speaking of Nick, dear sister, Dani already spoke to him about keeping an eye on me," said Whitney. "I've promised to let him know if I need his help. He's a good friend. Always has been."

"What about that summer you and he dated?" said Taylor. "I remember how love-struck you were. Crystal thinks he still has a thing for you."

"We're friends, that's all," said Whitney, but she couldn't deny the happy feeling that threaded through her when she was with him. He expected nothing from her except for her company. And that, she was more than willing to give.

CHAPTER FOUR
TAYLOR

Taylor heard the words Whitney was saying, but she didn't believe them. As skittish as Whitney was about a new relationship, a certain warmth entered her voice whenever she talked about Nick. Whatever that feeling was, Taylor hoped it would grow into something more meaningful. Whitney was normally so alive, so happy, so spontaneous. Lately, sadness and guilt had stolen Whitney's true self away. It was time to change that.

They walked the rest of the way in silence. As always, Taylor loved strolling down the pretty main street of Lilac Lake. She waved to a few of the shop owners she now knew and moved on. Though she and Cooper had decided to maintain homes in New Hampshire and New York City, Taylor had the feeling that they'd choose to spend more time in Lilac Lake. She hoped so.

They entered Jake's and stood a moment adjusting to the dim interior.

At the sound of her name, Taylor turned and saw Crystal waving at her. Smiling, Taylor grabbed Whitney's arm and led her over to a large round table where Crystal sat with several friends. She was pleased to see that Ross Roberts was there, along with a friend of his, Mike Dawson.

Ross was a former baseball star who'd played for the New York Yankees. He'd hurt his leg in an accident and had to quit the game, though he still had lucrative endorsements. With sandy-colored hair, blue eyes, and his famous boyish smile, he was adorable by most standards.

And nice too.

Mike Dawson, a long-time friend of Ross's, wore his brown hair back in a ponytail and was a one-time tennis pro, who'd given up the competitive circuit to open a tennis program.

Both men got to their feet as Taylor and Whitney approached, drawing attention to them

JoEllen rushed over. "Hey, do you have room for me?" she asked though the table was already overcrowded.

"There's a wait," said Crystal. "I'm not sure how long everyone is staying."

Sighing loudly, JoEllen walked away.

Taylor and Whitney exchanged looks.

"I'm not the only one who feels relieved?" Ross said quietly.

Taylor shook her head. "Not at all. She's trouble." At one time, JoEllen had gone to Cooper's rental cabin and undressed, hoping to launch a red-hot relationship and get things moving between them. It had had the opposite effect, and he moved out of the cabin next to her. JoEllen's actions made Taylor even more convinced that something was seriously wrong with her.

CHAPTER FIVE
WHITNEY

Whitney was pleased to see Ross among the group at Jake's. As a famous sports star, he understood the difficulties of being in the limelight. They'd enjoyed a pleasant evening together at Stan's restaurant and bar where Whitney had ended up singing one song on stage. He'd been as pleased by that as everyone else.

She turned to him now. "I'm glad to see you back in town. Are you staying long?"

"For the foreseeable future." He smiled. "You might say I'm hiding out after being named a part of a group of wild party goers in Miami. The fact that I wasn't even there doesn't matter to some people. But still, I'm accused of being inappropriate with women."

"I'm sorry to hear that," said Whitney, understanding his frustration. "Lilac Lake is soothing. I hope you find it so."

"Thanks. My lawyer is working to dispel those rumors, but it can be a nasty business," Ross said. "How are you doing? Things settling down for you?"

Whitney gazed into his blue eyes. "My relationship with Zane has been over for a couple of years, but the memory of what he used to be like is still painful."

"If you're looking to get out of the house, call me. I trust you, Whitney." His smile warmed her insides.

"Thanks, I might do that. How's your house coming along? You bought in The Meadows. My sister, Dani, was thrilled to help you design it."

"It's going to be fantastic," said Ross. "Come out and see it. The foundation has been poured, and they've started the framing."

"Very exciting," said Whitney.

"What are you two talking about?" asked Mike.

"My house," said Ross. "I'm trying to get Whitney to come and see it."

"I don't blame you, buddy." Mike grinned at her. "I'm Mike Dawson, in case you don't remember me."

Whitney held in a chuckle. She'd missed this playful kind of attention, even if it was superficial. She listened as Mike talked about the tennis school he was running for kids in Florida.

"I'm starting a theater program with kids. They're enthusiastic about doing a very short play here in Lilac Lake," said Whitney.

"Working with kids is special," said Mike. "It's their parents who are the problems. There's a lot of competition going on."

"I can imagine," she said, turning as the waitress arrived to take orders.

After ordering a glass of white wine and a Chicken Caesar salad, she spoke to Crystal across the table. "How was the play?" Crystal sometimes took part in plays at the Ogunquit Playhouse a short distance away on the coast of Maine.

"A lot of work to handle with running the café and all, but a load of fun. But after a couple of weeks of playing a minor role, I was ready to slow down and come home."

"Sorry I didn't make it over to the coast to see you," said Whitney. "Next time, I should be in a better position to do so."

"No worries," said Crystal. She waved to a young couple coming into the restaurant.

Whitney couldn't help the smile that crossed her face. As

the owner of the Lilac Lake Café, Crystal knew everyone in town, including visitors, it seemed.

The evening passed pleasantly, and then Taylor announced she was ready to go.

Content to leave, Whitney joined her, and they headed home.

The next morning, Whitney awoke with a new sense of anticipation. Today, she'd have her first meeting with the kids putting on the play. She didn't really expect them to have learned their parts; she simply wanted them to become acquainted with the story line—Lucy, the mouse, liked to brag about herself and runs into trouble when she loses her voice. It was a cute story, short, and doable.

When she went downstairs, Taylor was already up and sipping coffee at the kitchen table.

"'Morning," Whitney said. "You're up early."

"Yes, I wanted to get some words down after I thought of them as I lay in bed. I decided to get up and take a walk. That usually helps with plotting. What's on your schedule today?"

"I'm going to do some paperwork this morning for the foundation I'm setting up, and this afternoon I'm meeting with the theater kids to talk about the play. Maybe practice some lines. I can't wait."

"Sounds like fun." Taylor gave her a devilish grin. "By the way, this morning I also thought how perfect you and Ross would be together. He, more than many, understands what it's like to have public attention. That could be helpful to you."

Whitney shook her head. "Don't even go there."

Taylor held up her hands. "Just sayin'. That's all. He sure seemed into you. C'mon, you've got to admit he's nice ... and hot."

Whitney chuckled at Taylor's persistence. "Okay, okay. You

win. He's hot."

"Thought so," said Taylor. "How about a cup of coffee?" She got up and poured them each a cup.

"Thanks," said Whitney. "The best suggestion of the day."

Whitney took her coffee out to the patio. Mindy, who must have gotten up with Taylor, came racing toward her.

"Hey, little girl," cooed Whitney, stroking her silky head. She took a seat in the shade and took in a long breath of fresh air. It was going to be another hot day.

As she sipped her coffee, she thought about what Taylor had said. She did enjoy Ross's company. He wasn't fazed by being with her. In fact, she was the one slightly awed by him. Maybe after seeing his face on television so often. But then, she knew very well what played out on television wasn't the same as being with the real person or living in the same situation.

Later, she was washing her breakfast dishes when her cell rang. *Ross.*

"Hello," she said, "you're up early."

"Hi, Whitney. I have a big favor to ask. I understand you're the person who chose most of the furnishings for the cottage. I'm wondering if you could help me come up with suggestions for what would be suitable for my house. I'm tired of having decorators furnish my houses, making them look like no one would be comfortable living there."

"I'm flattered to be asked, but perhaps you should go ahead and hire a decorator, but use my input, if that's what you want. A decorator has better access to materials, fabrics, and furnishings at a better price. Our cottage was meant to be tasteful and simple. That's all."

"And that's what I want. A place where I can relax and be comfortable, maybe eventually settle down and start a family there," said Ross. "Just as Dani has helped make the renovation of the inn more in keeping with the area, I thought you could provide help to me."

"When is your house due to be completed?" Whitney asked.

"By the end of the year," said Ross. "I know from past experiences that furniture can take months to receive after ordering it, and I want to have Christmas in my new house."

"Okay, let's go over finishing touches in the house, materials to be used, different styles, and such. We can meet at The Meadow's Design Center at Collister Construction and begin there."

"That would be great," said Ross. "Dani showed me what you did at the cottage, and I really liked it. In fact, she suggested I ask for your help."

"I see," Whitney said, wondering if this was a set-up deal to make her feel useful. Even so, it sounded intriguing. "Okay, then, as I said, let's meet at Collister Construction. I'm available until mid-afternoon."

"Let's say 11 o'clock. And if necessary, we can talk it over at lunch, my treat," said Ross.

"That'll be fine," said Whitney pleased by the new project. She'd loved taking over the decoration of the cottage.

After she ended the call, she phoned Dani.

"Yes," Dani said playfully into the phone.

"I bet you're pleased with yourself," said Whitney. "I just got off a phone call with Ross, and now I'm going to help him with the interior of his new home. First Taylor, now you, thinking Ross and I should be doing things together."

Dani laughed. "It's a perfect project for you. And if a relationship forms out of it, so much the better. Anyway, you did an excellent job with the cottage. Even without all the furniture, it's obvious how perfect it's going to be because of the choices you made."

"Okay, then. I'll do my best. Thanks for giving me

something more to do. I didn't get the chance to tell you, but I'm helping a group of kids put on a short play over the Labor Day Weekend."

"How fun. I can't wait to see it," said Dani. "Sorry, but I have to go. I'm meeting with prospective buyers about the different designs we're offering."

"Okay. Hope to see you soon. With your living next door with Brad, Taylor and I don't get to see enough of you."

"Let's set up a girls' night out soon," said Dani. "I'd love it."

Whitney ended the call and smiled. Suddenly her days were becoming filled with things that had nothing to do with Zane. It felt good.

Promptly at eleven o'clock, Whitney pulled into the parking lot at the Collister Design Center. She picked up her leather-covered notepad and got out of the car as Ross pulled into the lot.

She waited for him to join her, and then they went inside together. It always enthralled her to see the various kitchen cabinets, countertop selections, paint choices, rug, and flooring choices. She loved coordinating items to create a distinctive look.

The office was empty, which was usual unless an appointment had been set up. It made it easier for Whitney to explore different options for finishing touches by pulling samples together from every section. Ross had a schematic of the interior of his house so they could better see how things could be laid out.

They started with the basics: trim pieces and an overall style that he wanted.

From there, wooden and tile floorings were chosen, cabinets, and even some lighting fixtures.

"We'll save some of the lighting fixtures for later, so you

can have something more dramatic in certain areas," said Whitney.

"You're really talented at this," said Ross, giving her a look of admiration.

She grinned. "We have very similar tastes, which makes it easy."

Rather than going with dark wood tones everywhere, they both liked soft, warm grays and the softest of yellows. She knew from the past how dark and cold some days in New Hampshire could be, and after describing it to Ross, he agreed with her suggestions.

Almost two hours later, Whitney set aside her notebook. "All basics are done. We can go to Boston and look at furniture. The fun will be decorating the house. That's where your personal touches will be on display."

"Thanks for helping me. The builders were urging me to take care of this. Now, I can't wait to do the rest of this with you." Ross smiled, and Whitney was once more aware of how his boyish grin lit his blue eyes. "How about lunch?" he said.

"I'm ready," she said. "Nothing like a café meal. Crystal has done such a fabulous job with her restaurant."

"She certainly knows her crowd," agreed Ross. "She wanted to start dating, but it was never going to work."

"Crystal is a very independent person. Very capable. Very kind," said Whitney, eager to defend her.

"Oh, yes. I know all that," said Ross. "But that special feeling wasn't there."

They remained quiet as they left the building and Whitney realized she and Ross were becoming friends.

CHAPTER SIX
WHITNEY

When Whitney walked into the café with Ross, Crystal waved at them from behind the counter. She was hard to miss with her short, messy, purple hairdo.

It amused Whitney that Crystal never failed to see her customers either coming or going. She made a point of greeting new people, giving them a welcome that made them want to come back again.

Ross waved at Crystal but kept on walking.

They were able to get seats inside facing one another in a corner booth.

"I already know what I'm having," said Whitney. "There's nothing like the Caesar salad here."

"I'm going for a Reuben sandwich," said Ross, looking up as an older waitress approached with menus and a pitcher of ice water.

"What'll you have?" the waitress said, pouring them each a glass of water, and handing out the menus.

Whitney and Ross quickly gave their orders and sat back.

Facing the doorway, Whitney smiled when she saw Dani and Brad enter. She waved at them.

Dani and Brad came right over.

"Care if we join you?" Brad asked.

"We'd love to have you," said Whitney. "We just completed the building information form for Collister Construction for Ross's house."

"Oh, good," said Dani. "I'm helping to coordinate that." She turned to Ross. "No more additions to the basic plan?"

He shook his head. "No, I'm pleased with what we did the other day."

"Good," said Dani. "With some materials so hard to get, we must have these selections of finishes made early in the game."

"Right," said Brad, "so we can hit a homerun with our customers."

The four of them laughed at his attempt to tease Ross with baseball lingo.

"Sorry, I couldn't resist that," said Brad, his eyes sparkling with humor.

Whitney could see why Dani loved him so much. He was such a nice guy.

Through lunch, they talked about the housing development and Ross's house, in particular.

"I've told Whitney I want it to be a home for a family. A couple of my friends can't believe it, but I'm ready to settle down. I've partied all over the world, but now I need something deeper than that. You know?"

Brad smiled and placed an arm around Dani sitting next to him. "I know exactly what you mean. Dani and I are building a home at The Meadows, too. There's something about the development that makes customers want to stay there."

"It's the best of both worlds—a luxury home and country living with easy access to bigger cities," said Dani.

Whitney nodded thoughtfully. "It's perfect for families too."

Dani's cheeks grew pink as she glanced at Brad. "We think so."

Whitney didn't dare look at Ross. He was intriguing, but she wasn't sure about a future with him. Maybe thinking something could come of it was simply her being unrealistically romantic, wanting a change from the past few months.

Later that afternoon, Whitney sat in the dance studio with the twelve children who'd signed up to put on the play, *A Mouse's Mistake*.
Looking down at the eager faces, her heart lifted.
Elissa Sawyer, the girl playing Lucy, the mouse, was a natural for the part. Her schoolteacher parents had helped her with her script, and she already knew many of the lines. Better yet, she was a natural actress, and her facial expressions matched the words. Whitney already loved both Elissa and her character, Lucy.
Tessa Knight, who was playing the cat, had her actions down but would need help on her words.
The other kids, playing smaller parts, would be fine.
Whitney turned to Jamie and Susan and the other two girls working on sets and stage enhancement.
"What ideas have you come up with for the stage?" she asked them.
"Well, the play takes place in a garden, so we need lots of flowers," said Jamie.
"And a place for Lucy to sit. So, I thought of a log," Susan said.
"A couple of trees," said one of the girls.
"Maybe some birds in trees," the other girl said.
"Wonderful," exclaimed Whitney, truly impressed with their thoughts. "I know where we can get some paper flowers or better yet, make them. And we can ask the florist in town to let us borrow some tall plants."
"Or ask my father's landscaping company for trees," said one of the girls.
"And I could bring in my pet parakeet as long as we keep

him in a cage," said another.

"I love all the thought you've put into it. Anything else?" asked Whitney.

"I could paint a picture to hand out to everyone with the program," said Jamie.

Unsure about that, Whitney glanced at Linda, the owner of the studio. She nodded emphatically.

"Okay, Jamie, that sounds perfect," said Whitney and faced the group. "How about we come back in two days for another rehearsal?"

The chorus of "Yeses" brought a smile to Whitney.

Jamie held back as the other kids raced for the door.

"Is there something I can help you with?" asked Whitney.

"I need to make sure my dad doesn't know I come here to dance class. Is there another place we can rehearse?"

"Mmm, maybe," said Whitney. "Why don't I ask and see if I can work something out."

"Okay, thanks," said Jamie breaking into a smile. "My father thinks dancing is for sissies. He doesn't know how strong you have to be to do it."

"Yes, I took dance lessons for years, and I know how true that is," said Whitney, filling with sympathy for him. "You have to be strong and fast on your feet."

She said goodbye to him and headed over to Beckman Lumber. Bethany Beckman had promised to look into approval for theater rehearsals to take place there. That would be a better place for Jamie and the kids to practice, giving Linda a break from having to keep the studio open.

As she drove into the lumberyard and over to the gift shop, Whitney was eager to see Bethany. The two of them working together had picked out several things from the store for the cottage—household items that were unique. She couldn't wait to see what might have come into the store since she'd last been there.

Opening the door and stepping inside was like walking into a bright wonderland of gifts, household items, and artwork. Whitney glanced around, checking for new items. Her gaze landed on an old-fashioned bird bath made of alpine stone. She checked the tag. Though it was pricey, she knew it was perfect for the garden Taylor was planning.

"Hi, Whitney," said Bethany appearing from her office. "What can I help you with?"

As they hugged hello, Whitney was careful not to crush Bethany's growing baby bump. "First of all, I want to buy the bird bath. Secondly, I need to ask you if I can use the storage shed for play rehearsals as we discussed earlier. It would be for only a couple of weeks or so. I've unexpectedly decided to do a short, trial play to put on over Labor Day."

"How exciting! Yes, I've checked on your use of it and the answer is yes. We open it in the morning and close it up at night. So, if this is for evening rehearsals, we'll have to make special arrangements."

"No, no, the rehearsals will take place in the afternoon. I'm thinking three o'clock."

"Perfect. No problem then." Bethany grinned. "Come on back to the storeroom. I've got some new things in."

"I'll look, but at the moment I want to buy the bird bath."

"Just look," said Bethany with a twinkle in her eye.

A short while later, Bethany rang up the bird bath and several other outdoor ornaments. "I knew you'd like the new shipment," she said with a pleased smile.

Whitney laughed. "I can't help myself. Some of the things you have here are totally irresistible."

"I love them, too. When I first married him, I kept telling my husband and his family that I could make a go of a gift shop here and they didn't believe me. It's taken some time, but it's working, just like I said."

"How do you compete with the stores on Main Street?" Whitney asked.

"I don't. But I do have a display of items in the bookstore. Estelle Bookbinder is happy to do that for me because I've always promoted the bookstore here."

"Nice. I love that," said Whitney. "Maybe she'd be willing to put up a poster about the play in her store."

"I'm sure she would. I will too. I have a special bulletin board for local events." Bethany gave her an affectionate look. "I'm glad to see you get involved in the community. I know it will be appreciated."

"Thanks. I'm hoping it's the start of a lot of new theater opportunities for kids in the area. I'll have Brad and Dani pick up the purchases later. The bird bath is too heavy for me to load, but Brad can put it in his truck."

"No problem. Everything will be kept safely here until they're ready."

They hugged again and Whitney left the store, thrilled that the rehearsal space she wanted was available to them.

At the house that evening, Whitney sat with her sisters on the patio catching up with one another as they sipped a wine Dani had picked out for them.

"You'll love the birdbath I bought for the cottage," said Whitney. "Taylor, you're doing a fabulous job of working with Graham Landscaping Company. The sketches you showed us look terrific. I can't wait for the house to be painted so those plans can be implemented."

"The Landscaping Company does a terrific job at The Meadows," said Dani. "I'm so pleased you're taking care of that end of things for the cottage, especially now that we're getting close to completing the project."

"I never thought I'd be so thrilled to own this house with the two of you," said Whitney. "But it's perfect for all of us."

"You don't mind that I'll be coming and going between here and New York City?" asked Taylor. "As long as one of us is staying at the cottage, it will meet the requirements arranged between GG and the new owners."

"Right," said Dani. "I figure if we get in a bind timewise, I'll simply move from my house here at The Meadows to the cottage for a short time. Hopefully, that won't be necessary. Either way, it's a win-win situation because the cottage is gorgeous."

"I intend to stay in Lilac Lake for the foreseeable future," said Whitney. "If the time comes for me to be away on a job, I could be gone for long periods of time. But we'll work that out when necessary."

"Agreed," said Dani. "So, what else is going on with the two of you?"

Whitney grinned. She loved girls' night with her sisters, whether it took place at a restaurant or like this evening, simply staying at home.

Taylor let out a long sigh. "Mom is going to get her wish that one of us have a big, lavish wedding. When Cooper and I marry, it will be a big wedding in New York. Mom and Grace Pritchard have agreed with everyone scattered away from Atlanta, it makes sense to hold it in a more central location."

"Are you okay with that?" asked Whitney. "After all, it's *your* wedding."

"Yes. Cooper and I talked it over, and we both agree the wedding doesn't matter as much as the honeymoon. We're going to Tahiti with a layover in Hawaii." Taylor clasped her hands together and a huge smile spread across her face. "It should be a fabulous trip."

"Oh-h-h, that will be lovely," said Dani. "Brad and I are

going to Paris for our honeymoon. The people at my old office gave me two tickets to Paris as my farewell gift." She beamed at them. "It couldn't come at a better time."

"What about your wedding?" Whitney asked Dani.

"Brad and I are talking about a Christmas wedding at our house so we can celebrate the holidays together as a married couple."

"That's a beautiful idea," said Taylor. "But it won't give you much time to prepare."

"Brad and I want our wedding and all the celebrations around it to be as simple as possible. We'll get married here in Lilac Lake at the Congregational Church. I've already warned Mom about it, and she understands."

"What about you, Whitney? What do you want for a wedding?" asked Taylor.

Whitney laughed. "Uh, you forget. There's one problem. I have yet to find a groom."

Taylor elbowed her. "You have two choices—Nick or Ross. Both men are into you."

A sting of barely formed tears surprised Whitney. Maybe it was being in this cute little town where everyone was so friendly, but for the first time in a long while, she was ready to see if she could find a man she might want to marry one day.

CHAPTER SEVEN
WHITNEY

Whitney decided to meet the parents of the twelve kids involved in the play right away, so they'd feel more comfortable about their children being involved in the project. Whitney was especially interested in meeting Jamie's parents and saved their meeting until last.

By the time she arrived at Jamie's house, Whitney was convinced that Lilac Lake held the best of American families—they all seemed like hard-working, law-abiding citizens who genuinely cared about their children.

Jamie's house, located in a small subdivision behind the one where she and her sisters were renting, was smaller than some, but neatly maintained. When his mother answered the doorbell, Whitney was surprised to see how young she was. She was holding a baby, and Whitney saw two toddlers in the background.

Whitney introduced herself to Jamie's mother and explained that she was getting a group of children together to put on a play, and that Jamie had offered to help with the staging of it.

The frown that had appeared on his mother's face deepened as she listened. "My husband, Bud, won't like hearing about this. The boy is supposed to be playing baseball this summer."

Whitney studied the tired-looking woman whose brown hair needed a shampoo and thought quickly. "What if I told you that Ross Roberts, an ex-Yankees player, was in town and might give lessons to the kids doing the play?"

Jamie's mother's eyes widened. "Well, now that would make a big difference. That would be no problem at all. Where are they going to practice for the play?"

Whitney explained about the space at Beckman Lumber. "If you'd like, I can pick up Jamie and drop him off after rehearsal."

"Thanks," she said. "It's hard for me to get all the kids in the car, even for a short trip like that." One of the children started to cry and then another joined in.

"I won't keep you," said Whitney smoothly. "I'll pick up Jamie at three o'clock if that's all right with you."

His mother nodded. "Fine by me. He's a good kid. But we've got to be careful to follow Bud's rules when it comes to him being around. As Jamie is the only boy, my husband has placed a lot of hopes on him."

"I understand he doesn't know about Linda's school," said Whitney, careful not to say anything that one of the smaller kids could repeat.

A look of terror crossed Jamie's mother's face and disappeared. "No, he don't. And we got to keep it that way."

"Of course. I understand," said Whitney. "Thank you for allowing Jamie to participate. He's going to be doing some drawings for programs, too."

"His father don't like that none," said Jamie's mother. "Just don't have him sign his name. Like I said, Jamie is a good boy. He helps me a lot. It's only fair he can do some stuff that makes him happy."

"Yes, I agree," said Whitney, catching a glimpse of Jamie in the background leading a little girl by the hand into the kitchen. "See you later."

As soon as Whitney was settled in her car, she punched in the number for Ross Roberts, hoping he'd understand.

Ross picked up the call right away. "Hi, Whitney. What's up?"

"Can you meet me at the café? There's something I need to talk to you about."

"Okay," said Ross. "I'm accepting the fact that it must be important."

"Yes, it is," said Whitney. "I need your help with something."

"No problem. I'll leave now and meet you there in a few minutes."

Whitney ended the call grateful for Ross's support. He hadn't asked for more information; the fact that she needed his help was enough for him. That was something she'd always remember.

Whitney was sitting on the patio at the café when Ross walked onto it looking for her.

She lifted her arm in a wave and waited for him to come to her. He was taller than average, with a ripped body, and the smile that was adored by millions. Yet, he did nothing to draw attention to himself even now, as other diners recognized him.

"What is this about? I can never refuse a damsel in distress," he said, smiling as he sat down opposite her.

"You mentioned once that you'd be willing to help me out with the theater project for kids. Well, it isn't exactly what I'm asking, but this might even be better for you." Whitney explained the situation about Jamie and said, "When his mother mentioned baseball, I knew that's how you could help not just one boy in town, but many. Are you willing to work with them however you want?"

He grinned. "Sure. Why not? I'm staying in Lilac Lake trying to keep a low profile until my name gets cleared from the scandal I wasn't even involved with."

"You've mentioned it before. What exactly is this scandal?"

"A group of us rented a hotel room in Miami. One of the guys invited a bunch of girls up to the suite. Alcohol was served and one of the girls got very drunk and had to be taken to the hospital. The thing was, I'd decided to go home and visit my dad. He's dying from cancer, and I had a feeling I should go see him."

"Oh, my god! How is he?"

"Not good. It's end-stage cancer. He still has some good days but not many. Lucky for me, it was one of his better days."

"So, you weren't even there?"

Ross shook his head. "No, but my name was on the reservation for the suite. They're trying to say I was responsible. It's a mess, but my lawyer says they have no grounds to blame me for the party. I will have to pay for damages, unless my so-called friends pitch in and pay for them."

Whitney sensed how betrayed Ross felt and automatically reached for his hand. "I'm so sorry," she managed to say suddenly feeling awkward as the touch of his skin caused her to blush. Good lord! Had it been that long since she'd socialized with a man?

"Are you alright?" Ross asked, gazing steadily into her eyes.

"Yes, I'm fine," she said, pulling her hand away from him. On screen she'd had to fake attraction. Compared to the nonchalant act she was performing now, that had been nothing. "What in heaven's name had happened? Maybe it was the heat," she told herself, but she knew the shock she'd felt had nothing to do with the hot day.

She gazed at Ross.

He was staring out at the street, watching the people stroll by.

Telling herself she was being ridiculous, she said to him, "So, you're willing to help out with a few baseball clinics?"

"Sure. I'll be glad to do that. Let's figure out how to tie it into your play rehearsals."

They talked about logistics and agreed that Ross would meet the kids today and set up a time for a Saturday morning session. In the meantime, the news would get out by word of mouth and with the help of various organizations willing to spread the information.

"Don't be surprised if you get a lot of the dads, too. I'm hoping Jamie's dad will be one of them. That poor kid has no chance of doing what he really wants unless he has a way to tie it into a sport. Baseball will be good for him."

"Glad to help out. Now, maybe you'll help me and agree to go out to dinner with me. I've been trying to do my own cooking in the house I'm renting, but what I really want is dinner at Fins."

Whitney smiled. "I'd be delighted." One good deed deserved another, didn't it?

Even before they entered the restaurant, a young couple recognized Ross and rushed up to him to ask him for an autograph. He politely did as she'd asked. Then, the woman noticed Whitney and said, "Oh, my god! Whitney Gilford! What are you doing here? You're with Ross? Wait until my girlfriends hear about this."

"Ross and I are simply friends," Whitney said, and realized that's all she wanted from him. A friendship with no complications. Understanding how it would be dating him, distaste made her stomach fill with acid. She'd had enough of that kind of behavior dealing with Zane. There was no way she wanted to be part of a relationship like that again. As attracted as she was to Ross, she'd stand firm on this.

Ross gave her a questioning look.

"Ross is doing something nice for the community and we're celebrating," said Whitney, smiling at him. "That's all."

Ross put an arm around Whitney's shoulders. "We're only friends, like the lady said."

When they entered the restaurant, Melissa Hendrickson's mother, Susan, acting as hostess, gushed a flirty welcome to Ross. Witnessing Ross's effect on women, Whitney knew she was right to banish any thought about a relationship with him. She couldn't do it.

Whitney was happy when Melissa, who was Whitney's age, came out of the kitchen to greet them wearing her chef's coat and toque. "The special tonight is fresh-caught cod. I can cook it any way the two of you want."

Ross grinned at Melissa. "Music to my ears. How about a typical scrod dish with lots of lemon?"

"Done," said Melissa returning his smile with flushed cheeks. "And you, Whitney?"

"I'll have the same," Whitney said. "I know how delicious it is." She and Taylor had splurged on dinner at Fins a few days ago.

After Ross had ordered a Napa Valley sauvignon blanc and they sat back facing one another, Ross gave Whitney a penetrating look. "Did you mean it? You want to be just friends?"

"Yes. I think it's best for both of us. I'm still recovering from a terrible relationship with a famous actor, and I have no idea what I'm going to do with my career or my life going forward."

"I understand. I'm in a state of limbo, too. At the moment, I'm busy doing publicity work and trying to get into the television side of things. So, it's best if I don't get involved with anyone."

"That's good," said Whitney, relieved. "If we should end up

living in Lilac Lake together for any period of time, I want to be able to count on you as a friend."

"Me, too," said Ross. He shot her a teasing grin. "In the meantime, if either of us changes our mind, let's talk about it."

Whitney laughed. "That's a promise." She loved that they'd been honest with one another from the start. That spark of attraction was there, but she wouldn't act on it. More than one thing was holding her back, and she'd learned to listen to herself.

They shared a delicious meal, with the scrod baked perfectly with a lemony bread crumb topping, fresh asparagus with a light lemon sauce, and boiled New England potatoes.

Now that they'd made the decision to be friends, Whitney found herself totally relaxed with Ross. He, in turn, told her about his time growing up in New Jersey and how baseball had kept him out of trouble.

She had no similar story. Compared to his tough life, hers was simple. Zane had once accused her of not knowing the darker side of life, and she couldn't deny it. She'd had a happy childhood with kind and loving parents.

By the time they left the restaurant, Whitney felt she and Ross were truly friends.

Ross drove her to her house, thanked her for a nice evening, kissed her on the cheek, and said, "See you on Saturday."

Taylor greeted Whitney at the door with a bright smile. "How'd your date with Ross go?"

Whitney sighed. She knew Taylor and Dani were anxious for her to find love like they had, but she needed time. "We've decided to be friends. We both agree it's best that way. His future is as uncertain as mine and we don't want to become involved with someone at this stage. Believe me, it's a relief. I'm attracted to him, but there are enough issues with him being famous and from a different background. I don't want another relationship with someone famous and in the public spotlight."

Taylor's look was crestfallen. "Oh. Well, then, I'm glad you both decided that's how it would be. I bet Ross doesn't have many, if any, girls turn him down."

"I think you're right. But he was a real gentleman about my honesty and was as relieved as I simply to relax and enjoy one another's company." Whitney shook her head. "A group of admirers saw us outside the restaurant. One of them said she couldn't wait to tell her girlfriends that Ross and I were together. I hope that goes nowhere."

Taylor made a face. "Me, too. Rumors like that can be dangerous."

Whitney blinked in surprise. "What do you mean 'dangerous'"?

"Oh, dangerous may be too strong a word. I meant unhealthy more than anything." Taylor gave her a hug. "I certainly don't want anything bad to happen to you."

"I know," said Whitney, laughing off the shiver that had crossed her shoulders.

After rain the previous day, sunshine welcomed Saturday morning with a brightness Whitney appreciated. Ross's baseball clinic was the talk of town, and she was looking forward to seeing Jamie and meeting his father.

Taylor had left for New York, and she and Mindy had the house all to themselves. She got out of bed and headed downstairs to fix a cup of coffee, enjoying the solitude on this summer morning.

Later, sitting on the patio with her coffee, she could hear Dani's dog, Pirate, chasing a ball next door, his feet pounding the ground with an undeniable rhythm. Rather than call over the fence to her sister, Whitney remained quiet. She knew Dani and Brad liked their privacy and could hardly wait to have a house together in Brad's new development.

After a refreshing shower, Whitney got dressed and headed to the local ballpark to join Ross at this first-ever baseball clinic. She hoped her decision to give Jamie a sport to talk about with his father would take the pressure off him for wanting to participate in the play's production.

On a leash beside her, Mindy pranced with excitement on her short, crooked legs, enjoying being out and about. A crowd of young boys and girls stood in a clump beside the baseball field. Whitney smiled at Ross in the middle of them trying to answer all their questions at once.

"Hello," Whitney called to him and approached a group of parents who were talking together. She noticed how many of the dads had shown up and was pleased to see them. She made a mental note to ask Ross to mention the play at the end of his clinic. With Ross's stamp of approval, perhaps Jamie's father would understand there was room for different kinds of activities for Jamie.

Even though many of them knew who she was, Whitney introduced herself to the parents and told them about the need for this clinic and other opportunities she hoped to offer the kids in the area. An average-sized man with broad shoulders and a thick midriff, balding black hair and hazel eyes approached her. "We don't want no theater stuff, no dancing, singing, and the like for our kids. We want them outdoors doing sports. That's what they need."

"I'm sorry, I didn't catch your name," said Whitney, stalling for time.

"Bud Thompkins," said the man drawing himself up. "My son, Jamie, is a talented ball player. I want him to keep at it, not wasting his time on indoor stuff."

"I'm glad we could put on the clinic today, but the opportunity for kids to try all kinds of healthy activities is what we hope to achieve. Some outdoors, some not."

"He knows what I expect," said Bud in a threatening tone that made Mindy growl.

Determined not to show her unease, Whitney stood her ground and waited for Jamie's father to step back.

As other parents spoke to her, Whitney took advantage of the time with them to talk about her plans for a children's theater program which she hoped would be tied into the schools and summer camps in the area. Most parents were receptive, a few not.

Ross approached them. "I'm going to start with a few tips on batting. My friend, Mike Dawson, will pitch and my pal, Ben Gooding will catch. I'll stand by and make notes for each of the boys and girls as they bat."

With everyone asking for autographs, Ross held up his hand. "No autographs right now. We're not prepared today. We're here for the kids' clinic. Maybe another time."

He and his friends took their positions, and then one by one, the boys and girls tried their hand at batting. Twenty-one children had shown up, which meant a couple of hours of individual coaching addressed to not only the batter but the others as well so they could all learn.

"Remember, no one is perfect. We all have a lot to learn." Ross patted Jamie on the back. "You're off to an excellent start."

Jamie's father met him walking off the field. "We'll have to practice a lot while I'm home. No more foolishness about dancing and other activities."

"But, Dad, I've promised to help with the play. I'm working on sets for it."

"No way," Bud said.

Overhearing him, Whitney confronted him. "Jamie's talent is needed for the play a new group is putting on. It won't take much time, I promise. But now that he's started, we need him to finish it."

"Who said you could do this? Your mother?" Bud said, narrowing his eyes at Jamie.

Jamie's face flushed with embarrassment. "I promised I'd still help with the kids. It only takes a short time between taking care of them. Mom said it was okay."

"We'll talk about it at home," said Bud, glaring at Whitney. If looks could kill, Whitney knew she'd be mortally wounded.

Just then, Ross's voice called out to everyone, "Remember to support the new play in town over Labor Day. It's really important."

Bud looked from Ross to her. "I suppose you got him to say something like this."

Whitney forced a smile. "I'm sure Ross Roberts wouldn't endorse anything he didn't believe in." She knew from Ross's interviews on television that he made a point of saying that.

"We'll see," said Bud. He returned a wave from Ross, who, bless his heart, was supporting Whitney's project every way he could.

"See you later," she said to Jamie. "Great job on the batting."

Jamie glanced at his father, frowned, and shrugged.

Whitney sighed. On his own, dancing or painting, Jamie was a joyful, smiling boy.

After everyone had left the field, Whitney thanked Ben, Mike, and Ross. "You don't know what a boost this is to my plan of offering other activities to the kids in the area. It means a lot."

"One guy isn't very happy about them," said Ben. "I noticed him glaring at you. Are you going to be all right?"

"There's a hothead in every crowd," said Ross. "I'll keep my eye on him at our next clinic."

"Me, too," said Ben. "There's something about him I don't trust."

"Can I buy you lunch at the café?" said Whitney. "That's the least I can do for your help."

"Sounds fine to me," said Ben. "I told Crystal I'd see her when I got back to town."

Whitney studied him. With his broad shoulders and sturdy body, Ben looked the part of baseball catcher in earlier years. She liked his upbeat manner, his easy smile. The thought of him with purple-haired, dramatic Crystal amused her. She glanced at Ross, and he winked at her as if he'd read her mind.

As usual, when Whitney and the others entered the Lilac Lake Café, it was buzzing with conversations and the sight of people enjoying their food.

Ben left them to say hello to Crystal behind the counter. The way Crystal's face lit at the sight of him brought a smile to Whitney. Maybe there was something more than friendship brewing there.

They elected to sit outside. Though the sun was high and the temperature warm, a gentle breeze cooled their skin. That, and iced tea were welcome after their busy morning.

Whitney was finishing the salad she'd ordered when Crystal walked over to them. "How's everything?"

"Delicious as usual," Whitney said.

Crystal's gaze went from Ross to her. "I understand the two of you are together now. I guess, it takes Instagram and TikTok to keep me up to date on things happening in my own town."

"What are you talking about?" asked Whitney, feeling a cold chill.

"Someone posted a photograph of the two of you together here in town," said Crystal. "She said that although you tried to tell her you were only friends, she could tell it was something more than that."

Whitney looked at Ross and sighed. "We were just being honest."

"Maybe my agent can stop the spread of that news," said Ross, giving her a sympathetic look.

"It might be too late," said Crystal looking concerned. "There is a group of Zane's fans who think you were to blame for his downfall, Whitney. Now, they're saying they're going to stop you from ruining Ross's career too."

Whitney hugged her stomach, feeling she might throw up. She'd thought those earlier threats were over.

Ross placed a hand on her shoulder. "I'll call my agent as soon as I get back to my house. I promise."

Whitney couldn't shake the fear that filled her. Fans could become obsessed by posts that weren't healthy or true.

"It's good that you live in a small town," said Crystal. "There isn't a person here who wouldn't help to keep you safe."

"I want this as quiet as possible. Otherwise, someone will make the problem even worse by saying something that could be spread. I've already experienced how that can work." Whitney couldn't hide the bitterness in her voice. She'd been blamed for Zane's drug use when she'd tried every way that she could to convince him to get help.

"I think you should tell Nick what's going on," said Crystal.

"I've already promised to let him know if anything happens to cause me worry," said Whitney. "Let's not overreact."

Crystal studied her, and though she silently agreed, her look of concern didn't disappear.

"You'd better tell him about that hothead father," said Ben.

"There's something going on with him and his family that I don't like. His son looked afraid of him."

"I know," said Whitney. "That worries me too."

CHAPTER EIGHT
TAYLOR

Taylor got off the phone with Whitney and let out a troubled sigh. She'd called because she'd decided to stay in New York for a couple of weeks while she and Cooper went over the novel she'd just finished. Meeting and critiquing the book in person was so much more convenient that staying there made sense. They were also having fun picking out furniture for his new condo, the home they'd soon share. A wedding date hadn't been set, but with both their mothers wanting a summer wedding next year, they were trying to choose one according to available venues.

Dani and Brad were planning on a Christmas wedding, which made a summer wedding for Taylor and Cooper workable. Whitney had no prospects in sight because she had no interest in a new relationship with a man after suffering from the dysfunctional one with Zane.

Taylor glanced over at Cooper. With his chocolate-brown hair and hazel eyes behind horn-rimmed glasses, he was the cutest book editor she'd ever imagined. He glanced up at her and smiled.

Taylor's heart pulsed with happiness and a surge of lust. She, who'd never experienced deep love, now knew what she and some of her characters had been missing.

Still thinking of Whitney, Taylor called Dani. "I'm really worried about Whitney. There is some crazy online chatter from the group of Zane's fans about how Ross Roberts is her next victim in her path of destruction."

"What? Why Ross?" Dani asked.

"Apparently a visitor to Lilac Lake took a picture of Ross and Whitney together, claiming they were now a couple. It's not true, but that won't matter. The photos and gossip have stirred up the anger of that radical group of Zane's fans, and they are threatening to make Whitney pay for what she's done. It's all crazy, of course."

"Crazy, but dangerous," said Dani. "I don't like it. I haven't spent much time with Whitney lately, but I'll make sure to see her today. And whether she likes it or not, I'm calling Nick. Weird things like this can turn deadly."

Taylor was shaken. The thought of anything happening to her beautiful, talented sister brought tears to her eyes. "Tell Nick I'll pay for any protection he thinks she needs. We need to keep her safe."

"I know some people will think we're worrying about nothing, but I don't want to be someone who wished she'd acted on such information and didn't. Know what I mean?"

"Oh, yes. I feel the same way." Taylor ignored the look of concern Cooper shot her way and said, "If necessary, I'll come right home."

CHAPTER NINE
DANI

As soon as Dani ended the call with Taylor, she decided to make a visit to police headquarters. What she had to say to Nick was something she wanted to be private. While she'd been living and working with Brad, her sister was facing possible trouble. Guilt made her catch her breath. She'd been so happy with her new situation she'd forgotten to keep an eye on her sister. Whitney might be older than she and very capable in her own career, but it didn't mean she didn't need emotional support.

Dani drove to the center of town to the red brick building that housed the police station and was happy to see Nick's car outside.

She parked next to it and went inside.

Nick, as usual, was happy to see her. Looking at his fit body, the blue shirt that matched his blue eyes, and the dark hair that made those eyes stand out, Dani had to admit that Taylor was right. He was the perfect, sexy guy on which to base any of her book heroes.

Nick offered her a chair in his rather spartan office, and she happily sat down in front of his desk.

"What can I do for you, Dani?" he asked, studying her face.

"It's Whitney ..." she began.

His eyebrows rose with alarm. "Is she alright?"

"I'm not sure," said Dani, and then explained the situation to him.

He frowned and stared out the window thoughtfully. "We

have no evidence of any real threat, but I don't like the sound of it. Often, before someone who's unbalanced takes action, she or he talks about it on social media. You say Crystal is the one who first mentioned it to Whitney?"

Dani nodded. "That's what Taylor said."

"Let me talk to Crystal and try to get a name. I'll do a little checking on the few people who've seemed to make threats and get back to you. Right now, as a police officer, I have no reason to do anything other than to keep an eye on things. But as an old friend of hers, I'll go see her."

Dani smiled at him. "I remember the summer you and Whitney dated."

His features softened. "Whitney's always been special to me."

"That's what we're counting on. Not that we want Whitney to know about my visit to you. She's very independent and would be furious for us intruding in her life."

"I'm not so sure that's true. The Gilford girls have always stood up for one another in times past. No reason to stop now. I remember summers when the three of you would visit. Those were good times."

"The best. That's why it's important to GG that we've returned to Lilac Lake to live for at least part-time."

"Anything more happening with that ghost of yours in the cottage?" Nick asked, unable to stop a smile from creasing his face.

Dani let out an embarrassed chuckle. "For the moment, no. But we're still trying to find out more information about Mrs. Maynard so we can figure out how to make sure she's not around."

"When are you planning to move in?" Nick asked.

"Not until the end of our lease at the end of September. Though we've moved in some things, most of the custom furniture won't be ready until then. Truthfully, we're in no hurry until the ghost issue is resolved."

"Understandable. I know Taylor, especially, is nervous about it," said Nick calmly, and Dani loved him for not making fun of them.

"I just thought of something. Why don't you come to dinner at Brad's house tomorrow? I'll ask Whitney to join us, and you can get a better sense of what's going on than from what I can tell you."

Nick's eyes lit with pleasure. "Sounds nice. I sure get tired of my own cooking."

"Well, then, that's settled." Dani stood, pleased with her plan. "Thank you. Come to the house around six. Brad and I are learning to cook together, and it should be good."

Nick walked her to the door, and Dani headed home to surprise Whitney with a visit.

CHAPTER TEN
WHITNEY

When Whitney went to answer the doorbell and saw Dani standing there, she let out a soft groan. She opened the door and said, "I gather Taylor talked to you."

"Yes, as a matter of fact, she did," said Dani, stepping inside. "Have time for a glass of iced tea and some talk?"

Whitney smiled. "I guess 'no' wouldn't be the right answer. C'mon in. It's nice to see you."

Dani returned her smile pleased they shared an easy friendship. She reached down and gave Mindy a pat on the head. "Hey, little girl. Pirate needs to come over one day for a play date."

"How is Pirate? I heard him running around the yard the other day but didn't want to intrude on your space. Having you and Brad living next door is nice, but I know how you feel about having your privacy."

"You and Taylor are welcome anytime. But yes, we're both excited about the possibility of having our own larger home at The Meadows. That will make it easier on Brad, especially, because memories of his life with Patti in his house can sometimes intrude."

"Understandable," said Whitney.

After fixing glasses of iced tea for them, extra lemon for her, Whitney led Dani outside to the patio. "Okay, sis, what is the visit really about?"

Dani sighed. "I had to get the news from Taylor about possible threats to you from that crazy group of Zane's fans who can't seem to understand what happened to him, how drugs took him down and finally ended his life. They still blame you. I understand they got riled up again after seeing a photo of you and Ross together."

Tears welled in Whitney's eyes, but she couldn't stop them. "It's all so messed up. I don't know why I'm the one they want to blame. Somebody says something that may or may not be true, and people cling to it even when it doesn't make sense."

"I know you may be irritated with Taylor and me, but I've told Nick about the situation, and he'll keep an eye on things. In fact, I've invited him to dinner at Brad's house tomorrow night and I want you to join us. We can talk more sensibly about the situation when we're together."

Whitney let out a long sigh. "I'm not mad at you for doing that. I simply don't want to be a bother to Nick. As Chief of Police of Lilac Lake, he's busy enough with real problems."

"I think he was delighted to be asked. He's always had a thing for you, and it makes him happy to think he's helping," said Dani.

"He's a sweetheart," admitted Whitney. She stopped and waved away Dani's grin. "And a good friend. Emphasis on friend."

Dani shook her head. "I'm not pressing the issue, just saying."

"Thanks for your concern. Now tell me about the progress on your house. Your goal is to have it done by Christmas in time for your wedding. Right?"

"Right. And I was going to ask you about helping me with the décor. You did such a nice job with the cottage. And I know you're helping Ross. Can you do something different for Brad and me?"

Whitney felt her wide grin. "I'd love to help. That will keep my mind off troubling issues w ith the play the dance group is putting on over the Labor Day Weekend."

"Troubles?" Dani frowned at her. "I thought it was going to be short and simple."

"Oh, it is," said Whitney, unable to hide her enthusiasm. "The kids are really enjoying it. Jamie Thompkins, a darling boy and dancer I've spoken about before, is working on the scenery for the play. But his father wants Jamie to concentrate on sports. Thank goodness, he doesn't know about Jamie taking dance lessons because he was upset about Jamie working on the play. He's not a nice man."

"I don't get why some parents are like that," said Dani. "If a child of mine were talented, I'd want him or her to continue with it. Like Mom and Dad did for you."

"I agree, but some guys are stuck in the past where thinking about special roles for genders still exists. Ben and Ross call him a hothead."

"Is this another thing to worry about?" asked Dani.

Whitney shook her head. "I can't go there. And I won't give up on presenting opportunities for Jamie. But I don't want to do anything to anger his father. Jamie is afraid of him."

"Well, one step at a time. Get through the play and sit tight to see what happens after that. His mother has already permitted him dance lessons. Right?"

"Yes, but like I said, his father doesn't know about them. It's pure defiance on her part, I guess, because I suspect she's a little afraid of Jamie's father too."

"Brad and I talk about having children. But the more I hear about other people's children, the more I want to wait a while after we're married until we've settled into our routines in our new house. Brad's mother, MaryLou, will have to be content with his sister, Amy's, new baby next winter. In the meantime, her little Will is one of the cutest baby boys I've ever seen. It

Love Under the Stars

makes me wonder what babies Brad and I make will look like."

"Mmm. Seems you've been doing a lot of thinking about it," said Whitney amused. Once Dani made up her mind about something it was all but a done deal. Hearing her now, Whitney thought she might become an aunt sooner rather than later.

They chatted a while longer, then Dani rose. "I've got to meet with a client out at The Meadows. I'd better go, but I'm glad we've had this talk. It's important for us to keep in touch. In fact, I'm sorry I've been so absent lately."

"No problem," said Whitney. "I know you and Brad have been working together on The Meadows and then cooking together in the evening. It's really sweet."

Dani's grin lit her blue eyes as she pushed a lock of brown hair behind her ear. "It's better than sweet. It's hot."

Whitney's laugh rang out and they hugged one another.

"You go, girl," Whitney said and walked her to the front door.

Whitney decided Dani was right. The family hadn't kept as close as they had in the past. She picked up her car keys and drove to The Woodlands, where GG lived. A talk with her grandmother always helped her perspective on things.

Whitney studied the complex as she drove into the parking lot. The structure spread across a fresh green lawn in front of a pretty, wooded area. The one-story building was handsome with gray-stained clapboards and stone accents. The building was a point of pride for the entire family because with GG's help, Brad and his brother Aaron had been the contractors for it.

Inside, the smell of fresh bread permeated the air, giving it a pleasing odor not usually found in assisted-living facilities. But The Woodlands was an exceptionally nice place. Whitney was pleased that her grandmother had arranged to stay there following a financial disaster and the sale of the inn. But then, after running the Lilac Lake Inn for so long, her grandmother deserved such a comfortable setting for her last years. Not that GG was about to die. Far from it. She still had a lot of energy and made friends as easily here as she had at the inn.

When Whitney reached the apartment, she found the door cracked open. A sign of friendliness. She knocked and peered inside. GG was on the sofa napping with a book in her hand.

"GG?" Whitney called softly, then wondered if she should come back another time.

Her grandmother sat up with a start and when she saw Whitney, she smiled and waved her inside. "I'm so glad to see you."

"I hope I'm not disturbing you. It looked like you were having a nice nap."

"I'd much rather be talking to you. I was going to call you. I understand you and Ross Roberts are seeing each other now."

Frowning, Whitney leaned down and kissed her grandmother's cheek. "Where did you get that idea?"

"Oh, ever since you started your acting career, I'm addicted to those Hollywood news programs. I saw it there."

Whitney sat down and took hold of GG's hand. "If I get serious with someone new, you'll be among the first to find out. Like always."

"Oh, good. I like knowing what you girls are up to. With Taylor and Dani's futures more-or-less settled, I'm anxious about you."

"No need to worry about me," Whitney said, forcing a nonchalance. The last thing she wanted to do was cause her grandmother to be upset.

"Good," said GG, getting to her feet. She checked her

watch. "You're in time for tea, if you choose."

Whitney heard the hope in GG's voice. "Sure. That sounds like fun." She turned as a knock sounded at the door.

JoEllen Daniels poked her head inside. "I heard you had company Mrs. Wittner and had to see who it was." She smiled at Whitney. "Heard you might be dating Ross."

"We're just friends. That's all," said Whitney. JoEllen's nosiness bothered her.

"Oh, that's good because I've been trying to get him to meet me at Jake's. Maybe now he can."

After JoEllen left, Whitney let out a sigh. Had she been too quick to end any thought of a relationship with Ross? No, she reminded herself. She had no desire to have a fling, and she thought that's all it might have turned out to be between the two of them.

"That young woman is a bother," said GG.

"I agree. Come on. I'll walk you down to the tearoom and we can catch up with what everyone in the family is doing. You probably know more than I do about them."

GG laughed. "Maybe not. We'll see. I just love hearing about my family."

After she got settled in her chair, her grandmother smiled at the waitress hovering nearby. "Alice, this is my granddaughter, Whitney."

GG's pride in her touched Whitney. She smiled. "Nice to meet you, Alice. Are you new here?"

"Yes," said Alice. "I love Genie and meeting you and everyone else in the family."

"I'm lucky to have them," said GG, giving Whitney a wink.

Whitney grinned. GG loved the attention she was getting. But then, she'd always had a lot of friends, The move to an assisted-living facility was a big change for her. Whitney was glad to see her so happy.

As they sipped their tea and nibbled on cookies, Whitney told GG about the baseball clinic Ross and his friends had held.

"What a superb opportunity for the kids. I'm sorry to hear that one of the fathers is a troublemaker. I believe a child is given a talent for a reason. What if your parents hadn't allowed you to dance or sing? What a disappointment that would have been for so many people."

"I was very lucky to have their support and yours. I guess that's why I feel so strongly about Jamie."

"Be careful about being too outspoken about it. His parents have the right to raise him as they see fit, as long as it's not destructive to him or anyone else."

"But I sense that Jamie is afraid of his father. I'm going to keep an eye on him. In a couple more weeks, the play will be over, and he'll be back in school. By then, I hope to have a better schedule for moving into the cottage and creating a new life for myself."

"One day at a time, my darling," said GG. "Now, how about passing that plate of cookies over to me?"

Whitney chuckled, took one for herself, and handed her grandmother the plate.

The next afternoon, Whitney waited anxiously for Jamie to appear at the storage shed at the Beckman Lumber company where play rehearsal was scheduled. She'd given up hope that he was coming when at last his father drove up to it. Jamie climbed out of the truck wearing a harried look.

Whitney went to greet him and gave a wave to Jamie's father, who stared at her and didn't return her greeting.

"Are you okay?" she asked Jamie gently.

He nodded and hurried into the building.

Whitney decided to heed GG's warning and not say

anything more to Jamie about being comfortable there. But she noticed the more Jamie got into the job of painting the backdrop, the more relaxed he became. Better yet, another boy had joined the production team and was chatting with Jamie about the baseball clinic.

After the practice was over and the kids had once again done well with their lines and were adding movements to their roles, Whitney was ready to go home and relax before dinner at Brad's.

She waited outside the shed for parents to pick up their children with a sense of accomplishment that things were going so well. Bud, Jamie's dad, was the last to arrive.

Trying to be cordial, Whitney said, "Jamie's a big help."

He grunted something unintelligible and then said to Jamie, "Get in."

Whitney waved goodbye and stood back as the truck roared out of the driveway. Staring at it, she decided she didn't like that man and never would.

CHAPTER ELEVEN
WHITNEY

Whitney took her time dressing for dinner. It had been a while since she'd been out, and though it wasn't a real date, she wanted to look nice. She studied herself in the mirror. Since leaving Hollywood behind, she'd gained a couple of pounds that she was forced to admit made her look better.

She checked to be sure her hair was in place. Most hot days she wore it in a ponytail, but tonight she wanted a different, softer look. Satisfied, she turned away, retrieved a bottle of wine to present to the cooks, and left the house with Mindy at her heels. Her dog would play with Pirate in the backyard while they had drinks on the patio.

Whitney could hardly wait for dinner because sharing food they'd prepared together was so important to Dani and Brad. It was cute how they were becoming even closer through cooking. They'd even invited GG to dinner several times.

She walked across the lawn to Brad's house.

Brad answered the door wearing a chef's apron. "Hi, Whitney. C'mon in. Dani's working in the kitchen. We're about ready, and Nick is on his way."

"Something smells delicious," said Whitney handing him the bottle of wine.

As she entered the kitchen, Dani looked up at her and smiled. "Hey, there. You look lovely."

"Thanks," said Whitney. She put Mindy outside and then turned to her. "What are you making?"

"Brad is going to grill some veggies that we've been

marinating, along with chicken breasts with a teriyaki glaze. What you smell is a pineapple upside down cake for dessert. Not too rich."

"I'll certainly have a taste. It smells too delicious to resist." Whitney smiled at the image of Dani wearing a frilly apron over the cut-off jeans and T-shirt she usually wore to the building site.

Dani noticed and grinned. "I haven't had the chance to change. I'm still learning how to time things better. I'm glad it's you and Nick for dinner and not Brad's parents or mine."

They laughed together and then Brad led Nick into the kitchen. "The gang's all here."

"Hi, everyone," said Nick. "Something smells delicious." He put a bag holding ice cream on the kitchen counter. "Here's the vanilla ice cream Brad asked me to bring."

Grinning, Dani shook her head at Brad. "That was sneaky. But we'll all enjoy it."

"A man's got to have ice cream with cake. It's a rule," said Brad laughing.

"Not in my house growing up," Dani said. "But working on the farm is hard, so I understand why it your family did it."

"Scoops has the best ice cream. Remember how we all used to end up there a few summer evenings every year?" said Nick.

"Yes. Especially after swimming at the lake," said Whitney awash in childhood memories. Summers in Lilac Lake had been a wonderful change for her sisters and her.

"How about some wine?" said Brad. "Whitney brought a nice Chandler Hill Chardonnay."

"Sounds perfect," said Dani. "Let's sit outdoors. It's cooled off nicely."

Brad opened the wine, and then they each carried a glass out to the patio.

Nick sat facing Whitney in the circle of chairs and smiled

at her. "I drove by while the baseball clinic was being put on for the kids. I heard it was your doing that made it happen."

"Yes, I thought it might help one of the boys on the production team for the play we're putting on for Labor Day."

"Oh?" Nick replied. "Which boy are you talking about?"

"Jamie Thompkins. His father doesn't like Jamie being associated with the play. Apparently, he doesn't know about Jamie's dance classes. After meeting his father, I understand why Jamie and his mother are keeping it a secret from him."

"Bud Thompkins is a troublemaker," said Nick. "His wife has called for help a couple of times when Bud's had too much to drink. But I understand he does a satisfactory job for the trucking company he works for. No alcohol allowed, of course. So, I think it's a way for Bud to let loose. But I've warned him that bad behavior will not be allowed in town."

"Wow! He must not have liked to hear that," said Whitney.

"He was very angry with me, but I won't back down. At the first sign of trouble, he'll be brought in." His deep voice, firm and steady, was comforting.

"I'm keeping an eye on him. Jamie is afraid of his father," said Whitney, filled with a determination to help.

"If you suspect anything, call me. Don't do anything on your own. That could be dangerous with a man like that." Nick's gaze bored into her.

"We might as well get the unpleasantness out of the way so we can enjoy the rest of the evening," said Dani. "Nick, what did you find out about that fan group of Zane's?"

Nick drew a deep breath and let out a sigh. "On the surface, it looks like a bunch of disgruntled fans who Zane had reached out to at one point in his career, sending photos, exchanging messages in social media, and the like."

"Something we were warned not to do," said Whitney, unable to hide the disgust in her voice.

"But there's a disturbing commonality among them. They're loners who've come together over a false belief and who are determined to take things into their own hands." Nick shook his head. "In this day and age, with social media promoting wrong information or even simply accepting statements that aren't true, I suggest we all keep eyes and ears open to any unusual activity in town that might be directed against Whitney."

A shiver traveled down Whitney's back and settled in her stomach causing her to feel nauseous.

Nick reached over and clasped her hand. "Don't worry, Whitney. You'll be safe. I'm going to see to it."

She looked into his startling blue eyes and saw something deeper than friendship. Uncertain what to say or do about it, she remained quiet.

"We'll keep you surrounded with people who care," said Dani. "No one wants anything bad to happen to you."

"Thanks," Whitney managed to say, remembering how alone she'd felt in L.A. Small town living sure had its advantages.

"Enough of all this worrisome stuff," said Brad. "We've got a great dinner ahead. Let's enjoy it."

Dani lifted her glass of wine. "Hear! Hear!"

As Whitney raised her glass, she looked around at the people with her and felt a surge of love.

After a meal in which compliments were well deserved, the four of them sat talking on the patio and sipping ice water. It was too hot even to think about coffee. Still, the thought of being so comfortable, so free to speak was rewarding to Whitney. Being in the spotlight with her work and with the uproar over Zane's death, she'd begun to feel as if no one was listening to her. Now, the reality of a group the press was calling Zaniacs was disturbing. Especially because they were ignoring all the facts.

The young man she'd fallen in love with had taught her a lot about love, life, even herself. Then it had become a tangled mess with an ugliness she'd never be able to forget completely.

Nick stood. "Guess I'd better head home. Busy day tomorrow."

"I should go too," said Whitney. She knew both Brad and Dani were up early to get to the building site during summer hours when work could start at first light.

Whitney got to her feet, hugged both Dani and Brad and waited while Nick said goodbye. Then they left together with Mindy.

Outside, Nick turned to her. "I meant what I said, Whitney. Call me any time day or night if you feel the least bit uncomfortable about being alone."

Whitney smiled and gave him a quick hug. "You're such a dear friend."

Nick studied her with those startling blue eyes and for a moment Whitney felt as if she were swimming in them.

He lifted her chin and very gently kissed her cheek. "Let me know if that feeling ever changes."

She nodded too shaken to speak. She'd admired him, his body, his steadfastness to doing an outstanding job for the community. She'd adored him as a teenager.

"C'mon, I'll walk you over to your house to be sure everything is fine." He took her hand.

The jolt Whitney felt from the way his fingers curled around her palm made her release a soft gasp. She glanced at Nick, but he didn't seem to notice. He was too busy studying the front porch of her house.

He dropped her hand. "Stay here."

He jogged over to the front steps and lifted a brick. Sliding the paper beneath it out, he read the bold, typed words: *I know where you live.*

"What is it?" asked Whitney joining him, Mindy at her heels.

He silently handed her the note. "I don't like this. I think I'd better stay. If you're okay with it, I can sleep on the couch. Tomorrow, we'll try to get some information from any of the neighbors about seeing an unfamiliar car or person."

"Where do you think that came from?" asked Whitney feeling a chill run through her.

Nick shook his head. "It could be anyone. We already know there are certain individuals who are trying to harass you. Sometimes a person can read or hear about something like that and add to it in a big or even small way. It's sick behavior, but it happens."

A burst of anger swept through Whitney. "I can't leave Lilac Lake or allow them to scare me. I've got the play to put on. I won't let the kids down."

"One day at a time, Whitney," warned Nick. "No need to panic. I'll have a patrol car assigned to drive by the house on a regular basis. And, like I said, until we get a handle on it, I'm willing to stay. No strings attached."

Whitney's shoulders sagged. "Okay, if you think that's best. I'm glad Taylor is out of town and Dani is with Brad. I wouldn't want them placed in danger because of me."

"It could be only a kid wanting to play a dirty trick. We don't know. Anyone could've seen all the furor on social media. And there was talk about it at Jake's recently."

"Or it could be a kid's father," said Whitney thinking of Bud Thompkins. She hadn't liked him from the start, had sensed his antipathy when she had done nothing wrong. But if she wasn't mistaken, Bud was used to being in control. All the more reason for him never to find out about Jamie's dancing lessons.

Whitney let out a long sigh. "Are you sure you don't mind staying the night? Dani's room is available. You won't have to sleep on the couch."

"Thanks, but for tonight, I'll take the couch. Seems more professional that way," Nick said, giving her a wink that sent a bolt of electricity through her.

"Okay, but I want to be sure you'll be comfortable," said Whitney.

Inside the house, she left him in the living room and returned with fresh sheets, a pillow, and a light summer blanket. With the air conditioner running, he might need it.

Together, they made a bed for him on the long couch. Whitney told herself to stop wondering what it would be like to sleep with him and hurried to the kitchen to get him a glass of water.

She handed the glass to him. "There. I think you have everything. Can you think of anything else?"

"Maybe a kiss goodnight?" His lips twisted into a lop-sided grin.

She laughed and allowed him to kiss her. When she pulled back, she could see desire in his eyes. Confused by her own quick arousal, she stepped away.

"Don't worry, Whitney. You'll be safe with me," he said, and she wondered if he knew what that kiss had done to her. It wasn't safe at all.

Later, as Whitney lay in bed, she stared up at the ceiling reliving Nick's kiss, his hand curled around hers, the wink that was filled with a promise she was pleased to consider. The way he made her remember what it felt like to share passion at the same time he made her feel safe was an interesting balance.

She recalled the summer they dated. She was a

sophisticated eighteen and he was in his early twenties. She was smitten with him, and though he returned her feelings, he'd told her from the beginning he'd never stand in the way of her doing what she wanted with her life, that he never wanted to hurt her. Life interrupted their young romance when Whitney got word that an acting school had accepted her application and she left New Hampshire early.

But now, thinking of him in this new light, she was intrigued by the possibility of a more sophisticated relationship with him. She knew enough about him to know she could trust him. Even though he and Crystal had married and divorced, the fact that they were still friends told a tale of its own. He was a very decent, kind man.

Moving Mindy away from her side, Whitney rolled over, relieved to know Nick was downstairs ready to protect her, if necessary.

CHAPTER TWELVE
TAYLOR

After receiving a phone call from Whitney, Taylor sat at her desk staring into space. This summer was turning out to be the strangest of all. She and Dani had quickly and forever found love, while Whitney, whom everyone adored, was being besieged by enraged fans who didn't really know her. It was so unfair.

But Taylor would do as Whitney asked and stay in the city longer than she'd planned. The upside was that she would get to spend some time on Long Island with Cooper and meet more of his friends. So far, the few friends she'd met had seemed very nice.

Taylor padded into the kitchen of her condo where Cooper was sitting at the table in denim shorts and nothing else. She settled her gaze on his broad chest and then at his questioning look, she said, "That was Whitney. Some crazy stuff is going on at home, and she asked me not to return. Some of Zane's fans are angry with her, blaming her for his death, the father of one of the boys helping to put on a play is upset with her, and now, someone has left a note on the porch saying: '*I know where you live.*' Pretty upsetting."

"Is this a matter for the police?" Cooper asked, giving her a look of concern.

"As a matter of fact, Nick slept over on the couch last night and will be looking into the matter."

"Good. It could be a joke, but it's important to be sure. Do you mind staying longer than you had planned?"

Taylor smiled at him. "Of course not. I prefer to be here with you, but I want to do my share to help my sisters."

He pulled her onto his lap. "Mmm, I smell flowers."

"It's my shampoo," she said, laughing when he nuzzled her neck, growling softly.

He lifted his head and kissed her on the lips.

Taylor couldn't contain the soft moan that escaped her. He made her feel so treasured.

Her phone chimed, and Taylor lifted herself off his lap. *Dani.*

"Hi, Taylor. Has Whitney talked to you yet?" Dani asked.

"As a matter of fact, I just got off the phone with her. What's up?"

"I'm trying to get her to leave Lilac Lake for a couple of days, but she refuses. She says she can't let other people rule her life by talking about making her pay for Zane's death."

"What about the note left on the porch?" Taylor asked. "That makes it seem very real."

"I talked to Nick about it and he's not sure it's a threat. He thinks it might be more like someone adding on to the news that's circulating. But, of course, he's on it and will be keeping a careful eye on her. If the way he looked at her last evening when the two of them were here for dinner is an indication, I'd say he was very attracted to her."

"Crystal once told me she thinks Nick has always loved Whitney. Do you think she'd be receptive to that?"

"Oh, yeah," said Dani. "It's sometimes hard to tell what Whitney is thinking, but she was definitely responding to his attention. They would make an adorable couple, don't you think?"

"I do," said Taylor. "But we can't push anything, or she'll put on her 'I'm-the-big-sister-don't-tell-me-what-to-do act.'"

Dani laughed. "True. Nick will be keeping an eye on her,

but Brad and I will, too. It's a good thing Whitney has Mindy to warn her about strangers. Dogs are effective deterrents to intruders."

Taylor had at one time thought she wouldn't know deep love because she was the only one of the three who didn't own a dog. She couldn't own one as long as she lived in the city. Maybe when she and Cooper were spending more time in Lilac Lake, that could happen. But she didn't need a dog to verify she knew true love. She and Cooper had found it.

CHAPTER THIRTEEN
WHITNEY

Whitney folded up the sheets and blanket Nick had used overnight and instead of putting them in the wash, she placed them on a shelf in the laundry room with the pillow in case Nick needed them again. Waking up to find him in the kitchen after protecting her all night had brought home the emptiness of the past couple of years in Hollywood. She'd liked seeing Nick there, sharing coffee with him, sending him off with a wish for a good day. It seemed so ... domestic.

She shook her head and reminded herself that it wasn't a normal scene, that Nick was there to protect her from what could be something serious or a simply a mean prank.

Mindy whined at her feet.

Whitney bent over and picked her up, enjoying cuddling the dachshund. With all the worrisome things that were going on, Whitney was happier than ever that she'd adopted the dog. Mindy might be small and have short legs, but she became a teeth-bared beast when anyone threatened Whitney.

Whitney had stepped from the shower when GG called.

"Hi, darling. Are you alright?" GG asked.

"Yes. Why are you asking?" Whitney said cautiously.

"I overheard the staff talking about some trouble you were having with fans of Zane's. One person even mentioned a note on your doorstep."

Whitney's heart stopped beating and then sprang ahead to

catch up. "What are you talking about? A note on my doorstep? Who said that?" That note hadn't been reported to anyone.

"I'm not sure where that started. I'll try to find out. But, Whitney, dear, what's going on? Should I be worried?"

"I'm fine. Nick Woodruff is going to investigate to make sure I stay that way." Whitney tried for humor. "Living in a small town makes it easy to get the attention of the Chief of Police."

"My darling, you can catch Nick's attention anytime. I remember what it was like between the two of you that one summer. Very special." GG's voice held a softness that made Whitney unexpectedly want to cry.

"Are you up for a visit?" Whitney asked her.

"That would be lovely. Maybe the two of us can find out about these rumors. A note on the doorstep. What will they think of next?"

Whitney remained quiet. No way did she want GG to worry about her. Besides, she had a pretty good idea where such a rumor might have started. Thinking she might need a witness, she called Dani.

Twenty minutes later, Dani accompanied Whitney to GG's room at The Woodlands.

When GG saw them, she rose from her chair on the patio and opened her arms. "Ah, two of my three grands. What a treat."

Whitney enveloped her grandmother in a hug. She stepped aside as Dani hugged GG and then Dani said in her no-nonsense way, "We're here to find the person who knew about the note left on our front porch."

GG's eyebrows shot up. "Then it's true?" She glanced at Whitney.

"I didn't want to say anything to you about it. We want to get to the bottom of it, so we don't have to worry. Nick thinks it might be a prank caused by all the social media gossip."

"But that's such a cruel thing to do," said GG.

"Yes, it is," said Dani. "That's why I'm here."

Whitney placed a hand on Dani's arm. "We can't go charging around here accusing someone of doing this. We need to know where the information came from. Right?"

"Yes, but I already know who the culprit is," said Dani. Her nostrils flared. "I'd bet money on it."

"Let me go speak to the receptionist and check to see who's on duty," said Whitney. "I'll ask in such a way she won't suspect anything. Then you can take over."

"Deal," said Dani looking grim.

Whitney left them and returned. Giving a smile to Dani, she said, "Ready."

"I'll be back," said Dani, leaving the room with a purposeful stride.

"What's this about?" asked GG.

"You'll see," said Whitney. She wanted GG's surprise to be real. But then again, maybe it wouldn't be a surprise at all.

In less than ten minutes, Dani returned with JoEllen. "Yep, we were right all along. What do you have to say for yourself, JoEllen?"

JoEllen clasped her hands in front of her and rocked from one foot to another. "I'm sorry. A group of us were at Jake's when all this stuff came on the entertainment show about the group called the Zaniacs. We'd had a lot to drink, and when someone came up with the suggestion, I told them I'd deliver it."

"Whose idea was it?" Whitney asked, her hands balled into fists.

JoEllen shrugged. "Probably all of us. It was a stupid thing to do, I now realize. At the time, we thought it was funny."

"I'm reporting the incident to the police," said Dani. "If Nick calls you, like you've always wanted, it'll be to give you a warning. I don't know what your game is, but you have some serious problems."

"I said I'm sorry," said JoEllen, crossing her arms in front of her, a look of fury on her face. "Because you Gilford girls are everyone's favorites, it doesn't mean you should be treated differently from anyone else, as if you're so special."

"Are you telling me you'd do this to someone else?" Whitney asked in a cool, controlled voice. Her icy stare made even Dani uncomfortable.

"No, no, I didn't say that," JoEllen said. "Look, I've got to go back to work."

"I'm prepared to tell the manager what has happened, what kind of person you are," said GG entering the conversation. "If I ever hear that you've done anything to harass my granddaughters, I will. Do you understand?"

JoEllen bowed her head. "I just want to make friends," she mumbled. "That's why I agreed to do it."

"Well, then, smarten up. Why would you risk getting into trouble to make friends? No spying on Brad and Dani, no mean tricks," said GG sounding as firm as she had all of Whitney's growing up years.

"Let your 'friends' know that this kind of thing won't be tolerated. I'm telling Nick about it, but that's all," said Whitney both frustrated by JoEllen and feeling sorry for her.

"You can go now," said Dani, opening the door to GG's room and standing by as JoEllen made her exit.

"What a story," said GG. "This calls for some lemonade and cookies. I've got some here already."

"A celebration of sorts," said Dani. "All this worry for nothing feels very good."

"Amen," said GG.

"Yes," agreed Whitney. "I hope it puts an end to it."

Dani elbowed Whitney. "One good thing though. We know Nick would do anything for you. That was worth the scare. Huh?"

Whitney laughed, unable to think of anything to say except "maybe".

When they left The Woodlands, Whitney and Dani drove directly to the police station and asked to see Nick. They waited for a moment before he approached them in uniform from the back of the building. Seeing him in this setting, Whitney understood why Taylor was basing the hero in her next book on him. He was drop-dead gorgeous even as he wore a look of concern as he walked toward them.

"Everything okay?" he asked Whitney.

"We thought you ought to have an update on the note situation," said Dani. "It's pretty unreal."

"Come on back to my office and we can talk there." He studied Whitney. "Are you alright?"

"Yes, but I'm mad as hell," said Whitney.

He led them into an office which could only be considered plain with its institutional yellow walls and lack of furnishings. Two chairs sat in front of a wooden desk. A long worktable sat in the middle of the facing wall. Framed documents noting the education and awards Nick had received decorated the wall above the table.

"It's not much, but it works," said Nick, indicating the office with a sweep of his arm. "Please have a seat and tell me what's going on."

Dani leaned forward anxious to tell the story.

Whitney let her take the lead. Dani was even more upset than she and rightly so. JoEllen had been a nuisance to her and Brad for weeks, claiming Brad had agreed to marry her to fulfill his deceased wife's wish. Another bizarre situation.

Nick listened as Dani told the story of how they'd gone to The Woodlands after GG mentioned knowing about a note left on the front porch.

"Anything to add?" Nick asked, focusing his gaze on Whitney.

"Though I'm livid about her actions, I understand them in a way. JoEllen has few social skills, has a particular way of irritating people, and wants desperately to be liked. It's an impossible situation. She claims someone else thought of the idea and she promised to carry through with it as a joke. But it's more problematic than that."

"You're too kind," said Dani, shifting in her seat with irritation.

"You can't legally charge her with anything other than harassment, perhaps, but I certainly can speak to her. She's called me a couple of times asking me to meet her, so I owe her a call anyway."

Whitney was relieved. She didn't want a major fight on her hands but did want JoEllen to know pranks like this were not acceptable. Something she should've been aware of on her own.

As someone knocked on the door, Nick checked his watch and stood. "Okay, then, I think we're done here. I'll report back to you, Whitney. And I'm going to continue to keep an eye on things."

The smile Nick gave her sent a flurry of longing through her. He was someone she definitely wanted to know better.

As they left the police station, Dani turned to Whitney. "You guys are so hot together."

"What do you mean?" asked Whitney.

"C'mon. That smile he sent you all but set you on fire." Dani wrapped her arm around Whitney. "I loved seeing that. It's about time you had some fun in your life."

Whitney was quiet, but she wasn't about to have a fling with anyone. She'd be careful with Nick because she knew now that she wanted more than that.

CHAPTER FOURTEEN
DANI

That night, when Dani saw Nick's car in the driveway next door, she couldn't stop a smile from spreading across her face. She hadn't been kidding when she'd told Whitney there was a spark between the two of them that anyone could see.

She glanced over at Brad, absently stroking Pirate's shiny black fur as he read something in the paper. They were sitting outside as usual and had finished a delightful meal of grilled filets of beef, a green lettuce salad, and fresh cut-up fruit for dessert. Dani was much more comfortable in the kitchen now, which pleased both her and Brad.

Brad looked up, saw her attention on him, and grinned. "What's up?"

"Nick's car is parked next door. That makes me happy. Whitney has been feeling down lately, and I want to see her enjoying herself."

Brad frowned. "Are you trying to be a matchmaker?"

"Not really. I just want my sisters to be as happy as I am," she said, rising and climbing into his welcoming lap.

She leaned against him, enjoying the solid feel of his chest and the way his hands circled her back in comforting strokes. Though they often worked at the development together she never tired of being with him. His enthusiasm for her plans at The Meadows and the new consulting company she was setting up meant everything to her after her work at the firm she used to work for in Boston was all but ignored.

Since meeting Brad and falling in love with him, Dani's

entire life had changed for the better. GG had always told her that life is one big circle after another. Dani believed she might not have even met Brad if GG hadn't gifted her sisters and her the cottage.

Thinking of it now, she wondered how soon the furniture would come and when she and her sisters could live there. The question of Mrs. Maynard's ghost had faded into the background with all their activities, but Dani was certain her sisters wanted closure as much as she.

CHAPTER FIFTEEN
WHITNEY

When Nick called to say he'd spoken to JoEllen, Whitney said, "Why don't you stop by after work to tell me about it, and I'll treat you to a homemade meal? You've been so nice, it's the least I can do."

"Sounds good. Thanks, I will. See you then."

After the call ended, Whitney was at a loss. She knew a lot about fixing small healthy meals for herself, but she needed a suggestion for a "guy" meal for Nick. In the end, she decided to stick to one of her favorites—a shrimp pasta dish that was easy to make. She got in her car and went to the market for shrimp. The lemon, butter, and caper sauce would be easy and refreshing on a summer day. That, French bread, and fruit and cheese for an appetizer would do nicely. She'd even splurge and choose a nice Chandler Hill rosé to accompany the meal.

While she was picking up what she needed, Pam Sawyer, the mother of Elissa who played the mouse in the play, saw her and walked over. "I want to tell you how thrilled Elissa is to be part of the play."

"She's not just part of the play, she's the star." Whitney grinned. "She's adorable and so bright. And she loves to act."

Pam laughed. "She's a ham all right. Feel free to tell her to calm down, if necessary. She can get carried away."

"No worries. She's perfect for the part. I understand you and your husband are teachers in the Lilac Lake school district. I'm concerned about Jamie Thompkins. He's working on the sets for the play and is doing a great job. His father, though, is against him doing any activity that doesn't involve sports."

"I'm familiar with the situation. I've found it best to be nonconfrontational with any parents like that. As long as no harm is done."

Whitney gripped the lemon in her hand. "I suppose you're right. But I've seen that Jamie is afraid of his father. It bothers me."

"I'm sure it does. Other people have concerns too and we're all keeping an eye on the family. In a small town, it's possible to do that."

"I'm learning a lot about small town living. I hope we can count on you to spread the word about the play and the baseball clinics Ross Roberts is putting on some Saturday mornings. He's helping me out by doing it, and I want to support him."

"It's a once-in-a-lifetime chance for the kids. Elissa's brother is very interested in attending Ross's clinic after missing the last one." Pam's kind dark-brown eyes matched her dark curly hair. She smiled at Whitney. "I hope we can be friends. I'd like to help you with the program you discussed with Angelica Hammond at the Community Center."

Whitney laughed. "This small-town interaction is unbelievable. I'd love your help and your friendship."

"Well, then," said Pam, obviously pleased. "I'll see you at next rehearsal to see how you're handling the program."

"Thanks," said Whitney meaning it.

They parted, and all the way home, Whitney thought how lucky she was to find someone like Pam reaching out to her.

Later, she was still feeling pleased about that connection when Nick pulled up in the driveway. Whitney didn't know who was more excited to see him—she or Mindy.

Whitney opened the door and stood back as Nick entered carrying a bottle of wine. "It's my night off so I can be a little more festive." He bent to give Mindy the attention she wanted.

"Two nights off in a row?" Whitney said grinning. "That's terrific."

"In some ways, I'm always on call. But for tonight, I've left word not to contact me unless it's a real emergency." He handed her the wine and grinned. "I want this time to be ... special. A chance to enjoy one another."

Her mind darted to the scene last night when he'd asked for a goodnight kiss. She'd wanted to give him a real kiss but had decided at the last minute not to. A pure case of nerves. Yes, she could act her way through anything but when it came to her innermost feelings, her first instinct was to protect them. Especially after the debacle with Zane. But then she'd allowed herself to kiss Nick and had thought about it ever since.

They walked into the kitchen.

When Nick saw the table set for two with a crystal vase holding a single yellow rose in the center, he grinned. "Very nice."

"Truthfully, I'm not much of a cook, but I do like setting a pretty dinner table."

"Being here is a real treat. I go to the café a lot for meals, but it's nice to do something different."

Nick opened the bottle of wine for her while she set out a plate of cheese and crackers decorated with a small bunch of chilled grapes. Then, instead of heading out to the patio where it was hot, they went into the living room. Soft music played in the background lending a little romance to the air. Whitney had decided Dani was right. It was time for her to enjoy being with Nick to see if the flames Dani had talked about were real. She was tired of being alone, scorned, and fighting melancholy.

As soon as they were seated on the couch, Whitney raised her glass. "Here's to us!"

He grinned and lifted his glass. "I like that."

They each took a sip and then Nick set his glass down. "I need to tell you about the meeting I had with JoEllen."

Seeing the seriousness on his face, Whitney immediately grew concerned. "How did it go?"

"I guess I could say it went well, but the situation is complicated. I've gone so far as suggesting that JoEllen speak to a professional counselor. I even gave her the name of Nora Schinberg, a woman I trust here in town."

"What's the story?" Whitney asked, placing her wineglass on the coffee table in front of her.

"It's a family situation of one daughter being perfect; the other always failing. JoEllen is trying to build friendships in a destructive way and is making a lot of mistakes that are adding to her problems. She says she's sorry she left that note on the porch, that she didn't realize how serious it was to do something like that."

"It's the trick of a kid, not someone her age," protested Whitney.

"Yes, I agree. That's why I think she needs help. I've seen bad guys in my job. She's not one of them. Mixed up, yes. Angry. Unhappy."

"I'll let it go, but I'm not going to tolerate more of her antics toward me or my family. I'm tired of the way people think they can say or do anything without any repercussions for their bad behavior."

"Understandable. And as I've said, I'm here to help in any way I can." He reached over and took hold of her hand. When he gave a gentle tug, Whitney leaned over and accepted the kiss he offered.

His lips were soft and yet confident as he deepened the kiss.

The world around Whitney disappeared. She fought to keep her mental balance for a moment and then gave in to the pleasure that filled her.

When they finally pulled apart, Whitney could only stare at him as memories of their long ago summer together met with the present in a heart-stopping moment.

He looked as thunderstruck as she felt. She'd never experienced anything like the feelings running rampant inside her—tenderness, lust, and peace. And hunger.

Nick reached for her, and she threw herself into his arms, wanting more, much more.

Later, lying together, Whitney stroked his naked chest, loving the hard muscle beneath his skin. She couldn't seem to get enough of him. Gazing up at him, she said, "That was nothing like our kisses of the past."

He grinned and hugged her closer, enough for her to know he was aroused again. "We're all grown up now."

Tears sprang to her eyes, startling them both. "Oh, Nick. It feels so right, us together."

"I wasn't sure how much longer I could wait to be with you. I've wanted this for a long time. Since we were kids, really. But I knew I had to let you go."

"And now? I'm not sure what's happening, but I don't want it to stop," said Whitney. "GG is always telling us that life is full of circles. Maybe this is one of them."

He cupped her face in his strong hands. The look in his eyes told her there was more than lust between them. "I'm here for you, Whitney. I know what I want, but it has to be right for you. And after this, I won't be all that patient."

She traced his lips with her finger before placing her lips

on his. She knew what she wanted too. Darned if it took her so long to realize it.

As they dressed and then ate dinner, they talked and talked.

Nick told her about his foolish decision to marry Crystal whom he'd always liked, but something had been missing. He explained it was more a marriage of convenience for both of them who were still living in town at that time when so many of their friends had moved on to other places and careers.

Whitney told him the gritty details of her relationship with Zane, how it had affected her decision to leave Hollywood.

"But that's not the end of your acting career, is it?" Nick asked with a look of concern. "Acting, singing, dancing is what you do, who you are."

"I'll always want to be able to do certain jobs if they're offered to me, but what I've realized is that I can have a full life away from acting. In fact, that's what I'm choosing to do. Lilac Lake is a wonderful community, and I can have a rich life here, working on Zane's charity, doing things I like. But if an opportunity comes up for a part that I want, I'll take it, providing everything is right with it."

"Good," said Nick. "That's one thing I learned from Crystal the hard way. I don't want to repeat that mistake. But my life is here in Lilac Lake. My mom is still here, and I'm keeping an eye on her."

"As you've done since you were a child. I remember that," said Whitney, giving his hand a squeeze.

"Yeah, I guess that's how I got started in police work," said Nick, pulling his fingers through his dark curls. As a kid, he'd protected his mother from her violent husband until she found the strength and courage to end the marriage.

They took ice water out to the patio and continued talking.

Whitney noticed with amusement that Mindy stretched out by Nick's feet, a sure sign of trust and affection.

When at last, Nick stood and said, "Guess I'd better go."

"Do you want to spend the night?" Whitney asked, feeling suddenly shy. When had she ever said that to a man with so much hope?

"Are you sure?" Nick said, and she knew he was asking for more than the invitation she'd extended.

Whitney decided not to mince words. "Yes, I want to see where this relationship takes us."

Nick wrapped his arms around her. "Me, too."

Whitney looked up at him. "But I don't want to make a big announcement about our being together. I want to be free of any expectations from others so we can enjoy ourselves at our own pace."

"As police chief I'm privy to a lot of information about folks in town. No need for us to be part of that kind of gossip."

Satisfied, Whitney snuggled against Nick's chest, wondering if this was the new beginning GG had hoped for her.

CHAPTER SIXTEEN
WHITNEY

In the early hours of the morning, Whitney stood in her robe at the front door watching Nick quietly back his truck out of the driveway. What a fabulous night it had been, with more talk and more loving. Now that she'd committed to dating him exclusively, she realized how much she'd missed spending time with a man she not only admired but could see herself falling in love with.

She looked over at a figure hurrying toward her and sighed.

"What are you doing up so early?" Dani asked, hugging her. "Where's Nick going?"

Whitney hid a groan. There went the plans to keep her new relationship with Nick private. "He's gone back to his house to get ready for work. Dani, please, we want to keep this quiet for as long as we can."

Dani grinned and shook her head. "Then you'd better not show yourselves around town. The two of you together are hot, hot, hot! Besides, what's the problem? You're both free to do what you want." Dani elbowed her. "So, how was it?"

Whitney couldn't help laughing at Dani's enthusiasm. "Nick is the wonderful boy he was times a hundred now that he's a man. We've always had that certain connection, you know?"

"Oh, yeah. We all do." Dani grinned at her. "I'm so happy for you, Whit. You and Nick are perfect together. But I won't spread any gossip about it except to Taylor. She'll be thrilled for you both."

"Don't say a word to GG. I want to be sure this relationship is one Nick and I both want to continue. We've each made mistakes in the past."

"Okay, but you know how this town is. If she asks you about it, it won't be because of me. But the glow on your face tells a story of its own." Dani became serious. "Did he tell you about his meeting with JoEllen?"

"Yes, and it's pretty sad, actually." Whitney gave Dani the details and then shook her head. "I don't want to pursue this issue with her, but JoEllen had better understand the Gilford girls stand together, so she'd better stop bugging you and Brad."

"Amen," said Dani. "I've got to go. Have a good day, sis."

"You, too," said Whitney. After sharing a goodbye kiss with Nick earlier, the day was already fabulous.

Later, Whitney received a phone call from the company in Boston where she'd ordered most of the furniture for the cottage. Another delay. Sighing with frustration, she decided to go to the house to make a list of the smaller items she still needed for the cottage. She'd set aside some of those choices, waiting until the furniture arrived. But now, she decided to go ahead and select a few more final touches for the décor. The house they were renting was going on the market at the end of September, and they needed to be out a few days earlier.

She drove to the Lilac Lake Inn and paused to see the progress on it. Aaron was overseeing construction there. Noticing him, she got out of the car. The exterior of the main lodge was pretty much the same, although skylights had been added along with a kitchen addition that any chef would love. The two former guestroom wings had been replaced by larger ones that were more modern in design but would retain some of the more rustic interior features of the main building to make them compatible. Things like paneled walls in the hallways and pine trim in the rooms. The result of the renovation so far was a major improvement from the simple, rustic inn GG had successfully overseen for years. And the lakefront setting amidst evergreens and lilac bushes couldn't be more beautiful.

"Looks like things are moving along," Whitney said to Aaron.

He smiled at her. "It's going to be spectacular when it's done. The exterior is almost finished. Then the tedious work on the interior will begin. That's the part that guests will notice most, and the finishing touches have to be done carefully."

"I can't think of a better company to do it than Collister Construction."

He grinned. "You sound like Dani's sister, all right. She's our biggest cheerleader."

Whitney returned his smile. "She loves being part of the team. You're lucky to have her."

"I know it," said Aaron agreeably. "Where are you off to?"

"The cottage. I need to figure out some finishing touches myself."

"Want me to go with you to keep you safe from the ghost?"

She laughed. "No, thanks. I'm fine. We haven't seen any sign of the ghost lately."

"But you still haven't done the attic yet. Mind if I make a suggestion?" At the shake of her head, he continued. "Why don't you open up that space by ripping out the exterior wall facing the lake and add a balcony for some additional sunning space? Think of the views you could have from there. You don't really need an extra room, and you haven't decided on a screened porch. This could be an easy fix to a space whose use has always been questionable."

Whitney felt her eyes widen. "What a super plan."

"Something to think about. Brad and I wanted to buy the cottage at one time, and it's an idea I once had."

Elated by the thought, Whitney said, "Let me talk it over with Dani and Taylor. Opening up the space would be one way to get rid of the ghost hiding up there."

"It's not as easy as it sounds. We'd have to cantilever the balcony and decide how far back into the cottage structure the beams would have to go in order to meet all the building codes. Some sliding-glass doors to close the room off in colder weather would add a nice finishing touch. But it can be done."

"I love the idea—a private nest overlooking the world around us."

His dark eyes flashed approval. "That's how I see it too."

Whitney was still thinking about Aaron's suggestion when she pulled up to the cottage. It still hadn't been painted the warm gray she'd chosen, and now she was glad. Best to wait until the entire work was completed before doing that. And until the painting was done, the landscaping would have to wait. At the cottage, she parked her car and decided to look at the attic space before calling her sisters. She wanted to be able to envision how it would look so she could sell them on the plan.

She entered the house and stood a moment by the front entrance. Studying the interior now, no one would guess how awful it had looked before. Gone were the ordinary closed-off rooms, replaced by openness and sunshine that combined to give anyone a warm greeting.

Dani had done a fantastic job of rearranging space. Whitney knew her contributions of color inside helped to show it off.

She headed upstairs. There, too, she took a moment to look

around. Now, the master bedroom and two bedrooms were spacious and adaptable. For the bedrooms, Whitney had chosen a woodland theme with green walls and light-wood furniture. The wooden floors would be covered in part by a handwoven rag rugs in various blues and greens, reflecting the colors of the woods and the sky.

She moved to the door to the attic. As she'd learned to do from her sisters, she said quietly, "We wish you no harm," as she opened it. She didn't know whether it was necessary, but she chose to honor the words Aaron had first spoken when entering the house with Taylor.

She flipped on the light and climbed the stairs feeling a coldness wash through her. "Stop it," she told herself and walked onto the landing. The three windows facing the lake allowed sunlight through them in lemony slices. Thinking of what Aaron had suggested, she imagined the outer wall and windows gone, an expanse of sliding glass doors with a cantilevered balcony beyond it and sighed with pleasure.

She walked over to the windows and peered outside to get a better view. A shadow reflected in the glass moved behind her. She whipped around. Seeing nothing, she once again told herself to calm down and realized a cloud had passed by the sun causing shadows.

Able now to visualize it, she couldn't wait to tell her sisters about it. No doubt there'd be extra cost, but she was willing to donate the difference between what had been set aside and the actual expense. If all went well with her conversation with her sisters, maybe the work could start right away.

She sprinted down the stairs and closed the attic door behind her. At the sound of someone walking on the first floor below, she froze.

"Whitney? Are you here?" came a voice that set her heart racing.

She went to the stairway and looked down at Nick's smiling face. "What are you doing here?"

"Aaron called me on personal business and when he told me he met up with you as you were heading to the cottage, I thought I'd surprise you."

"Thanks," Whitney said, hurrying down the stairs to greet him.

He opened his arms, and as she rushed into them, she saw sparkles of light around him. He kissed her and a warmth rushed through her.

"I've thought about you all morning," he murmured, cupping her face in his hands and gazing at her with such love tears swam in Whitney's eyes. She thought she heard a sigh and realized a breeze had entered the house through the open door.

"Are you cold?" Nick asked her.

"What? No, but thanks." She nestled closer to him wanting to feel every inch of his body next to hers.

"How about lunch at the café?" Nick asked, rubbing her back.

"Dani says once everyone sees us together, they'll know about us. Are you ready for that?" she asked him.

"The better question is, are you ready?" Nick asked, his gaze penetrating her.

She drew a deep breath. After being with him like this, feeling whole with him, she didn't care who knew they'd chosen to be together. "I am."

"Good. Then let's go," he said, kissing her once more.

They walked to the front door and outside.

As Whitney turned to lock the door, she noticed a streak of sunlight falling across the floor of the living room where she and Nick had stood. It seemed appropriate, as if their love were still shining there.

When they walked into the café, Crystal and several others turned to them. Whitney smiled at Nick, who winked at her, and they found seats outside on the patio in the shade. She loved being able to eat in the open air like this.

Excited about the idea Aaron had come up with, Whitney told Nick about the plans.

"The views of the White Mountains from there should be fabulous. It's going to be a very special house when you're done with it."

"I think so too," she said. With Dani moving in with Brad and Taylor moving to New York City, it would be up to her to make sure the house was lived in. That brought a smile to her face. Telling herself to slow down, she nevertheless wondered how Nick would feel spending time there with her.

After their order had been taken and food delivered, Crystal walked up to the table, pulled out a chair, and sat down, beaming at them. "I see this has finally happened."

"What do you mean?" said Whitney, unable to stop a smile.

"The two of you together are perfect. It shows on your faces—that certain satisfaction that comes from choosing right." She turned to Nick and said quietly, "I'm thrilled for you, Nick. You know I am. I hope I find my Mr. Right soon. I've got a sudden yearning to make something work."

Nick covered Crystal's hand with his. "I know you will, Crystal. It just wasn't me."

"You're such a good man, but not right for me. I always knew it was Whitney."

Whitney remained quiet listening to the interchange. It was rare for exes to talk like this, and she was grateful that both Crystal and Nick were such kind people. In this small town, Crystal's acceptance of their new relationship was important.

Crystal turned to her. "I'm happy for you, Whitney. I guess this means you'll be staying in town for a while."

"Yes. My career is presently on hold. And I still have all that work to do for Zane's foundation. In fact, I'm hoping for some input from you this winter when things calm down for you."

"The ski crowd shows up then, but it isn't busy like summers," said Crystal. "And you know I'm always glad to help however I can. You're the one friend who understands my need to be involved with the theater."

Whitney grinned. "That's why I'm hoping to talk to you about a couple of ideas."

"I'll be ready when you are. I'm hiring someone to help me with the café in the fall. We'll see what happens from there." She glanced around the restaurant. "Better get back to my customers."

After she left the table, Nick said, "Crystal and I are friends who married for the wrong reasons. I admire Crystal for her achievement with the café."

"She deserves it after all the work she's done to change her life."

Nick reached across the table, and squeezed her hand. "You're a success too. I don't want to be the one to ruin it for you."

Whitney gazed into his eyes and smiled. "I appreciate that, and there is no way you could ruin it for me."

They finished in companionable silence and then Nick said, "I'd better get back to work. It's been quiet, but it won't stay that way with a weekend coming up."

Whitney gathered her purse. "I've got to be in touch with my sisters so we can make a decision about the balcony idea Aaron mentioned. You're welcome to come for dinner. It won't be fancy, but I'd love to have you."

He chuckled. "In that case, I'd love to come and have you."
They laughed together.

CHAPTER SEVENTEEN
TAYLOR

Sitting on the beach along the south shore of Long Island with Cooper and his friends, Taylor was relieved to get a call from Whitney. She picked up her phone and walked away from the group.

"Hi, what's going on?" she asked Whitney.

"Aaron has come up with a suggestion that I want to pursue at the cottage." Whitney told her about the plans and promised her willingness to pay any extra fees associated with it.

"I love it," said Taylor. "No need to worry about you paying for it until Dani does a budget for us. We can all chip in. What does Dani say about it? She's the architect."

"I haven't spoken to her yet. I thought I'd drive out to The Meadows and see her there. How are you? Where are you?"

"I'm at the beach with Cooper and his friends. We're staying at his family's home, more like an estate, in Southampton on Long Island."

"Nice. How are things going?"

Taylor hesitated and then she blurted out, "His friends hate me. At least the women do. They're catty. They think I'm a dumb Southern Belle from Georgia who's managed to snag him after one of them tried and failed."

Whitney's voice was soft but firm. "Taylor, you're one of the Gilford Girls. Don't forget it. You're bright, creative, and capable. No one can take that away from you. The fact that Cooper chose you should be a sign of it, not a failure on his part. Don't let petty women try to destroy the magic you and Cooper have. Has he noticed any of this?"

"No. He and his male friends are playing volleyball while we women watch," said Taylor.

"But you're an excellent volleyball player. Why aren't you playing?" said Whitney. "Get out there."

Taylor grinned. "I was trying to follow the crowd, be accepted. But now, hearing you say this, I might join the guys."

"Go, girl," said Whitney. She hated when people tried to take advantage of Taylor because she was shy. "Let me know what happens."

"Will do," said Taylor, sounding more like her spunky self. "What's up with you?"

"Something big, actually. Nick and I are dating exclusively."

It took a moment for that to sink in, then Taylor exclaimed, "Oh my god! That's terrific!" She knew Whitney wouldn't casually mention something like this. It had to be very real.

"We'll see where it takes us, but we're very happy with the decision. It somehow feels right," said Whitney, and Taylor could hear the happiness in her voice.

"You bet it's right. One of GG's full circles," Taylor said.

Whitney chuckled softly. "That's what I thought too. Have fun, Taylor, and don't let petty women get to you. You're better than they are for staying away from that kind of behavior. Tell Cooper hi from me. Talk to you later. Thanks for the input."

Taylor clicked off the call, and with a new energy to her step headed back to the group and called out to Cooper. "How about me joining the game?"

He grinned at her. "Really? That's so cool. C'mon. You're on my team."

Soon all the women were on the volleyball court where Taylor could prove to them and herself that she had no need to apologize for who she was.

That evening, instead of going bar hopping with a group, Cooper and Taylor opted to stay home. Cooper had a sunburn and didn't feel like going out. Taylor offered to heat the meal the housekeeper had made earlier and left for them, content to have some private time with Cooper.

"How did you like my friends?" he asked as they lounged in the pool at the house.

"They were not friendly to begin with. Tabitha, especially. But now I know she was the woman you broke up with before you met me. Why didn't you mention her to me?"

Cooper looked at her with confusion. "She wasn't anyone I was ever serious with. Why would she indicate she was?"

"Maybe wishful thinking," said Taylor, leaning forward and kissing him on the lips.

He grinned and started to pull her closer and stopped. "Don't touch my back, okay?"

She raised her hand. "I promise. Just your lips."

"That's my girl," said Cooper, leaning forward.

CHAPTER EIGHTEEN
WHITNEY

Whitney waited until after play rehearsal to seek out Dani. Taylor had been right to mention Dani's role and the need for her approval.

Though it was close to dinnertime when she arrived at The Meadows, Brad and a crew of men were still working on Ross's house. Dani, she could see, was acting as gofer for them, bringing them different tools, helping in any way she could.

When she saw Whitney, Dani raised her hand and waved.

Whitney hurried over to her. "Got a minute?"

"Sure. The crew wants to get the roof done now because showers are expected later. But come sit with me under the tree. We can talk there."

Once they were settled on a blanket, they faced one another. "What's going on?" Dani asked.

Whitney drew a deep breath, hoping she'd be successful. "I want to tell you about a plan Aaron suggested for the cottage. As you are the architect in the family, Taylor and I feel you should have the final say, but we both love the plan. I've even offered to pay for any extra costs as it seems I will probably be living there more than the two of you."

"It must be fantastic if you're willing to pay," teased Dani with a twinkle in her eye.

Whitney laughed. "Hear me out." She told Dani about adding a balcony and sliding-glass doors. "I even went up to the attic to get a better idea of what it would look like."

"Hold on. You went up to the attic alone in the house?"

"Yes. We've got to get over this story a of a ghost living there."

"Did you see any special signs anywhere?" Dani asked.

Whitney thought for a moment. "Not until Nick came to surprise me. When I went to meet him, I did see those sparkly lights everyone has talked about. But that's it. Remember, it's a sunny day."

"Okay. Just asking. As to the balcony, I love it. But, Whitney, it's going to take quite a bit of extra money to do it right. We'd need to cantilever the balcony like Aaron said, redo the entire floor, think about some structural things and all. And remember, we don't want to destroy the character of the cottage, so we want to keep the proportions exactly right."

"Yes," agreed Whitney. "That's why I want you and Brad to talk to Aaron about it. The only problem I see is getting the work done quickly. We're running out of time. Our lease is almost up."

"Leave that to me," said Dani. "If I'm not mistaken, the challenge of doing this will be enough for them to focus on the work. That, of course, is something I'll encourage."

"I love you, sis," said Whitney, giving Dani a quick embrace.

She grinned. "Love you too. How's everything else going? Nick surprised you at the house?"

"He did. Oh, Dani, I think I know what you must feel being with Brad. If I'm very honest with myself, being here in Lilac Lake has brought back lovely memories of that summer with Nick and how special he was. Now that Nick and I are both grownups, our relationship is so much better, much deeper, even at this new stage."

"Be careful not to hurt one another," said Dani. "It's happening pretty quickly."

"In some ways, yes. But in other ways, it's continuation of

what we once shared. We still respect each other's wishes as far as career choices go. Even though I've stepped back from Hollywood, I love acting, and if a chance for something worthwhile comes up, I need the freedom to choose."

"Absolutely. I'm glad Nick appreciates that," said Dani.

Brad approached them. "What are you two up to now?"

"Building a balcony," said Dani. "Wanna help?"

He grinned. "Maybe. What are you talking about?"

As he stretched out on the grass beside them, Dani filled him on the details.

He sat up. "Sounds intriguing. When Aaron and I were looking at the house to buy, he never brought it up. But it's perfect. You've given the house an open, airy look, and this will complement that."

"That's what I think too," said Dani. "There's one problem. We'll need to divert some of the crew to get it done. Please?"

Brad put an arm around Dani. "For you, anything. We'll work it out."

Whitney gave Dani a thumbs-up sign, impressed by Dani's ability to get Brad to agree. But then Brad was so in love with her sister that anything was possible.

Brad left them to do some clean-up work at the site, and Whitney turned to Dani. "When I talked to Taylor, she was a little stressed by the way some of Cooper's friends were treating her. You might want to give her a call. I gave her a pep talk, but I'm curious to know how things are going."

"I'll get right on it as soon as I get home and take a shower," said Dani.

"Good, that's what sisters do for one another," said Whitney, grateful for hers.

The next morning, Whitney got out of bed and wandered down to the kitchen.

She made herself a cup of coffee and carried it out to the patio. The showers that had been promised had left drops of water on the grass and landscaping. When a burst of sunlight emerged through lingering clouds, Whitney gasped with pleasure. A thousand rainbows were reflected from raindrops acting like crystals. Mother Nature could sometimes be cruel, but she also delivered moments of awe like this.

Staring out at the yard, Whitney reflected on how her life was changing. She'd gone from feeling guilty about Zane death's to discovering new purpose with kids and now to finding love. Life seemed perfect.

Whitney clapped a hand to her heart and told herself to erase that thought. Every time life seemed perfect to her, something bad happened.

She was still feeling that way when her cell phone rang. Without checking the caller information, she snatched it up thinking it was Nick. "Hi, darling."

There was a pause at the other end, then a gruff voice said, "I've got you in my sights."

"Hello? Who is this?" she asked.

"You'll find out soon enough. Zane might be gone, but he's not forgotten. I'll make sure of it. You were the cause of all his troubles."

"Who is this?" Whitney said.

But all she heard was silence. She checked her phone for recent calls. An L.A. phone number. Feeling a coldness wash through her, Whitney decided to call her agent. She knew Barbara Griffiths well enough to know what an early riser she was.

Sure enough, Barbara answered on the third ring. "How's my favorite actress?"

"At the moment, I'm not so sure. I need your help. There's apparently a fringe group of Zane's fans who are blaming me for his death. I just got an upsetting call from what I think was one of them. A call from an L.A. number." She told Barbara what the man had said and continued, "I'm worried. There are so many crazies out there. And for some reason he has his sight on me. Can you spread some positive PR about me to counteract this kind of crap?"

"How did he get your cell phone number?" Barbara asked. "That alone is cause for concern. I suggest you change it. And why would a man be so angry with you?"

Whitney paused and then said, "Toward the end, Zane was into everything. I think he had several one-night stands with both men and women. Maybe he's one of them."

"Good heavens! I loved that boy, but he certainly got messed up with drugs," said Barbara. "If he were here now, I'd want to kill him." She laughed without mirth. "Guess it's too late to do that. But still, for such a talent to be lost to a life like that is enough to break anyone's heart."

"I know. The whole thing is enormously sad," said Whitney.

"I admire your wish to treat the memory of Zane kindly, but maybe you're doing yourself a disservice by not speaking up. As his agent, I can't badmouth him."

"I can't either. What we had in the beginning was very precious. I have to remember the man he once was, or the last four years of working with and loving him become a joke." Whitney heard the bitterness in her voice but didn't care. It was a struggle to remember those early times. Especially now with a group of his fans blaming her for driving Zane to his death.

"Is there something you can do? Maybe talk to them?" Whitney asked Barbara. "Or maybe make another announcement about Zane's death indicating his drug use?"

"I'll make some calls and see what I can do. In the

meantime, is there someone you can talk to there about this?"

"I'll speak to Nick, our police chief. I know he'll help at this end," said Whitney. She didn't tell Barbara about their relationship. That could wait until later.

"Okay, keep me informed. Call me anytime. I'm concerned and will do what I can at this end."

"Thanks." Whitney said.

"Kiss, kiss," Barbara said and ended the call.

Whitney sat back in her seat, feeling totally lost. What had Zane told others to make them so upset? Or was this a case of someone wishing they could blame her for something gone wrong in his life? Either way, it hurt.

She punched in Nick's number.

"Good morning," Nick said cheerfully. "Did you miss me as much as I missed you?"

"More," she said smiling. She told Nick about the phone call. "I'm worried that this is a real crazy person who somehow has gotten his life mixed up with Zane's and wants to do me harm."

"Give me the phone number. I'll put a trace on it," said Nick crisply, indicating his concern. "And if you see anything unusual, anything at all, let me know. We can't pretend this isn't serious."

"I know. I'm relieved you understand my concern."

Nick's voice softened. "I love you, Whitney. I never want anything bad to happen to you. I'll do everything I can to make sure you're safe."

Whitney's eyes filled. She loved him too but hadn't told him.

They talked a few more minutes and then after she ended the call, she went online and changed her Verizon cell phone number. With some thought, she decided to drive into Portsmouth to get a new phone. She needed an upgrade anyway, and the thought of that nasty message on her old phone was disturbing to her.

Portsmouth was an interesting port city on the coast at the southeastern corner of the state, leading into Maine. For a small city, it was quite remarkable. Lovely 17th- and 18th- Century homes in town included several within the "Strawbery Banke Museum" where costumed staff demonstrated traditional crafts. GG had made sure the girls visited the museum several times as they were growing up, so they'd have an appreciation of how history had changed things. And that's not all Portsmouth offered tourists. A submarine was on display in a park, and Market Square had cute shops and restaurants.

She'd been driving awhile when Whitney remembered the unfamiliar car that she'd seen parked outside their cul de sac. She hadn't paid attention to it and knew only that it was a dark gray color. She'd tell Nick about it, and next time, she'd be more observant.

It bothered her that she was being unjustly blamed for Zane's death. Any sane person could follow his career from the height of success and see where drug use had led. Didn't this man understand that? Was he a druggie too? Was that why he was being so unreasonable?

Whitney's thoughts flew to Zane's behavior when he was stoned and worse. He was like a Dr. Jekyll and Mr. Hyde creature come to life, his goodness blocked by his inner demons. She sighed and drove on.

In town, Whitney drove to the Verizon store and went inside. It took less time than she thought it would to purchase a new phone and have all her information from her old phone transferred to it. Leaving the store, a new sense of comfort filled her. No one would be able to call her except the few people who had to have her new number—family, friends, and her agent, Barbara.

Whitney decided to go to the waterfront for lunch at an old favorite of hers, the River House on Bow Street. She already knew what she was going to eat. Her mouth watered at the thought.

As usual, the restaurant was busy with tourists and locals alike. On a beautiful day like this, it was the perfect place to eat.

She was seated on the outdoor deck next to the railing. As she waited for her waitress to come to her, she breathed in the smell of the river water and let out a sigh of satisfaction. A few boats were on the water, and the decks of a nearby restaurant were also crowded with people for her to watch.

She smiled as the waitress approached. "I already know what I'm going to have. You do have the lobster roll and chowder special today, don't you?"

The waitress grinned back at her. "It's our special every day. And what would you like to drink?"

"Lemon water, please," said Whitney, her mood upbeat. What had been an upsetting day was turning into a nice one. No one had recognized her with her straw hat and sunglasses, which made things so much easier.

Whitney took the time to send messages to her parents, GG, and her sisters, giving them the new number. She hesitated and then sent another message to Barbara, reassuring her that the old number was gone.

Her lunch, when it came, was delicious—Maine lobster served on a toasted brioche roll, a cup of seafood chowder, and hand cut potato chips. Whitney was very full by the end of her meal, but it was a good feeling. She'd promised herself she wouldn't go crazy eating a lot while she wasn't working, but a splurge like this was worth every calorie.

She'd paid and was about to leave when a young woman came over to her. "You're Whitney Gilford, aren't you?"

Whitney nodded and then braced herself.

The woman shook a finger at her. "What's the deal with you and Zane? How could you wreck his life? He was doing fine until he met you and then you broke up."

Tired of this kind of bullshit, Whitney said quietly but firmly, "I wasn't the cause of his death. Drugs were. He was deep into them when he overdosed."

The woman's eyes widened. "Really? That's not what all the Instagram posts say."

"Well, it's time to put a stop to that. Will you help me?" Whitney said.

"Me? How?" The woman edged away from her.

"Don't believe everything you read on some site. I tried to convince Zane to get help. I begged and pleaded, but he wouldn't listen to me," Whitney pleaded. "Now, I'm getting unfairly blamed." She got up from the table and moved quickly to the exit, anxious for others not to recognize her. The lunch that she'd loved roiled in her stomach. She was so mad she could hardly breathe. It had been several weeks since Zane had died. Who kept those rumors going?

On the way home, Taylor called her. "What's up with the new cell phone number? Are you in trouble?"

"Not really. This morning, I got a nasty call and decided to change my number. I don't know what's happening, but someone is spreading rumors about Zane dying because of me and our break-up. It was the drugs. He overdosed and though we thought it was intentional, it was decided it wasn't. The news reports all said that."

"I didn't realize this was going on. Are you safe?" Taylor asked, her concern evident.

"I've told Nick and my agent about the issue. Nick's trying to trace the number now. If things get really bad, I'll move in with him."

"It's great that he's on it," said Taylor. "Keep me informed. By the way, thanks for the pep talk earlier. I ended up organizing a whole new volleyball game and getting everyone, including the women, involved. It turned out to be a good move. Cooper's old girlfriend and I will never be close, but I made friends with some other people."

"I'm glad, Taylor. I need to remind myself that we Gilford sisters are strong, and I shouldn't let gossip mar my happiness. But it's easier said than done."

"I can imagine," said Taylor. "Dani called me, and she's excited about the balcony idea. I'm glad that's going to happen. And sooner rather than later. If things get worse for you, maybe you can hide out at the cottage. No one could find you there."

"Not even Mrs. Maynard's ghost?" said Whitney, trying to inject some humor into the situation.

"You know, like it or not. I think we should have one of Crystal's friends who's into such things help us get rid of our unwanted ghost in the cottage."

"We might have to do that soon," said Whitney. She didn't want either of her sisters to feel uncomfortable in the cottage. It was turning into a beautiful property.

On a whim, Whitney decided to call Barbara to ask her to make a new announcement about Zane's death in the hope of stopping the hurtful blame games that were going on.

A male voice answered. "Barbara Griffith's phone."

"Is Barbara there?" Whitney asked, puzzled by a man answering her phone.

"Yes, but she's busy with a client. I'm her new assistant. Her old one has left."

"Oh, I see," said Whitney. "I'll call later."

"May I take a message?" the man asked.

"No, thank you," she said, suddenly wary. She ended the call and sat back. Barbara's assistant, Diana, had been with her for almost five years. It seemed strange that Barbara hadn't mentioned a new assistant. Must be a recent change.

A few minutes later, Barbara called her. "Sorry, I couldn't take the call. Todd told me you called."

"Todd? What happened to Diana?" Whitney asked.

"She and her boyfriend are moving to Hawaii," said Barbara. "He's got work there, and she agreed to go with him. She's hoping to marry him, but I don't see that happening. Not that she's listening to me."

"That's too bad. I called to ask you to put out another notice about Zane's death, telling the real story once more, that it was due to an overdose caused by a long drug habit." Whitney sighed. "Apparently there are a lot of rumors on Instagram and other social media outlets. We need to stop this. I was confronted by a fan when I was having lunch in Portsmouth, New Hampshire, for god's sake."

"Okay, dear girl, I'll do what I can. Any news on the caller this morning?" Barbara asked.

"Not yet. I'll let you know."

"Okay. Must run. Kiss. Kiss." Barbara ended the call.

Whitney made her way back home, each mile closer brought a sense of relief. When she drove by the lake and entered the outskirts of the town of Lilac Lake, she felt as if it was a haven for her.

CHAPTER NINETEEN
WHITNEY

Whitney was ready to have a quiet evening with Nick. The trip to Portsmouth had given her a break she needed but had twisted into something unpleasant. More than ever, it felt good to be at home in Lilac Lake.

Nick arrived a little late but handed her a bottle of wine as he apologized. "I wanted to wait until I had time to trace the phone number you gave me. Unfortunately, the number came from a burner phone, so it won't be of much help. I'm glad you had your phone number changed. That might take care of the situation."

"I hope so. I didn't do much on social media in the past, but now all of my accounts have been taken down. Others may hear what they're saying about me, but I won't be able to respond."

"Yes, any response you might make would add fuel to the situation," warned Nick. "Aside from that, any unusual activity around?"

"I forgot to mention I saw an unfamiliar car parked by the cul de sac recently. I didn't pay much attention to it. All I know is that it was a dark gray sedan."

"Has it returned?" Nick asked.

"No," said Whitney. "But it's usually quiet enough here in the neighborhood that I noticed it. I'll let you know if I see it again."

"Okay. Deal. I'm inclined to think it's a disgruntled fan, nothing more. But as I told you, I'll do anything to keep you safe." He came over to her and put his arms around her. "I love you, Whitney. I always have."

She hugged him to her, loving the shape, size, and smell of him. They were perfect together, Whitney thought, as their lips met.

A few minutes later, Nick pulled away and smiled at her. "You make me feel like a horny kid again."

She laughed. "I sometimes feel the same way when I'm with you. We had a special relationship back then. This is even better."

He drew her to him once more and whispered in her ear, "I love you, Whitney."

She looked up at him and smiled. "I love you, too." It felt so satisfying finally to say it.

He cupped her face in his hands and gave her a loving look. "I'll always be here for you."

"I know," she said softly and met his kiss.

At their feet, Mindy growled for attention.

Laughing, Whitney pulled away from Nick. "Guess who's jealous?"

"Okay, little lady. Let's see what's for dinner," said Nick, picking up Mindy and chuckling as her kisses covered his cheek.

"I thought we'd have a green salad with cooked eggs, tomatoes, bacon, and sliced chicken. That, and some fresh bread from the market. Is that going to be enough for you?"

"Sounds good. I don't like to eat too heavily at night," said Nick. "I never know when I might have a call to deal with a problem. It doesn't happen often, but when it does, I want to be ready."

"Good. Why don't you pour the wine, and I'll fix a plate of cheese and crackers as an appetizer. You liked that the other night."

"Perfect." He set Mindy down and accepted the wine opener she handed him.

Later, after their simple meal, Nick got a call about a fight at one of the bars outside of town. Apologizing for having to leave, he tugged her into a hug and kissed her deeply. "I'll make this up to you."

"No problem," Whitney said, hiding her disappointment. "I understand. It's all part of your job."

Left alone, Whitney decided to look up some items online. She knew what she wanted for a lamp in her bedroom but hadn't found it yet.

Later, she was sitting in the kitchen when she heard a car approach. Thinking it was Nick, she went to the front window and looked out. A dark-gray sedan drove by, circled, and drove past again. Whitney hid behind the curtain and tried to search for a license plate number, but it was too dark to see. She could tell it was a New Hampshire plate, though she couldn't tell whether the driver was male or female.

After the car left, she locked the front door and called Nick.

"As soon as I can, I'll finish here and come stay at your house. There was no hesitating in front of the house? Anything that was out of the ordinary except driving by twice?"

"Nothing. They simply drove away."

"Though it could be nothing more than someone looking at the house that will be going up for sale, I'll come as quickly as I can."

Whitney ended the call and slumped into a kitchen chair. She didn't want to make it seem worse than it was, but something was going on. Against her own advice, Whitney did some research online and found the group called The Zaniacs. Whitney's impression of the people she saw in a few posted photographs was one of surprise. She'd expected to see young people, mostly women, but some middle-aged women and a lot of men were shown. She wondered how much of a secret life Zane had lived. It felt surreal to see her name bandied about carelessly with such anger. There was no mention of last names, but a few first names showed up, among them the name Todd.

Whitney's thoughts flew to Barbara's new assistant. She checked the time and called Barbara, hoping to get her at home.

Barbara answered on the first ring. "Whitney, how are you? Anything happening with that group of Zane's fans?"

"I'm not sure, but I wanted to ask you about your new assistant. The name Todd came up in the group. Do you think he'd be part of them?"

"I can't imagine it. I checked all his references before hiring him. He's an ambitious young man who wants to get ahead in the industry and become an agent one day. He was very open about that."

Deflated, Whitney said, "Okay, it was just a thought. If you ever hear or see anything that might link him to the group, will you please let me know?"

"Of course. Things okay there?"

"I guess. Thanks." Whitney ended the call glad Nick was staying the night.

The next couple of days were busy. Ross and his friends put on another clinic for the kids. Joining them at the park, Whitney was happy to see so many boys and girls participating. Parents, mostly fathers, stood around watching, silently urging their children to do well.

But as Ross had done earlier, he emphasized the importance of trying and a willingness to learn. Jamie's father stood aside watching the activity. Jamie was next to him looking miserable.

She walked over to them. "Hi, Jamie. Hi, Bud. Nice to see you here. Ross and his friends are doing a great job of giving everyone a chance to show their skills."

"Some of us need to practice," growled Bud, nudging Jamie.

Jamie glanced at her and turned away, embarrassed.

"Practice is important for everyone," Whitney said. "Not only a few."

Bud focused his gaze on her, his brown eyes darkening.

Whitney stepped back. Then, before she could change her mind, she said to Bud, "Jamie's a talented boy."

He grunted and glared at her.

She said, "See you later, Jamie," and left before she could make the situation with Bud worse.

When she had a moment with Ross, she reminded him to talk about the upcoming play. "And Jamie. How did he do with catching balls?"

Ross frowned. "I can see that he's a good player, but his father makes him nervous."

"That's what I thought. Thanks for doing this, Ross. It's really nice that you and your friends are willing to give this kind of time to the kids."

"No problem," said Ross. "It's a rewarding way to keep busy."

They smiled at one another, and then she left to get the storage shed ready for a dress rehearsal. Time was drawing near.

After seeing that things were set, Whitney went to the cottage. Dani was there with Brad and Aaron, who were taking an initial look at the attic.

As she drove up the driveway, she studied the house. It was

beautifully situated on the land, facing the lake on a slight knoll. She was pleased to see Brad's truck was already there. She parked her car, got out, and went to the front of the house. Whitney gazed up at the third floor of the house and gasped. The windows had been torn out and some of the front wall as well.

She hurried onto the porch to the front door. It was open. Whitney stepped inside and called out, "Hello? Dani, Brad? Aaron?"

"Here," said Dani, coming to the top of the stairs. "I heard you drive in. Come on up."

Whitney moved quickly up the stairway, her pulse racing. The most unusual room in the house was about to become reality.

Dani greeted her at the head of the stairs. "Wait until you see what a difference it makes to have this open space."

Brad and Aaron were cutting through the exterior wall.

"They'll have to rip up the flooring to determine how best to cantilever the balcony," said Dani. "It's making an awful mess, but it'll all be worth it. The room looks brighter already."

Whitney stood beside Dani grinning as broadly as she. It was such a cool difference. She stepped back and stood in the shadows, watching the men work. As she was about to leave, she noticed a piece of white paper stuck under a floorboard and bent over to see what it was. She tugged on it and pulled out part of a ripped envelope.

"Dani, look," she cried, holding up the fragment.

"What is it?" Dani asked, coming right over to her.

"It's part of an envelope. The name R. A. Thomas is visible but that's all. The rest has been torn away."

Dani took the envelope and studied it. "The postage stamp is dated August 2001 in Portsmouth, New Hampshire."

"A new mystery," said Whitney, feeling a sweep of cold

behind her.

"We're going to have to do more investigation," said Dani. "It might be tied to our ghost."

"That's a long shot," said Whitney. "R. A. Thomas could live anywhere. All we know is the letter was sent from Portsmouth, not Lilac Lake. That's not a lot to go on."

"I know," said Dani. "But each little piece of information might help us. In the meantime, we're creating a gorgeous house for ourselves, something GG will be thrilled about."

The men stopped working and came over to them. "We'll bring a couple more guys over here and see what we're dealing with," said Aaron. "I can't wait to see how this puzzle is going to fit together."

Whitney grinned. "If it weren't for you, this might not even be taking place. Thanks for the idea."

Aaron tipped his baseball cap. "Anything for the Gilford girls."

Still chuckling, Whitney followed Dani down the stairs.

CHAPTER TWENTY
WHITNEY

As promised, Pam Sawyer showed up at play rehearsal with her daughter. Whitney was happy to see her because she hoped to get her input on ideas for future productions both in the community and hopefully within the school system.

A buzz of excitement rose from the children as they took their places on the stage in their costumes. The five kids working on sets had painted a large canvas with bunches of flowers, a blue sky, and a vibrant yellow sun.

"It's wonderful that the children have had this summertime activity. It's kept them busy with a creative, positive experience," said Pam, smiling at Whitney. "I'm so glad you decided to come back to Lilac Lake after your troubles in Hollywood."

"Thanks. I like it here," said Whitney.

"It must be difficult to deal with all the recent negativity your career has brought you. I'm here if you ever want to talk about it."

"Thanks, but what are you referring to?" Whitney asked. Was there more trouble from the Zaniacs?

"I'm sorry, I don't mean to intrude. It's simply that I've seen some of the online comments and threats about your part in Zane Blanchard's death." Pam gave her a worried look.

"Yes," said Whitney grimly. "People love to blame me for something I had no control over. It's pretty scary."

Pam placed a hand on her shoulder. "They'll find another victim for their venom. Give it a little more time and, hopefully, the worst will be over."

"I certainly hope so. I don't understand how people can be so hateful," said Whitney.

"Mom, we're ready," said Elissa, looking adorable in her mouse costume.

"Okay, honey," Pam said. She turned to Whitney. "I'll help with the costumes."

Whitney went over the script with the young actors, delighted by their growth and enthusiasm. They would be performing for a younger audience. Whitney was confident those kids were in for a treat.

When at last she felt the performers were ready, Whitney said, "Okay, everybody. On Sunday afternoon we'll meet at the community center at two o'clock for a quick rehearsal and at three thirty, we'll put on the play. It's going to be a long, exciting afternoon, so get plenty of rest."

"Afterwards, Elissa and I will host a cast party at our house for you kids and your parents," announced Pam.

"How nice," said Whitney.

"It's the least we can do for all the work you've put into this project, Whitney. We know most of the families through teaching in the schools and have already talked to them."

"Can I help in any way?" Whitney asked.

"Just bring yourself and Nick," Pam said, grinning when Whitney's face turned pink. "You can't hide anything in Lilac Lake. I'm very happy you two have found one another."

Whitney shook her head. "Nothing goes unnoticed, huh?"

"That's about the truth," Pam admitted. "But the people here are generally lovely and very supportive, and Nick is a favorite in town."

Later, as Whitney told Taylor in a phone call, "Small-town living is totally different from anything I've known. But I'm growing to like it."

"I'm glad, especially knowing how much you care for Nick," said Taylor. "How are you going to feel being married to the police chief?"

"Whoa! We've agreed to date exclusively, but marriage hasn't come up. It's a little early for that," said Whitney.

"Dani and I have proven how fast a decision like that can be," said Taylor laughing. "But each in her own time. Gotta run. I'm going sailing with Cooper."

"Sounds like fun. Thanks for the call." Whitney ended the conversation and smiled. This summer was proving to be a thrilling one for all three Gilford girls.

Labor Day weekend arrived with a burst of late summer heat. But Whitney could already smell a bit of fall in the early morning air that Sunday. She sat on the patio sipping her coffee anticipating the day ahead. Nick had left to go to work. Though it might be a holiday for some, for him, the weekend would be busy.Dani called over the fence between their houses, "Are you up for company? We're starting late today, and I'd love to see you."

"Come on over," said Whitney pleased. "Coffee's ready anytime you are." It pleased her to be able to see her sister so often. For years, their schedules and locations had meant spending time together only at the holidays and little else.

Dani came over with Pirate. The black lab and Mindy, best of friends, were soon chasing each other in the backyard.

Whitney and Dani watched them, chatting easily.

"I'll try to come and see the play today, but I promised to help Brad's mom with the farm stand this afternoon. It's a super busy time for them."

"No problem. How are you and Mary Lou getting along?"

"Fine. She's a warm, loving person. She and Mom are

talking every so often and seem to like one another, which makes it very nice for their talks about the wedding."

"Thank goodness Taylor is planning a fancy one. That takes some of the pressure off you for having a small ceremony here," said Whitney.

"Brad and I are working hard to get our house done. Working on three or four houses at once makes it easy because the subcontractors know what we expect and can work at the site in one house or another without wasting any time."

"Sounds good," said Whitney. "The fact that you can give them a steady stream of work is helpful too, I would imagine."

"Yes, we sold another lot. Aaron and Brad are looking into buying more land there. We'll see," said Dani. "I'm so proud to be a part of their development. And, of course, I'm setting up my own consulting company, too."

"You told me Anthony Albono was pleased with your work and may want you to do more for him," said Whitney.

"Yes. He's such a strong supporter of mine. I've promised to invite him and his wife to my wedding. They've been very sweet to me."

"That's nice," said Whitney. She was pleased Dani was finally getting some recognition for her talent.

"I hope things work out between you and Nick," said Dani. "I saw him downtown the other day, and he was beaming."

"We're being open with each other but careful, too. We aren't going to be foolish by moving too fast. It's a huge leap of faith for us to be together again, but it feels so right. Looking back, we had a very special relationship as kids."

"Yes, that's why everyone is happy to see you two together. Like you said, it seems so right," said Dani. She lifted her coffee cup. "Here's to the two of you."

Laughing, Whitney raised her cup. "Here's to all the Gilford Girls."

"Amen," said Dani. She got to her feet. "Guess I'd better go. I told Mary Lou I'd get there by ten." She whistled for Pirate.

Whitney walked them to the door and then returned to the kitchen, wondering what Nick's mother was like. She had a vague recollection of a quiet, pretty woman who adored her son. Once abused, she'd never remarried and lived in a modest home in the same neighborhood as Jamie's family and still worked in the regional library.

When Nick was ready, Whitney knew he'd ask her to meet with his mother. Until then, Whitney would let it remain Nick's decision.

When Whitney arrived at the community center, the kids were all but jumping around in their excitement, bringing a smile to her. She greeted Pam and another mother, Susan Jenkins, whose son, Samuel, was in the play.

"This is a day we've all waited for. I know it's going to be good," said Whitney.

"Samuel is so pleased to be part of this, even if he has only one line," said Susan.

Whitney grinned. "'Look! There she goes.' is an important line. That's the thing about plays. Each line is part of the whole."

Susan laughed. "I love what you're doing with the kids."

Whitney gathered the kids in a circle around her. "Okay, let's work together to get the scenery and props ready, then we'll do a quick read through and then you can get in your costumes."

The large painting of flowers and blue sky was mounted on a portable white board, plants and potted flowers were placed about, and the pet bird of one of the girls chirped in his cage.

Whitney stood back and looked at the scenery with satisfaction. "You kids have done a marvelous job." She held up the programs which someone in the community center office had printed up. They were decorated with pictures of flowers and an outdoor scene. "And, Jamie, your drawings on the program really dress them up. Thank you."

A huge grin broke across Jamie's face. "I like drawing."

Linda, from Linda's Dance Studio, arrived. "Anything I can do to help?"

Whitney smiled. "All we need to do now is run through the lines. Then you can help kids with their costumes."

"Okay. Can't wait to see how my dance kids do. They've planned a little surprise for the end. I hope you won't mind."

Whitney studied her. "You approve?"

"Oh, yes. It's very touching."

"Then I won't worry about it. After all, the play would never happen without your encouragement."

By three thirty as the play was about to begin, the floor in front of the stage held at least two dozen toddlers sitting with older siblings. Adults sat in chairs behind them, seeming as eager as the kids. Whitney noticed Jamie's mother and his siblings enter the building. His father didn't join them.

Whitney stepped onto the stage. "Welcome to the first production by the Lilac Lake Children's Theater Group. We're pleased to present the play *'A Mouse's Mistake'*. Lucy, the mouse, loves to brag about herself. But what happens when she loses her squeak? Sit back, relax, and enjoy the show." She held up a finger to her lips. "Everyone quiet now."

Pam pulled the curtain open, and the play began.

Later, after what seemed no time at all, applause rang out.

While people were clapping, the actors and crew lined up across the front of the stage and began to do a soft-shoe dance.

Whitney watched, as amazed and pleased as the rest of the audience.

"Thank you to the kids at Linda's Dance Studio for that

little bit of entertainment," said Whitney. "A surprise for us all."

As applause filled the room, Whitney watched the kids take a bow, their faces aglow with accomplishment. She could remember times like this when as a child, she had participated in a theatrical event, and she filled with joy at the thought of providing the same opportunity to these children.

Backstage, she reminded everyone about the party at the Sawyer's house. "Remember, you and your families are invited."

Linda helped the kids with their costumes, and a few of the parents quickly helped dismantle the stage.

Whitney turned to see Jamie, his mother, and his siblings waiting for her. "Sorry, I took so long. Mrs. Thompkins."

"No problem. I just wanted to thank you for all the work you've done. And please, call me Sandra. The girls and I enjoyed seeing the play, even when Lily fell asleep." Sandra gave Whitney a shy smile. "I'm glad Jamie could be part of this."

"Your husband wasn't here to see it?" Whitney asked.

Sandra's lips thinned. "He's at home sleeping. He got in last night."

"I see. Well, I hope you're coming to the picnic at Elissa's parents' house."

"Thanks, we are. Pam spoke to me about it."

As Whitney helped load the three little ones into Sandra's car, she wondered if that's what it would be like if she and Nick married and had kids. When at last, they took off to go to the Sawyer's house, Whitney's admiration for Sandra knew no bounds. She was a kind, patient mother who dealt with fussing kids calmly.

Whitney drove up to the Sawyer's house, pleased to see the colorful balloons tied to the mailbox. Their house, a two-story white colonial in a new neighborhood on the eastern side of town was pretty, with green shutters and a side porch.

She parked and helped Sandra and Jamie with the little girls and walked with them to the backyard. Pam's husband, Tyrone, was at the grill, surrounded by other fathers. The kids were playing croquet at the far end of the yard. Some of the boys were shooting baskets in the driveway. A circle of chairs had been set up beyond the picnic table laden with food. Whitney realized to her chagrin the chairs and food were donations from the other mothers and wished she'd thought of it.

Pam hurried right over to them. "Hi, Sandra and Whitney. Come take a seat in the circle of chairs we set up over there. I've asked a few girls from my school class to be here and help babysit some of the younger kids." She waved a teenaged girl over. "This is Lisa. She can help with your girls."

Sandra smiled at Lisa. "Thank you for your help. That would be lovely." She put a hand on Jamie's shoulder. "Go ahead and play with the other kids."

As he ran away, Sandra said, "He's such a good boy. I depend on him a lot. That's why I can't deny him the lessons he wants."

"What would his father think of the kids dancing at the end of the play?" Whitney asked, curious.

Sandra shook her head. "He wouldn't like it at all."

"Well, I, for one, am glad you're allowing Jamie to study what he's passionate about. Dancing is hard work."

"Thank you for your encouragement. You and Linda Forrest are important to this community because not every kid wants to be a sports star." Sandra watched Jamie playing with the others and then turned to Whitney, her eyes shiny with tears. "Like I said, he's a good boy."

Whitney drew a breath of satisfaction. She couldn't let

someone like Bud Thompkins derail her efforts to give children a chance to participate in theater work. She left Sandra, walked over to Tyrone, and introduced herself to him.

"Thanks for having everyone here. It's such a nice thing to do."

He smiled. "Pam and I enjoy meeting and being with people outside our jobs at the schools. It's nice to have you here. Pam told me you might be bringing Nick Woodruff. Where is he?"

"He has to work, but said he'll try to join us later," said Whitney.

Tyrone smiled. "Great. He's one of the good guys."

Whitney went inside to see if Pam needed help. She was in the kitchen when they heard a commotion in the backyard.

She and Pam peered out the kitchen window.

Bud Thompkins was standing in front of Sandra shouting at her as he waved a beer can in the air.

Whitney followed Pam out of the kitchen and stood aside as Tyrone and another father moved toward Bud.

"Hey, there, Bud. What's going on?" asked Tyrone in a calm voice.

"I told Sandra she couldn't go see that stupid play Jamie was helping with. But when I fell asleep, she went anyway. What kind of wife would do that? I didn't give the boy my permission."

"This was a special occasion for all the kids in town. You wouldn't deprive your son from participating in that, would you?" Tyrone asked calmly.

"Damn right I would. A wife has to obey her husband. And she can't be raising some pansy kid because I'm not here to stop it. I work hard for a living driving a rig around the country."

"Yes, I know. And I'm sure you do a good job of it," said

Tyrone, putting a hand on his shoulder.

"Don't touch me," said Bud, slapping Tyrone's hand away. "I don't need you to tell me what my son can and cannot do. I just want to get my wife and the kids home."

Another father stepped up. "I can smell your breath from here. I don't think it's a smart idea for you to be driving anywhere. Why don't you sit down and cool off?"

Bud sank onto a chair and finished off his beer. And then he looked around. "Boy? Where are you, boy?"

Whitney had seen Jamie hurry behind the garage. She waited for anyone to point him out but realized they knew how frightened Jamie was and remained quiet. Even the kids.

Nick arrived. "Hello, everybody? What's going on?" he asked brightly and then noticed the men standing around Bud.

"I think Bud needs someone to drive him home," said Tyrone. "He's had too much to drink."

Bud jumped to his feet. "I'm going to drive my wife and my kids home. I didn't give them permission to be here."

"I told you, Bud, the children and I want to stay here," said Sandra.

Nick shook his head. "No one is going to drive anyone home if there's alcohol involved. I'll be glad to take you home, Bud. That will make it easy and safe for everyone."

"I can drive on my own," said Bud stubbornly, crinkling the beer can in his hand.

"My offer was more than a suggestion," said Nick firmly. He placed a hand on Bud's shoulder. "Come on, pal. Let's go."

As they walked away, Bud stumbled, unsteady on his feet.

Nick caught Whitney's eye and she said quietly, "See you later."

Bud whipped around at the sound of her voice. "You! It's all your fault. Better stay out of my family's business."

Pam walked up beside Whitney and faced Bud. "You're drunk. Go with Nick now."

"You're going to pay for messing in my business. I promise," said Bud, stumbling once again as Nick took hold of his arm and moved him away from the crowd.

As soon as Bud left the yard, Whitney went over to Sandra. "Is there something I can do for you?"

Sandra shook her head. "He's impossible to deal with once he's had too many beers."

Whitney drew a deep breath and let it out slowly, hoping she wasn't crossing any lines. "Are you and the kids safe with him?"

"So far. He's going through a rough time. The company he works for has threatened to fire him if he doesn't make some changes and get his temper under control." She shrugged. "He might be mean from time to time ..."

Whitney gave Sandra a steady look. "If you ever feel unsafe, you'll let someone know, won't you? There are lots of people able to help you. Just call me and I'll be there. Or better yet, call Nick."

"I will. I'll do anything to protect my kids."

"Jamie, most of all, I hope," Whitney said quietly as Jamie approached them.

"Is he gone?" Jamie asked his mother.

"Yes, the police chief is driving him home," Sandra told him.

One of the other mothers came over to them. "Jamie and my son, Jake, worked together on sets and he's asked me if Jamie could spend the night. He's welcome at our house if it's okay with you."

Sandra's face brightened. "That would be nice." She turned to Jamie. "Do you want to have a sleepover with Jake?"

"Yes," said Jamie. "Jake and I are friends." He ran off

shouting, "Jake! I can spend the night! My mom said it's okay."

The two boys fist bumped one another and took off toward the croquet game.

"Okay," said Pam. "That's settled. How about food? We have plenty of it."

Soon the yard was full of the sounds of adults chatting and kids playing.

Whitney and Pam gave one another looks of relief. But Whitney didn't think either one of them would forget to keep an eye on Sandra and her family.

CHAPTER TWENTY-ONE
DANI

Dani was amazed at the number of customers who came and went at the Collister's vegetable stand. Mary Lou handled the cash register, while Dani bagged the produce, jams, honey, and other items customers bought. In between sales, Dani and Mary Lou freshened displays and chatted with people. Usually, one of Brad's two sisters or the high school kids hired for the summer would help. But it was a holiday weekend, and they had made plans with their families. A well-deserved break for them.

Dani was happy to help. The Collister family was close knit, and she wanted to be part of it. Both of Brad's parents, Mary Lou and her husband, Joe, were kind, decent, hardworking people who freely gave their love and support to their children.

The time to attend Whitney's play came and went. Though Dani was disappointed, she didn't show it. There was no way she could leave Mary Lou with only one other helper.

"It'll slow down after suppertime," said Mary Lou. "Then we'll be busy getting food on the table for you and Brad, Joe, and me. A real quiet time with only the four of us, but sometimes that's nice too. Gives us a chance to talk. And I thought you might like to see some of our family photos."

Dani brightened. "I'd love that. Thanks."

Mary Lou's prediction came true as fewer and fewer people arrived at the vegetable stand as the afternoon lengthened and then drew to an end.

"You stay and close up and I'll go start dinner, okay?" said Mary Lou.

"No problem," said Dani. Mary Lou was a terrific cook, and Dani couldn't wait to see what she'd come up with next.

She closed the barn door and went to work straightening displays, removing any vegetables that wouldn't last another day, and placing them in a bag to carry up to the house. She made sure the refrigerators were working properly and the displays inside them were fine. Next, she swept the floor. Then, certain no late customers would arrive, she put the cash and receipts in a special bag provided by a local bank and carried it and the sack of veggies up to the house.

When she entered the kitchen, the smell of fried chicken was tantalizing. She handed the vegetables and money to Mary Lou and said, "What can I do to help?"

"Carry the cheese and crackers out to the porch. Brad and his father are having beer, but I thought you might like a glass of wine. I'll be out as soon as I take these last pieces of chicken out of the frying pan. The rest of the dinner is already done."

Dani walked through the lovely, restored farmhouse to the wide front porch, eager to see the men. They'd been working on a project in the fields. Dani admired Brad's commitment to his family. Joe and Mary Lou worked hard, but they were beginning to age and needed help.

"Ah, here she comes," said Brad, smiling at her. He stood and offered her a place on a two-seat couch. "Sit. I'll go get the wine for you and Mom."

Dani set down the plate of appetizers on a table beside Joe and lowered herself onto the couch.

"How'd it go in the store today?" he asked her.

"It was busy. But that makes it fun," Dani said. She smiled as Brad returned with wine for her.

"Mom will be here shortly," he said, handing her the glass

and taking a seat next to her. He swung an arm around her and squeezed, making her laugh as she balanced the glass of wine in her hand.

"Sorry," he said, and winked at her.

Mary Lou walked onto the porch and sat in the rocking chair next to Joe's. She lifted her glass in the air. "Here's to us. Happiness and health."

"To us," Dani said with the men.

"Many thanks to the two of you for stepping in to help us this holiday weekend," said Joe.

"We really appreciate it. Aaron and the girls had other plans for today and this evening, and it's only right for them to have time to themselves. We realize as time goes by and families have their own plans, the day will come when Joe and I will need to sell the farm," said Mary Lou. "But not for years to come."

"We're thinking of hiring more help," Joe said. "All in time."

After a delicious summertime meal of fried chicken, potato salad, fresh sliced tomatoes with chopped basil, and slices of cold watermelon for dessert, Mary Lou took Dani aside.

"I thought you'd like to see old family photos. Joe's mother did that for me one time, and I've never forgotten how treasured that made me feel. And, Dani, you are a true treasure. We're so happy you and Brad are engaged and will marry soon."

Dani's vision blurred. She accepted the hug Mary Lou gave her and then stood back. "There are so many awful stories about mothers-in-law, but none of it could ever be true for you. I'm so lucky."

Mary Lou gave her a pat on the shoulder and a wide smile. "We both are."

She walked over to a bookshelf in the living room and lifted down a wide leather book.

"The album begins twenty years ago after we first bought the farm. Joe and I were in a mid-life crisis and wanted to do something different with our lives. We had the family we wanted—two boys and two girls—and wanted them to have a better life. So, we moved from Boston to the farm and haven't looked back with regret."

They sat together on the couch, and Mary Lou began pointing out the kids, who were in their teens in the photos. Dani loved seeing pictures of them and imagined what children she and Brad would have one day would look like.

She came upon a couple of photos of the group with a young man who looked to be in his twenties. "Who's that?"

"Alexander, my sister's son. Such a sad story. He came to help us one summer between the end of college and his first job in New York City. Everyone loved Alex. He was a great young man."

"What happened?" Dani asked, intrigued by the handsome man smiling at the camera.

"His job was in the twin towers in New York City and started right after Labor Day in September 2011."

Cold chills ran over Dani's body. "Oh, my god! He was in one of the buildings that went down on September 11th?"

Mary Lou nodded solemnly. "My sister never got over it. He was far too young to die in such a horrible, horrible way. It was a huge shock to all of us. He was the kind of person you can never forget."

"I'm so sorry. I remember the videos and how shocked we all were. It changed so many things," said Dani.

"Yes, it did. It made me realize how happy I was to have changed my life from comfortable housewife and mother to a farmwife. I think it made a lot of people think differently about life and happiness." Mary Lou shook her head. "My parents thought Joe and I made a big mistake by buying the farm. But it's proved to be an excellent choice for us and our kids."

"GG kept running the inn even when others thought she was crazy. I'm glad she did. For her and for all of us," said Dani.

"Life sure is funny," said Mary Lou. "Full of surprises."

"This summer has been full of a lot of surprises for me and my sisters," said Dani. "Happy ones."

"I'm so pleased for you," said Mary Lou, giving her a warm smile.

That night, as Dani cuddled with Brad in bed, she talked about the photo album and the people she'd seen there.

"Your mother told me about your cousin, Alex. It's such a tragic story," said Dani. "It makes me wonder how I'd feel if a child of mine were to die. I can't imagine such a tragedy. She said your aunt was never the same."

Brad rubbed her back. "Life is about taking chances. You have to live with the good and the bad. That's why I'm so happy we found one another."

"Me, too," said Dani lifting her face to his. Soon all her worries dissolved into gratefulness for all the love they began to share.

CHAPTER TWENTY-TWO
WHITNEY

Labor Day was quiet for Whitney. With the play behind her she could relax. Sitting on the patio reading a book filled her with a sense of peace. *When was the last time she'd read a book?* she asked herself. Life at this slower pace was pleasing. She'd asked Barbara to let her know of any other threats, but to date, had heard nothing. Even Taylor was quiet about such social media news.

She thought of Bud Thompkins and his behavior. When she and Nick talked last night, he told her that Bud might be a bully but only seemed to show those colors when he'd been drinking. Still, he promised to keep an eye on him.

The day became better when she received an email from the furniture company that shipment was underway for some of the pieces. And then that afternoon, Nick called.

"I'm covered for the rest of the day. How about we take a picnic to the cottage and have a swim there?"

"That sounds perfect," said Whitney. "Pam sent me home with a lot of leftovers, so we have a variety of food choices. I'll add some things to it, along with a bottle of wine, water, and a thermos of coffee."

"Sounds great. Why don't I meet you up there in a half hour? I'm ready to relax and enjoy being with you. It's been a busy weekend."

"Okay, see you soon." Whitney set down her book and went into the kitchen to begin packing for the picnic. She filled a cooler with containers of food, water, plastic wine glasses, and all necessities for eating. Then she placed the thermos of coffee and a bottle of pinot noir in a canvas bag with her beach towel. After she dressed in a bikini and a coverup, she loaded the car, called to Mindy, and took off for the cottage, thinking Nick might already be there. She was pleased he enjoyed the cottage. They'd had some special moments there, sitting on the rock talking and kissing like the teenagers they'd been. It pleased them both to continue something that had started years ago.

At the house, she was disappointed not to see Nick's car there. She went inside, stored the food in the kitchen, and went down to the rock to sunbathe while she waited for Nick.

After some time, she checked her watch and sighed. Nick was late. She'd left her phone in the kitchen which meant missing any message he might have sent.

She was dozing with Mindy beside her when a voice said, "Hey, sorry I'm late."

Whitney sat up and smiled. Nick had changed into his swimming trunks. Seeing that body, knowing what he could do with it, her heart sped up. He was gorgeous, and hers.

He sat beside her and took her face in the palm of his hands. "Hi, beautiful." His lips met hers and she lost herself in his embrace. He always made her feel so safe.

They were still kissing when Mindy began to growl.

Whitney pulled away from Nick and jumped to her feet.

Bud Thompkins was headed their way down the grassy slope, and it didn't look like a friendly visit.

Nick got up and pushed Whitney behind him. "You stay here. Let me handle this."

He climbed the slope. "Hey there, Bud. How's it going? What are you doing here? This is private property."

"I have as much right to be here as you do," growled Bud.

Rocking unsteadily on his feet, he lifted his arm.

"Oh, my god! Nick! He has a gun!" Whitney cried moving toward them.

Bud turned to her. "Stop and shut up. Nick and I have personal business. No one makes a fool out of me and gets away with it. After the barbeque, when I went to get my car, he'd had it towed. Then he said I couldn't get it until I got some help for my drinking. And now my wife is talking about leaving me. It all started with you. Both of you."

"Whitney, I want you to go back to the rock," said Nick calmly. "Move slowly but go. And take Mindy."

Whitney remembered the phone Nick had brought with him and scooped Mindy up into her arms. Then she began to move backwards, careful of her footing. She had to get to the phone and call for help.

As she moved, she heard Nick speaking to Bud, trying to convince him to put the gun down. "That's it. Give the gun to me," Nick said, quietly, evenly. "You've had too much to drink. We can talk later when you sober up."

She neared the rock and saw the phone sitting on his towel.

"No, Bud. Don't," cried Nick, drawing her attention.

Whitney watched helplessly as Bud lifted the gun and aimed it at Nick.

"I got you now," Bud cried. "You and all the other people against me."

Whitney thought she saw a shadow behind him and blinked, confused by what she was seeing.

The sound of the gun going off roared in her ears.

She screamed as Bud was thrown off his feet, dropping the gun away from him as he toppled over.

Nick fell back and lay on the ground.

"Bud! You bastard!" Whitney cried. She snatched the phone up and ran as fast as she could up the slope, punching in 911 as she moved.

Bud jumped to his feet, trying to fight off Mindy who was attacking him. Kicking her away from him, he turned and ran away. Yapping, Mindy chased him.

Helpless to chase after them, Whitney cried into the phone. "Help! Please help! There's been a shooting at the cottage at the Lilac Lake Inn. The police chief is down."

"Hold on," said a calm voice. "You say the police chief has been shot? I want you to stay on the line while I call for police and ambulance service."

Whitney reached Nick, knelt beside him, and dropped the phone. "Nick! Nick! Are you alright?"

Nick sat up and grabbed hold of his left shoulder. "A lucky miss. Just a flesh wound, I think. Where's Bud?"

"He ran away. Mindy is chasing him."

"The gun?" Nick asked.

"There," said Whitney, pointed to it lying on the ground. "Bud dropped it when he fell."

Nick took the phone, called his dispatcher, and issued orders before disconnecting the call.

Whitney handed him her coverup to staunch the flow of blood from his wound. "Please don't die," she whispered, feeling sick to her stomach.

"Hey, I'm going to be alright," Nick said. "It's lucky Bud was unsteady on his feet."

Whitney remembered the shadow but didn't speak of it. "Thank God, he only wounded you. You might have been killed." Looking at the bloody garment Nick was holding to his arm, Whitney felt faint. She bent her head, trying to erase the spinning inside it.

"Stay here. I'll look around for Bud," said Nick, getting to his feet.

"No! I'm going with you. You're hurt, for god's sake. You

can't be running after him. Chances are he's so drunk he won't get far," said Whitney.

"You're right," said Nick, settling on the ground beside her.

Mindy came trotting back to them, her tongue hanging out from the exercise.

Several sirens sounded nearby and three police cars and an ambulance pulled into the driveway and skidded to a stop.

The three of them were sitting together when the first policeman ran down the slope to them. EMTs were close behind, and three other police ran off starting to search the area.

After checking Nick over, one of the EMTs announced, "We're taking you to the hospital."

"Would you like go come along, Whitney?" asked one of the policemen. "It's not safe for you to be here until we catch the man who did this."

"Yes, thank you," said Whitney getting to her feet. They hadn't reached the ambulance when an announcement came that the suspect had been apprehended and was in custody and heading to the jail.

"The damn fool," muttered Nick. "Now he's going to be facing serious charges. Putting him in jail might be the wakeup call he needs. It was so not necessary. We need to check on his wife."

"Do you want me to go see Sandra?" Whitney asked. "She trusts me."

"In time. Now, I need you to fill out a police report about what you saw. We need all the evidence we can get to get this guy some help," said Nick.

"What about you? You say it's only a minor wound but, Nick, you could've been killed." Tears filled Whitney's eyes and overflowed. "And there was nothing I could do to save you."

Nick put his good arm around her. "It's all part of the job, Whitney. Don't worry. I'm in great shape."

Whitney shook her head back and forth, crying in earnest now. "I don't think I can do this."

"Let's get you both in the ambulance," said one of the EMTs, glancing at Whitney.

"First things first," said one of the policemen. "Help for you, Nick. Then we can get to the reporting and you two can work things out with your cars and all. We'll take the dog to headquarters until Whitney can pick her up. She's quite the hero."

Nick gave Whitney a pleading look. "You okay, now?"

Whitney nodded, but she wasn't at all sure she'd ever be okay after what had happened.

At the hospital, Whitney sat beside Nick's bed in the emergency room, holding onto his hand, waiting for a doctor to inspect the wound. The EMTs had already cleaned and bandaged it and had told the staff that stitches were in order. A nurse took Nick's vital signs.

A few minutes later, a man pulled aside the privacy curtain and stepped inside.

"Ah, my pal, Nick," said an older man wearing a white coat, a stethoscope hanging around his neck. "What do we have this time?"

"Just a scratch on the shoulder," said Nick. "Only needs a stitch or two."

"We'll see," said the doctor whose name tag read, Dr. Johnstone.

Whitney rose from her chair to give him room. "I'll wait outside."

Feeling wobbly, Whitney went back to the waiting area. She couldn't block the image of Nick getting shot and falling. She'd thought he was dead as she'd stood by helpless.

A short while later, Nick emerged from where he'd been treated, his arm in a sling. He gave her a weak smile. "There goes our picnic. Sorry about that."

Whitney got to her feet and rushed over to him wanting to hang on to him, keep him safe.

Later, As Whitney gave her story to the policewoman taking it down, she felt as if she were reliving every moment. To Nick, it had been a scare. To her, it was the most frightening moment of her life. Guilt filled her. Nick could've died, and she'd been powerless to help him. She had, instead, caused Bud to become even angrier. She couldn't stop her flow of tears.

"Are you alright? Need a drink of water? Coffee?" the policewoman asked.

Whitney shook her head. "No, thanks. I'll be fine once I get over the shock of it all."

"Nick's an exceptional cop. He'll be fine." The policewoman smiled at her.

"You don't mind working in a job that could kill you so easily?" Whitney asked.

"Danger is part of the job. That's why we train," she said. "Working in Lilac Lake isn't the same as working in a big city, but we have to be prepared for anything at all times."

Whitney lowered her face into her hands. She'd always felt as if Nick made her feel safe. Now, after seeing how vulnerable he was, she'd constantly worry about him. She wasn't sure she could live a life like that. The thought sickened her.

Dani showed up at the police station. "I got here as soon as I could. Are you alright, Whitney? How about Nick?"

"Nick's going to be fine," Whitney said, and burst into tears.

Dani wrapped her arms around her. "Look, let me take you

and Mindy home. You need some time to recover from this shock."

"Nick is with some other officers," said Whitney. "Let me say goodbye to him."

"Okay. I'll wait here," said Dani.

Whitney went to another interrogation room and knocked on the door.

Nick looked up at her and smiled. "Are you done with your statement?"

"Yes. Dani is here to take me and Mindy home. Promise me you're alright."

"It's just a flesh wound. A couple of stitches, that's all," he said, giving her an encouraging smile.

The smile she returned to him was uncertain. "See you later."

"I'll come by when I can," he replied. "Tell Mindy she performed like a champion. One of Bud's pant legs was chewed up a bit."

Trying not to cry, Whitney kissed him, lingering a moment, and left the room, so upset she couldn't speak. She loved Nick, had wanted to live with him. Now, she wasn't sure she could.

CHAPTER TWENTY-THREE
DANI

It was silent in the car as Dani drove Whitney home. It bothered Dani. Usually, people were talkative after a shocking incident. Whitney sat staring out the window of the car with such a somber expression that Dani ached to stop the car and hug her.

"What can I do to help you?" Dani asked Whitney.

Whitney faced her. Fresh tears rolled down her cheeks. "I love Nick. I really do. But I don't think I can live this way. All the violence, the danger. My life is filled with threats against me. And now, because of me Nick was almost killed. How can I handle all that?"

"Hold on," said Dani, shocked to the core. "You're blaming yourself for Nick being shot? Don't go there, Whitney. What you and Nick have is special."

"So special that he'd die protecting me?" snapped Whitney, her green eyes flashing. "I can't do that to him. Don't you see?"

"What I do see is that you've had a terrible shock, and that you foolishly are blaming yourself for what happened," said Dani, growing more and more concerned. She pulled the car into the driveway of their house and faced Whitney.

"If I hadn't pushed for Jamie to be involved with the play maybe none of this would've happened," said Whitney.

"Jamie's helping with the play is such a small part of the problem with Bud. You know from your experiences with Zane how alcohol can affect someone's brain. He's a bully, and he's had some bad luck recently, I heard. It all adds up to a firestorm of emotions. It's not your fault, not Nick's, nor his family's."

"I can see how it has all played out, but he's been angry with me from the moment we met. Surely that has added to the situation," protested Whitney.

"Who knows what was going on in Bud's alcohol-addled mind? But it's wrong to blame yourself for the incident with Nick."

"But he was at the cottage," said Whitney. She stopped. "We need to talk about that. When I've had more time to think about it, I want to tell you and Taylor about something that happened there. I'm not sure, but I think our ghost might've helped us."

"What? Don't wait to tell me. What happened?"

"As Bud was aiming for Nick, I saw a shadow. I blinked and it was gone. But I think it might've knocked Bud off his feet. Of course, he was very drunk, and it could've happened anyway. But it was very strange." Whitney felt a shudder go through her.

Dani reached over to squeeze Whitney's hand and found it ice cold.

"Let's get you inside," said Dani. "You need some rest." Whitney's face was white.

Dani helped her sister inside and got her settled on the couch with a light blanket. Mindy jumped up and nestled close to Whitney as if she knew how much Whitney needed comfort.

"How about a cup of coffee or hot tea?" Dani asked.

Whitney shook her head. "Nothing thanks. I just need to rest."

While Whitney slept, Dani called Taylor.

CHAPTER TWENTY-FOUR
TAYLOR

Taylor ended the call with Dani and turned to Cooper lounging on the couch beside her reading a manuscript.

"I have to go home," she said. "Whitney needs me. Dani is with her, but Dani thinks I should be there."

Cooper sat up. "What's going on?"

Taylor told him what happened. "Now, Whitney's blaming herself. Dani thinks she might end her relationship with Nick over the fear of something like this happening again."

"Sounds like Whitney could use all the support she can get. Do you want me to ride up there with you?"

"No, but thanks. I think this is a Gilford girl time. I also have to help with the arrangements for the cottage. I promised to do my share. Construction is nearing the end, and I'm in charge of landscaping, which will be put in as soon as the house is painted."

"How long will you be gone?" said Cooper, drawing her close.

"I don't know. A couple of weeks at least," she said, lifting her face.

He lowered his lips to hers.

She reveled in his kiss, allowing all her angst to be swept away in a wave of desire. It was always this way.

When they parted, she smiled up at him. "I won't last more than a couple of weeks without you. Maybe you can arrange to join me in Lilac Lake."

"Definitely," he said. "I'm going to miss you like crazy. It won't be the same without you here." Since he'd furnished his condo, she'd opted to stay with him. She still hadn't decided whether to sell hers. Time would take care of that decision.

Driving to Lilac Lake, Taylor filled with determination. She'd help Whitney and make sure the cottage would be ready for them to move into by the end of the month. It was a challenge, but they could do it.

The one thing she and Dani hadn't talked about was the ghost. They wanted to be sure Mrs. Maynard or whoever it was had gone before making the cottage theirs.

CHAPTER TWENTY-FIVE
WHITNEY

The morning after another restless sleep, Whitney headed to a visit with Bud's wife, Sandra. She wanted to personally apologize to Sandra for any inconvenience because of her. Though Nick had told her it wasn't necessary, Whitney wouldn't feel right until she met with her.

Whitney parked in front of the house and headed for the front door. Jamie opened it and smiled at her. "Mom's waiting for you inside."

He held the door open, and Whitney stepped into the front entrance.

Sandra approached her, holding onto the hand of a little girl. "Jamie, will you take Eloise into the backyard to play? The others are still asleep."

Jamie picked up the little girl and carried her away.

"He's so helpful with his sisters," said Sandra. "Come into the kitchen. I appreciate your phone call and am glad you stopped by."

Sandra led Whitney into the kitchen and offered her a seat at the oblong wooden table.

"How about a cup of coffee?" Sandra said.

"That would be lovely," said Whitney. She'd already had a cup that morning but knew this was more than an offer for coffee. It was an extended hand of friendship.

After Sandra served coffee and offered cream and sugar that Whitney didn't accept, she took a seat at the table.

"I want to tell you how grateful I am for your concern, but

I don't want you to believe in any way that you're responsible for Bud's actions. I've been attending a few Al-Anon meetings, and Bud's incident with Nick was his own foolish reaction to his frustrations. He's agreed to go to a rehab center for a couple of weeks. Beyond that, who knows? I've told him I won't stay with him if he continues to drink."

"Oh, good," said Whitney. "I've attended a few meetings of my own in California. I know how helpful they can be. But in this case, I think I aggravated a situation, and I'm sorry."

Sandra reached over and squeezed her hand. "You've made our lives much better by encouraging me to stick by Jamie and his talent. I've said before how important your work with the kids and Linda's dance school is to the community."

After going through such self-incriminations, Whitney couldn't help the tears that stung her eyes. "I'm so happy you feel that way. I was beginning to doubt myself."

"Well, don't. Things happen for a reason. I'm very sorry that Nick was injured. It was so wrong of Bud to do that."

"Will you and the kids be alright with Bud gone?" Whitney asked.

"Better than ever. I'm used to being alone with Bud gone on road trips. This will be a little longer, a little calmer." Sandra smiled. "It's hectic around here, but that's nothing new."

A child's cry came through the speaker in the kitchen. "There's one of the girls now. Soon, the other will wake up. Then, the fun begins."

Realizing Sandra meant it, Whitney looked at her with surprise.

"I love being a mom," said Sandra.

"You're so good at it," Whitney said, realizing she wasn't ready for motherhood. She wasn't even sure she was ready for marriage.

Whitney said goodbye, intending to go to the dance studio to talk to Linda about future projects. Instead of going there, she turned around and headed to The Woodlands. She'd talked to GG but wanted to visit her in person.

It had been three days since the shooting, and she needed some advice. Anytime Nick had tried to talk to her about it, she'd put him off.

She knocked on GG's door and entered the apartment. GG was sitting outside on the patio and rose as Whitney approached her.

"Whitney, darling, I'm so happy to see you. Come sit with me. This cooler weather is so agreeable, don't you think?"

Whitney smiled. "Yes, but remember, I'm a summer girl. Not a winter one."

"Ah, I do remember," GG said, smiling. "Hopefully, with the cottage available to you, you'll enjoy some fine winter weather too."

"We'll see," said Whitney. She stared out at the green lawn leading to the woods behind the building.

"Why are you here? You know I love to see you anytime, but I know something's bothering you," said GG.

As Whitney turned back to GG, her eyes filled. Though she felt as if she'd been weepy for days, Whitney couldn't help herself. The life she'd imagined was turning out to be very different from reality.

"Oh, darling, you're still upset by the attack on Nick. I'm sorry. Did you know he called me?"

Whitney felt her eyes widen. "He did? When?"

"Last night. He wanted me to know you were safe, he kept you from danger like he once promised me."

"But he put himself at risk to do it. GG, Bud could've killed him. He had a gun pointed at him. He missed, but only because he was drunk. It was awful seeing Nick get shot. I don't think I'll ever get over it." Whitney realized her voice had risen with anguish, but she couldn't stop it.

GG gave her a steady look. "That's why you're here."

Whitney nodded. "I was going to go to Atlanta for a couple of weeks, but furniture is about to be delivered, so I couldn't leave. But I've told Nick I need space."

"Seems to me you've got some hard decisions to make," GG said quietly. "Nick has chosen his profession. He's good at it and we all appreciate it."

"Yes, but it's dangerous. He never knows if that morning when he wakes up will be his last. What an awful way to live."

"Life is uncertain for all of us," GG reminded her. "We can't predict when something horrible is going to happen."

"I know, but this is different. I love Nick, I really do. But I don't think I can live this way. Sending him off in the morning, never knowing if I'll see him that night."

"Do you remember the summer you were dating Nick? He let you go to follow your dreams. You can't take his away from him," GG said quietly.

"I know. That's why I need time to think. I've told him I need space," said Whitney wringing her hands.

"You must be totally honest with him," GG said.

Whitney lowered her head and let out a long breath. "I know."

Later, as Whitney left The Woodlands, she put in a call to Nick. "Can we meet? I need to talk to you."

"Sure. Tell me where and I'll be there," he said. "We need to settle things between us."

"I know," said Whitney. "Meet me at the cottage. A counselor told me I should face that site again if I hope to live there."

"Okay, I'll meet you on the rock," said Nick. "I'll head there now."

As he ended the call, Whitney swallowed hard, hoping she'd have the nerve to do what she knew she must.

When she arrived at the cottage, Nick's car was already there. Whitney got out and stood a moment looking around. She couldn't let a bad memory prevent her from enjoying the home she and her sisters had created for themselves.

She walked around to the front of the house and stared up at the balcony extending from the old attic room. Turning it into an indoor/outdoor gathering place was a genius idea of Aaron's.

In another couple of days, the sliding glass doors would be installed, and the trim work done.

She walked across the lawn and down to the rock where Nick stood looking out at the lake. The wind brushed the top of the water sending shimmering light across the surface, giving it a magical feel.

He turned to her and lifted his good hand in a greeting.

Swallowing a sob, she met him.

"May I kiss you?" Nick asked gently.

She nodded, though it might be the last one he'd give her.

Tears welled in her eyes as his lips met hers.

When they pulled apart, he thumbed the tears off her cheeks. "What's going on, Whitney?"

"I love you, Nick. You know that. But I can't be with you, watch you take off in the morning and wonder if you'll return to me that night."

"Police work is my job. I love it, and I'm good at it," said Nick.

"I know. I would never ask you to leave it. But if we're together, you'll know how afraid I am. And that one time when you shouldn't, you might hold back in a dangerous situation because of me. I couldn't bear it if something like that would ever happen."

"So, you're saying you don't want to be with me?"

"I'm saying I love you enough to step away," said Whitney.

Nick's lips thinned. "Sounds like a bunch of bullshit to me."

"I mean it, Nick. For now, I need my space and time to think it through. But I want to be totally honest with you. I'm not sure I can get past thinking you were dead."

"But I'm not dead. I'm here, very much alive and in love with you," said Nick. "It's the kind of love that doesn't often come along. Don't ruin that, Whitney. Stay with me."

"Just give me time, Nick. I love you and always will. But I need to think about supporting your career when I'm terrified." She clasped her hands, prayer-like, and wondered if she was doing the stupidest thing ever.

Nick settled his gaze on her, reaching deep inside her. "It's your decision. But if you decide you want to move forward with me, you'll have to come to me. I won't be seeking you out." He tipped his cap at her and walked away, leaving her to stare at the mountains in the distance, feeling more alone than she'd ever felt in her life.

CHAPTER TWENTY-SIX
WHITNEY

Whitney sat on the patio with her two sisters thinking back to the early days of the summer. Everything seemed so peaceful then, so full of hope. Ever since meeting Nick at the cottage, she'd felt empty. Even now, with her sisters chatting happily, she felt alone.

Taylor had arrived and was regaling them with stories of her summer weekends at Cooper's family summer home on Long Island. "Most of the people were nice; some were spoiled brats. One woman, in particular, was downright mean to me every chance she got. I admit she was gorgeous, but that's as far as it went."

"When you work with so many gorgeous women as I have, you soon realize that in real life, looks mean nothing," said Whitney. "Some of my favorite people were the ones working hard behind the scenes so we on screen could look good."

"Yes, I agree," said Taylor. "I love the fact that authors are judged by their words, not their looks."

"As it should be," said Dani. "Now, let's talk about the strange thing that happened at the cottage when Nick was being attacked. Whitney, tell us what you saw."

Whitney again recounted what happened, feeling as if her real self was set aside, watching from a distance. "Just as Bud aimed his gun at Nick, a shadow appeared behind him as he was firing the shot. He toppled to the ground, then got up and ran away. But it was really spooky. I was in a state of shock, but that's what I saw."

"I've been thinking about it a lot," said Dani. "None of us has seen an actual ghost, but we've felt and seen strange things. What do you think about trying to get someone who's trained to come take a look at the house to see if she can sense anything there? The furniture is arriving soon, and I want the house to be cleared before then."

"I talked to Crystal about it one time. She has a friend who has special abilities to sensing and hearing things from people in the past. Let's ask her for the name of her friend," said Taylor. "I won't feel comfortable unless we do."

"Okay, tomorrow we'll go to breakfast at the café, and we'll ask her then," said Dani. "Deal?"

"Deal," said Whitney. After witnessing the latest incident, she, too, would feel better living at the house after it was rid of the ghost.

The next morning the three of them walked to town. It felt comforting to Whitney to have her sisters with her. Especially now that she was on her own after telling Nick she needed space.

The café was as busy as usual, but Crystal waved at them from behind the counter. They selected a table outside on the patio and waited for a waitress to appear.

"I love eating outside here," said Taylor. "Such a difference from the city. I love it there, too, but the fresh air, friendly people, and cute shops and restaurants here make this a very special place."

"Agreed," said Dani. "Oh, look, here comes Nick."

Nick saw them, waved, and moved on keeping his gaze away from Whitney.

Whitney sighed. Seeing him with his arm in a sling, she knew she was doing the right thing. She needed time and he was giving it to her. Still, it hurt.

A waitress came for their order and filled their cups with coffee.

After she left, Dani leaned forward. "Taylor, go tell Crystal we need to see her when she has a moment to spare."

Taylor got up and left the table.

Dani leaned forward. "Did you see JoEllen? She came in while you were looking at the menu and now, she's sitting with Nick."

Whitney glanced at them and turned away. It wasn't fair to judge him. He'd told Whitney about getting help for JoEllen, and she knew he wasn't interested in a romance with her.

Taylor came back to the table as the waitress arrived with their food. "Crystal says she'll help us. She'll be out soon."

They ate quietly and then JoEllen appeared at their table. "Hello. Whitney, I'm sorry you and Nick have broken up. I wanted to tell you that."

She moved on and Dani said, "Wow! Maybe JoEllen is changing. She told Brad she was getting some help. She didn't even acknowledge me, which is what I've wanted all along. Otherwise, it feels as if she's spying on me."

"But, Whitney, you haven't broken up for real, have you?" said Taylor. "You're only taking some time apart. Right?"

Whitney shrugged. "We'll see." Her lips turned down of their own accord.

They didn't have time to dwell on it because Crystal appeared.

"Okay, tell me what's going on with you and the cottage?"

"We want to see if your friend who has what you call 'special abilities' can tell us about any spirits at the house," said Dani.

"We want her to make sure no ghosts are there," said Taylor bluntly.

"You mean Mrs. Maynard's ghost?" said Crystal, grinning.

Her violet eyes gleamed with intrigue, matching her purple hair almost perfectly.

"Aaron thinks spirits from the past are a possibility, and we want to have the house cleansed of them."

"I see," said Crystal. "I'll call her and let her know." She turned to Whitney. "Don't give up on Nick. That's all I'm going to say."

Whitney bobbed her head grateful Crystal was leaving the sensitive subject alone.

They finished breakfast, and then Dani said, "You two can linger. I have to get to work."

After Dani left, Taylor said, "Let's look in some of the shops for things for the house. Now that the attic has been opened up, we need to make it special."

"Dani told you about the envelope she found, didn't she?" Whitney said to her.

"Yes, she did. R. A. Thomas. A name we must remember. There's a story behind it. I wish I knew where to start."

They sipped their coffee and watched tourists walk by, getting an early start to the day.

"We'd better go. It's getting crowded," said Whitney. She got to her feet, glanced over at Nick's table, and then quickly looked away.

On the walk home, she and Taylor stopped in several stores to shop and chat with the owners. It was that kind of town.

Weighed down with candles, some serving dishes, and a wall hanging for Taylor's room, they walked slowly back to their house. The owner was pleased that it wouldn't be a problem to put the house on the market in early October because she'd decided to move close to her family.

It had been a wise plan, Whitney decided, for the three of them to rent the house together. It gave her a sense of what it might be like to share the cottage from time to time.

###

Later, while Taylor worked on her writing, Whitney drew up a draft of a business plan required for establishing a foundation. Now that she'd put on one short play, she wanted to do more. Again, she'd use Lilac Lake as a testing area. She still liked bringing theater opportunities to some of the summer camps in the area.

Her cell phone rang. She picked it up and clicked onto the call before realizing the screen said: *caller unknown.*

"Hello?"

"I haven't forgotten about you. Beware." The man's voice was low, threatening.

Whitney ended the call and dropped the phone, feeling as if she was touching something poisonous. Alarmed, her stomach churning, she stood and gazed out at the back lawn and garden, needing something to center her. How had the man gotten her new phone number? Only a few people knew it. Running down the list of those who did, Whitney came to Barbara's name and stopped.

She immediately called her.

A pleasant male voice answered. "The Griffith Agency."

"Is Barbara there?" she asked. "It's Whitney Gilford calling."

"Hold a moment please," the man said.

Barbara came on a few moments later. "Hi, girlfriend. How are you?"

"I'm not sure. I just received an ominous phone call on my cell. Very few people have my new number. Who in your office would have access to it?"

"Only Todd and me," said Barbara.

"Can you do me a favor? Can you go into my records and change my phone number to this number?" Whitney gave her the number of the landline in their rental. "If I get a call on that line, I'll know it's Todd. In the meantime, please keep an eye on him. There's something very wrong with him if he's the one threatening me. Who knows what else he might be doing? And for heaven's sake, don't let him know I suspect him of anything."

"You've really thought this through. I checked him out before I hired him, but that doesn't mean he didn't hide something from me," said Barbara. "I'd feel awful if he was causing you to feel threatened."

"Maybe someone else is putting him up to it. I don't know. It may be nothing, but when I go through the list of people who have that number, yours is the one that I suspect."

"Okay, doll, will do. I hope you're wrong, but I can't take a chance that you're not. Talk to you soon. Kiss. Kiss."

Whitney ended the call and sat back in her chair. Why would someone in Barbara's office be after her? Was he associated with the Zaniacs? The man who'd answered the phone was as pleasant as one could be.

She let out a sigh. GG liked to say life was one big circle after another. In this case, Whitney hoped to close this one quickly. Her nerves were on edge because of Nick. She didn't need to add to her distress.

CHAPTER TWENTY-SEVEN
WHITNEY

After talking to Crystal's friend, Summer, Whitney joined her sisters at the cottage one evening for a séance.

Summer was a woman in her fifties who wore a voluminous caftan. There was an air of peacefulness about her. Her gray hair hung in a braid behind her head, and her dark eyes were alive with interest as Dani explained some of the goings on at the house.

Taylor told Summer the story of Mrs. Maynard.

Whitney listened to the conversation. At one time she would've laughed at what they were doing, but after the shooting, she wasn't sure that a spirit wasn't living there.

Summer formed a circle of white candles on the kitchen floor and then indicated they were to sit inside it. "I can only tell you what I feel or what comes to me. Nothing more. I ask you to remain quiet and very still. Sometimes something comes through to me. Other times, not. But from what you told me there already is a pattern. Let's see. Shall we?" Summer lowered herself onto the floor, pulling the caftan behind her for a comfortable seat.

Whitney sat with her sisters. Dusk lent an eerie orange color to the grayness outside. As instructed, they hadn't turned on any lights inside the house.

Summer lifted her arms into the air. "We bring you no harm. Please show us who you are." She lowered her arms, held her hands in a prayerful pose, and closed her eyes.

They all sat quietly for several minutes.

Then Summer spoke. "Yes, I know. Love is all." She bobbed her head again and again as if she were listening to someone and then her shoulders slumped, and she sagged in her seat.

Whitney exchanged worried glances with her sisters but didn't speak.

After a few minutes, Summer straightened and looked around as if she didn't know where she was. "Ah, I remember. There is a spirit here, but it's not Mrs. Maynard. It's a young woman named Carol. She was supposed to meet someone here. Someone close to her. She has suffered many losses and is waiting for a sign that she can leave. It has something to do with love in this house."

"Wow, she told you all that?" Taylor said. "Do you think she'll do us harm?"

"No, exactly the opposite," said Summer. "But she told me one of you is still not sure about love. Does that make sense?"

Whitney squirmed as all eyes turned to her. "It's me. I'm taking some time to figure things out."

"Are you saying that once we all find love, Carol will leave?" asked Dani.

Summer shook her head. "I don't know if that's what she meant. But you did mention seeing sparkling lights when each of you was inside the house kissing your special person. Perhaps her energy is causing them."

"But what about the incident I told you about when Nick was in danger?" said Whitney.

"Well, if you think of it, perhaps she was protecting the love she knew you shared," said Summer calmly. "The one thing I do know is that she's not going to hurt any of you. She wants you happy."

Taylor sighed. "But how can we get her to leave? I'm uncomfortable with her here. I'm grateful she means us no harm, but it's still ... I don't know ... weird."

"Understandable to feel that way," said Summer. "Why don't the three of you do some investigation to try and find out her story? Then, when you're ready, we'll ask to speak to her again. Maybe help her find her way back to where she should be."

A shiver streaked down Whitney's back. Her sisters looked as spooked as she felt. In some ways, discovering that there really was a spirit or energy source in the house, a young woman named Carol, was terrifying.

She helped Summer get to her feet. Summer's dark eyes studied her. "Your heart will give you the answer you seek." She turned to the others. "Now, I must go. This work is very draining. All my senses need rest."

"I'll drive Summer home," said Dani.

"Okay, I'm leaving," said Taylor nervously glancing around.

"Me, too," said Whitney. "I'll take you to our house."

As they stepped outside the house, stars began to be seen in the sky which had grown dark. Gazing at them, Whitney thought as she had so many times how miraculous life seemed.

Dani joined Whitney and Taylor at the house. "I'm going to Brad's for the night, but I wanted to make sure the two of you were alright. Pretty strange stuff we're dealing with."

"Right," said Taylor. "But what is Carol's story?"

"That, dear sister, is what we need to find out."

"Do you think she's been hanging around that house for twenty years?" Whitney said. "That's downright creepy."

"Yeah, I know. But then I've read stories that say that time as we know it can be different in varying dimensions. So, maybe twenty years isn't so long for Carol." Dani shook her head. "This is all woo, woo stuff, but we're going to have to play along if we want her gone."

"It could be a very sweet story," said Taylor. "A love story of some kind."

Whitney and Dani exchanged smiles.

"You're such a romantic, Taylor," Dani said. "But I like it. I think we need to research Mrs. Maynard's daughter. Whitney, are you willing to go to the newspaper and see what you can find out there? I'll go back to the Historical Society. Taylor, why don't you see if GG can tell you anything."

Whitney briefly rankled at Dani taking charge and then sighed, grateful Dani wanted to see this project through because Whitney was still wondering how "Carol" could know about her indecision when it came to Nick.

The next day, Whitney was excited when a large truck from the furniture distributors pulled into the driveway of the cottage. It was one thing to buy something and another to see it in place. And it had been so long since she'd ordered it she hoped she hadn't made any mistakes.

She'd decided to stop thinking about "Carol" and concentrate on getting her life organized both with work at the cottage and setting up Zane's foundation.

The men parked the truck and opened the back, exposing the furniture inside.

Whitney peered inside and grinned. This was like Christmas morning. Maybe better because these pieces would be the final touches to the cottage and would be used for years to come.

Taylor arrived and then Dani, as eager to see the furniture as she.

They stood aside as Whitney directed the men where to place each piece. The living room, once empty, morphed into a stunning room with comfortable furnishings. Upstairs, beds and bureaus completed those rooms. One last minute purchase, a couch for the attic room, was carried upstairs. Whitney followed behind the men carrying it and thought she saw a shadow behind them.

"This is a cool room," said one of the men. "What a view."

Whitney smiled. "We're very pleased with it. Collister Construction did the work quickly as a favor to us."

"Yeah, I've seen some of the houses they're building," said the other man. "Cool stuff."

Downstairs, Whitney offered water to the men and tipped them for their work.

After they left, she stood with her sisters in the middle of the living room as delighted as they.

"Group hug," said Dani. "The cottage is ready for us."

As they hugged, Whitney told herself to ignore the sparkling lights around them.

CHAPTER TWENTY-EIGHT
TAYLOR

Taylor pulled up to The Woodlands, eager to talk to GG about the Maynard family. She had a feeling that the real story behind Carol wouldn't be found at the Historical Society or in a newspaper. Besides, she loved seeing her grandmother.

When she entered GG's apartment, she was chatting with her new friend, Betsy Norris, who'd moved to the area to be near her son.

"Hi. I don't mean to interrupt. Do you want me to come back later?" Taylor asked.

"Not at all. Come join us."

"Actually, I have to leave for a doctor's appointment shortly. I'd better go get ready. But it's always lovely to chat with you, Genie."

GG rose and walked Betsy to the door. "You come back soon. Good luck with your appointment."

She returned to her. "Taylor, dear, how nice to see you. What brings you here?"

"A ghost," said Taylor, grinning. "Actually, I wanted to talk to you about the Maynard family."

"Oh? I don't know how much help I'll be. I wasn't close to them. But sit down. We'll talk."

After GG got settled in her favorite chair, Taylor sat on the edge of the couch at the end closest to her. "We had one of Crystal's friends hold a séance at the cottage to see if she could tell if a ghost actually was there."

"And?"

"She said a spirit, a young woman named Carol, was present. That she'd had a lot of heartache. That Carol wanted us to find love and be happy." Taylor couldn't stop her shoulders from shivering. "It's eerie, I know."

"Strange, indeed, but possible," said GG. "The older I get the more open-minded I am. Life is a mysterious gift."

"What do you know about Carolyn Maynard?" Taylor asked, taking out a pen and notepad. "We're wondering if she's really the young woman called Carol."

"Not much. As I said, I wasn't close to the family. As a matter of fact, I didn't care for Milton Maynard. I thought he was a bully to his family. Very controlling. Carolyn was never allowed to date like other girls her age."

"But you reached out to Mrs. Maynard after he died," said Taylor.

"Of course. Women must support one another, and she needed housing. It was the least I could do. And I know that while Addie Maynard lived at the cottage, she did the same for others who needed help."

"Did her daughter move in with her?"

"I believe so," said GG. "But there was some sort of painful rift between her and her mother, and she left. Addie wouldn't talk about it. That's all I know."

"We know Carolyn died in December of 2002, and that Mrs. Maynard died Christmas Eve of that same year. But we don't know anything else about her."

"Look her up in the school yearbook," said GG. "Perhaps her picture is there."

"I wish I'd thought to go to the high school," said Taylor. "Now, how about you? How are you?"

GG's smile lit her blue eyes. "I'm fine. Just glad to be here when all you girls are finding love."

Taylor frowned. "All except Whitney. She's not sure she can

be with Nick because his work is dangerous. She was very shaken by the shooting. And she still is receiving phone calls from some jerk threatening her."

"Our lyrical, emotional Whitney will be fine," said GG. "I'm not surprised she has second thoughts, but I think it'll all turn out the way it should."

"And how's that?" asked Taylor.

GG chuckled. "With love, of course."

Taylor shook her head. "And my sisters think I'm such a romantic."

GG grinned. "Nothing like a little romance to make life full."

Taylor threw her arms around GG. "I love you so much."

"Love you too, sweet girl," GG murmured giving her a strong hug back.

CHAPTER TWENTY-NINE
WHITNEY

Dani sat with her sisters at the café for lunch and an update of what she'd found out about Carolyn. It was nothing more than they already knew.

Taylor spoke. "I talked to GG about Carolyn, as you asked. She didn't' really know the family well. She thought Mr. Maynard was a bully to his family and didn't like him. She said that Carolyn was not allowed to date like other girls her age, and she suggested I look her up in the high school yearbook."

"And what did you find?" Whitney asked.

"Nothing. A big fat zero," said Taylor.

"She probably was homeschooled," said Dani. "Funny, Brad's mother mentioned she wasn't a fan of Mr. Maynard, either. I think it's odd that he was able to act that way and remain a minister at one of the churches in town."

"Both GG and Mary Lou are strong women," said Whitney. "Maybe that's why they didn't like him. But perhaps others didn't see anything wrong with his behavior."

"Yeah, that could be," said Dani. "But I can tell you my future mother-in-law wouldn't let any man walk over her."

"GG said there was some kind of rift between Carolyn and her mother after Mr. Maynard died," said Taylor. "After Carolyn left, Addie would never talk about it."

"I can well imagine why Carolyn might have left," said Whitney. "She probably wanted to spread her wings a bit. Twenty years isn't that long ago. For her to be so restricted must have been very difficult for her."

Dani checked her watch and stood. "Sorry, ladies, but I've got to go to the site. They're doing some work on the house for Brad and me, and I want to be there. Keep gathering information. In the meantime, I assume no one is ready to move into the cottage?"

Whitney and Taylor shook their heads.

"They're supposed to start painting the cottage tomorrow," said Whitney.

"I've got the landscapers lined up for a week after they're done," Taylor said.

"Okay, so we have another week or so before we'd better start moving in," said Dani. "We have to make that time count."

After Dani left. Whitney turned to Taylor. "I've got an appointment with Linda at her dance studio. I'm going to ask her to be on the board of the foundation I'm forming."

"It's helpful to have a local community member on the board," said Taylor.

Whitney checked her watch. "Oh, I'm late! See you later." She jumped to her feet and rushed away, bumping into Nick, who was entering the café.

"Sorry," she said automatically and then looked up into his face.

His blue eyes were without their usual sparkle as he moved out of her way.

She wanted to reach out to him, but she didn't dare. She couldn't hurt him more than she already had.

She climbed into her car and sat a moment, fighting tears. It was difficult to do the right thing by being so honest with Nick. But her entire body cried out for him. Maybe it was time for her to go home to Atlanta for a couple of days.

That evening, Whitney told Taylor she was thinking of

going to Atlanta for a break.

"I understand how you feel," said Taylor, "but running away isn't going to help. You must decide for yourself what you want to do about Nick."

"I'm afraid if I try to get back with him, he'll think of me when he's in a dangerous situation and it may cost him his life."

Taylor shook her head. "That's crazier than thinking we have a ghost at the cottage. I'm going to New York to spend some time with Cooper. That will give you time alone to sort things out."

"Okay. You're right. I can't run away. I only hope I can make the right choice."

Taylor gave her a steady look. "You've hurt Nick, so you need to be careful. He's not going to hang around for too long while you make up your mind."

Whitney made a face. "How'd you get to be so smart about love?"

"Research," said Taylor quickly, making them both laugh.

The next day, Whitney was working on plans for the foundation when her cell rang. *Her agent, Barbara.*

"Good morning, Barbara," said Whitney trying for a cheerful tone. "What's up?"

"I had a talk with Todd earlier and discovered that a friend of his roommate is the one who got your private cell phone number."

"What? How?" Whitney asked.

"It seems I sent him a message with your information in it, asking him not to give it to anyone else. She, someone named Cynthi Desmond, looked through his phone. Todd says he didn't know it happened, that it must have been during a party at their apartment. I'm so sorry."

"Why would she want my number?" Whitney asked, uneasy.

"I asked him the same question. It seems she's part of the Zaniac group. He didn't know that either. He's severed all ties with her, but I wanted you to be aware that she has the new number you gave me."

"I haven't received a recent call on that line," said Whitney. "But that doesn't mean I'll rest easy. It's odd to me that someone would care so much about getting back at me for something I didn't do."

"Todd is very upset about it, which is why I'm keeping him on. But if I see any signs of activity through him, I'll let you know right away. How is everything else?"

"Not great. I have a few things I need to sort out. I'm not ready for any jobs at the moment, but I might be sooner than I expected."

"Good news for me," said Barbara. "In the meantime, I'll keep people from you for a while longer."

"Thanks," said Whitney, waiting for Barbara's "Kiss. Kiss." before ending the call.

She sat in the kitchen, absently rubbing Mindy's ear. She had to come up with a plan.

Whitney sat on the rock outside the cottage, sifting through her thoughts. At the moment, her life was as adrift as the small branch she saw floating atop the lake water at her feet. She couldn't go on living this way, afraid of what lay ahead. While she still needed time to think about her relationship with Nick, she knew there was something she could do to change things.

Feeling better, she walked into the water and floated on her back. Looking up at the clouds drifting above her in a bright blue sky, Whitney thought of her life going forward. If she didn't make a move now, she might be trapped in a life she hated.

Mindy barked, reminding Whitney that she'd better do what she'd planned. She climbed out of the water and leaned back on a towel she spread across the rock's surface. Allowing the sun to dry her, she knew what she had to do. Quickly, before she changed her mind, she made a couple of phone calls.

Then, satisfied, she headed up the slope to the cottage. Standing outside the building, the memory of Bud aiming a gun at Nick flashed in her mind. Shaking off the bad feelings, Whitney called to Mindy and headed to her car. She stopped and looked up at the deck, pleased that their plan had come together so quickly. But then, GG's working with Collister Construction had turned out to be excellent in so many ways.

At her car, she gazed at the garage and reminded herself to look into identifying the owner of the items in the box she and her sisters had found there. Maybe it belonged to one of the people Mrs. Maynard helped or one of the refugee families. She didn't have time to dwell on that now.

At home, she quickly packed her clothes. If she left right away, she could catch an evening flight to the west coast. Dani had already agreed to watch Mindy.

Whitney picked up the dog, gave her a kiss, and told her she'd be back soon.

Then she locked the house behind her and left with her carryon suitcase. She couldn't get away fast enough. She had to get her life in order.

Whitney surprised herself with a long nap on the plane. But then she'd been so stressed about everything that she was emotionally and physically exhausted and probably could've slept anywhere.

As promised, Barbara picked her up at the airport. Seeing her, Whitney filled with gratitude. Barbara hadn't hesitated to offer her a place to stay. Unlike her last visit following Zane's death, this visit promised to be a happier one for her. Or so she hoped.

"Hi, Whitney," said Barbara giving her a hug. "I'm so glad you decided to come. I've arranged a few things for you to do."

"Okay," said Whitney. "I want to make a splash, make sure everyone knows I'm back in town."

"Well, we still need to make sure you're safe. You'll meet with Todd's friends at some point. But we don't have to worry about that tonight."

Whitney smiled. She never would have agreed to it if she didn't believe this visit and the activities Barbara had planned would set her free from her past.

As usual, Barbara had a limo waiting for them. They headed out to Beverly Hills.

Sitting in the back with Barbara, Whitney said, "Thanks for putting me up for a few days. Both my condo and Zane's house are rented out."

"You wouldn't want to stay at Zane's house, regardless. It's become a shrine of sort for him." Barbara shook her head. "You have your work cut out for you."

"I don't see any other way to put things to rest," said Whitney. "As much as I love living in Lilac Lake, I don't want to give the Zaniacs the impression I'm hiding out."

"True," said Barbara giving her a soul-searching look that made Whitney want to squirm. "But I know you well enough to know there's something else going on."

Whitney fought the sting of tears. "Nick Woodruff, the police chief in town, and I are in love. But he was almost killed by a drunk man, something I witnessed. In a way, I was partially to blame for it. I don't know if I can ever forgive myself or move forward with the relationship."

"That's something we can talk about while we're relaxing later on. Tomorrow, I have an appointment for you at the spa you like. You're to get the full treatment so you'll be ready for your grand entrance at The Golden Eye."

Whitney's stomach knotted. There was a part of her that wanted to be back in Lilac Lake where she knew she could be herself.

The next morning, Whitney sighed when the limo pulled up in front of Henri's. It had been a while. She used to come here for pre-red-carpet treatments.

She got out of the limo and blew a kiss to Barbara. "Thanks. I'll see you later."

"Relax and enjoy it," Barbara said. "You'll be happy you did this. I've lined up some paparazzi to add to your moment and you'll want to look good."

Whitney swallowed hard. Then, straightening her shoulders, she walked into the salon.

A tall, beautiful Eurasian woman named Kali greeted her. "Whitney, it's so nice to see you again. We're going to make sure your stay is as wonderful as always. Henri knows you're here and will attend to you and your hair later. Amberleigh is set to do your makeup. But we'll start with a massage and facial before attending to your other needs."

"That sounds delightful," said Whitney, realizing how tense she was. A massage at Henri's was exactly what she needed to ease back into Hollywood life. An image of the cottage and the sunning rock flashed in her mind, but she pushed it away.

Whitney changed into the special spa robe that would be hers for the day and went for her massage. Lying in the dim lit room with soft, relaxing music playing, Whitney lost herself to the sensation of being totally relaxed while the attendant massaged away the tenseness of the last couple of months. She thought of the way Nick touched her body and sighed. He was such a wonderful lover. The thought that she might've caused him physical injury ate at her. Logically, she knew she wasn't the one who'd aimed a gun at him, but maybe if she hadn't been so eager to help Jamie and cause Bud to be upset, he might've let go of his beef with Nick with a simple argument.

After her massage and facial, Whitney sipped lemon water as the manicurist did her toes and fingernails. Then it was time for a calorie conscious lunch. Hardly worth calling it a meal, but it was tasty nevertheless, with a few slices of fruit atop a collection of lettuce leaves.

The best part of the day was meeting with Henri. An older man in his fifties, with a headful of gray hair that he upswept in a style of his own, he had an uncanny ability to know how best to style someone's hair.

After kissing her on both cheeks, Henri said, "One of my favorite customers. Lovely to see you, Whitney. I heard you'd escaped and are now living a simpler life."

"Yes, and no. I do have a home in New Hampshire, but I'm here to show the world I'm not afraid of what Zane's followers are accusing me of, that I have no reason to hide."

"Ah, I see. We'll make that very clear." He stood back and studied her. "Please turn."

She turned in a circle slowly wondering what style Henri would come up with.

"I think we'll do something simple, something classic. Trim the hair to your shoulders and let it move naturally. Your natural blond is beautiful, but we'll add a couple pops of lighter color for contrast. You'll love it. I promise."

Whitney smiled. She'd always loved what Henri had done for her in the past. There was no reason not to trust him now.

Later, examining herself in the mirror after Henri and the makeup artist, Amberleigh, had finished their work, Whitney could hardly believe it was her. She'd become used to wearing little or no makeup. Now her bright-red lips seemed almost garish, but it went with the classy look Henri had wanted for her.

Henri, standing by, clapped his hands with approval. "*Magnifique!*"

Going along with his accent, Whitney smiled. "*Merci beaucoup.*"

The limo driver Barbara had hired arrived to take her to Barbara's house for a rest before they went out to dinner.

Sitting in the back of the limo, Whitney felt like a fraud. She'd wanted to come to California to prove a point, but her heart was still in Lilac Lake. Still, she'd put on a good show. She was an excellent actress.

On a whim, Whitney asked the driver to take her to Zane's house. She still owned it, but would eventually sell it and put the money into the funds for the foundation.

"Please drive by slowly," she told the driver.

He complied and while she sat in the back, she gazed out at the front lawn of the house. Flowers were placed in front of a sign that read, "We still love you, Zane." Another sign said, "You're my hero, Zane." Still another said, "The Zaniacs will prevail."

The people renting the house must be so frustrated, Whitney thought. They'd complained to her, of course, but until she saw the tributes herself, she'd had no real appreciation for the mess all this adoration created.

"Okay, thanks," said Whitney. "Please drive on."

Whitney felt sadness hit her like a blow to her belly. It was all so senseless. But then, unless someone decided to fight it, the drugs always pulled a person down. For Zane, a handsome, talented, vibrant man, to fall so drastically was painful. To be reminded of him in this way hurt her to the core.

As they continued to Barbara's house, Whitney filled with resolve. She had to be honest in a way that still respected the man she'd once loved.

The Golden Eye Hollywood, no affiliation to the restaurant in Santa Barbara, was the place to be seen. The entrance to it had a short red carpet in front of the brass double doors leading inside. A uniformed staff member held the door open to the interior while those who wanted to be seen posed on the carpet before entering. Inside, discreet photographs were taken of those who were either famous or were on their desperate way to achieving it.

Barbara, who tended to be flamboyant anyway, was in her glory as she posed in front of the restaurant for the paparazzi she'd hired and others who usually hung around the restaurant hoping to catch sight of stars coming and going. She put an arm around Whitney and held up the other arm in triumph announcing that Whitney Gilford was back on the scene.

Whitney was glad she'd been at Henri's most of the day, but she still she'd never gotten used to the fact that strangers cared what she looked like or what she was doing. It struck her as invasive.

Yet, if she was going to complete her mission, she had to play the game.

Dinner was delicious even if she didn't dare order much. You never knew what would be reported.

Barbara circulated through the room chatting with new clients, old ones, and a few she hoped to make hers. Whitney didn't mind. Barbara was talented at what she did, and

Whitney was grateful for her help.

She looked up in surprise as the star of the latest Robot Hero movie, a tall blond from Australia sat down beside her. "Hi, Whitney. Glad to see you back in town. I hope we can get together sometime. I'd love to catch up with you."

Whitney couldn't hide a smirk from appearing on her face. "Did Barbara ask you to stop by?"

"Actually, she did," he said honestly. "But I jumped at the chance. I'd really like to see you sometime." He beamed at her just as cameras flashed.

"We'll see," said Whitney. "I'm here to take care of business with the group called the Zaniacs. It's an apt name. They're maniacs when it comes to Zane's memory. I have to straighten them out."

"Yeah, I've heard about them," he said, rising and kissing her on one cheek then the other.

Whitney was aware of more picture-taking, but she could do nothing to stop it.

Barbara walked over to her table. "I see you've made some progress on your comeback. It does my heart good to see it. I was talking to Harry DeLeon at Sunrise Productions. He's interested in having you read for a part."

Whitney shook her head. "I'm not ready for that. But tell him to keep me in mind."

Barbara studied her and finally nodded. "Okay. But you don't want to stay out of the mainstream for long."

"It hasn't been that long since Zane died. People will understand I need time to do as he asked. Besides, I have a life I like in Lilac Lake."

"Including a certain police chief," said Barbara.

Whitney let out a long sigh. "I'm still trying to figure that out. But I don't want to make any rash decisions."

"Okay. Are you ready for the next stop?"

"Not really," said Whitney, "but I know you've worked hard for this, so I'll go along with you."

The next stop was Wilbur's, a classy nightclub with music, beautiful women, and men considered big shots in the industry. One was as likely to see a couple making love in one of the private booths as two men shaking on a business deal that would impact the industry.

She and Zane had come here with other couples for a few times until Whitney figured out what Zane was really doing in the men's room. She'd been shocked at first, then disappointed and angry when she realized it was only the beginning of doing drugs for Zane. She still hated the place.

Barbara led her inside and went right to one of the booths near the dance floor. "We can watch from here. Or better yet, others can watch you."

Whitney placed a hand on Barbara's arm. "I'm warning you that I'm not staying long. It brings back too many bad memories."

"Okay," said Barbara. "We'll make sure you're noticed and then leave. Between here and the Golden Eye, you'll have made a splash."

CHAPTER THIRTY
WHITNEY

The next morning, Whitney was lounging by the pool at Barbara's house when Barbara emerged waving her iPad in her hand. "We made the news. Good job. I've got an interview lined up for you this morning before you meet with one of the Zaniacs group.

'Okay. I want to get this over with," said Whitney. She glanced at the images on the iPad Barbara showed her and sighed. It was a picture of her and the movie star smiling at each other at The Golden Eye.

She'd just laid down the iPad when her cell rang. *Dani.*

"Hi," Whitney said, happy to hear from someone she considered steady, sane.

"What's going on?" said Dani. "The entertainment sites are showing pictures of you at a restaurant and in a club. And is that hot guy with you really Troy Atkins? You sure know how to make a return to Hollywood."

"Hold on, Dani. This is only for show, remember?"

"Oh, right. But it sure doesn't look that way. I'd better go. Just wanted to say you're looking good, sis. Enjoy."

Instead of being pleased by the phone call, Whitney was irritated. And when she got a text from Nick she fought to keep from crying.

His text read:

> "I understand now where your heart truly lies, and it isn't with me or Lilac Lake. I'm disappointed, but as I

said all those years ago, all I can do is simply wish you luck. Have a good life."

This time, Whitney couldn't hold back her tears. What she'd had with Nick was so special, so full of the kind of love one can only dream of. Yet, he thought she'd thrown it away. She punched in Dani's number.

"Hey, what's up?" Dani said.

"You've got to help me," said Whitney. "I haven't made up my mind about Nick, but I'm not here in California to do anything more than meet with the Zaniacs and let people know I'm not hiding anymore. They will have to learn the truth about Zane. It's only fair. I was sure Nick would understand that I have to clear my name. But, apparently, he doesn't."

"So, you're not going to date that hot guy, Troy?"

"Dani, you're my sister. Why on earth would you say that? You know me better than that," sputtered Whitney.

"Sorry. It's the way the report on Hollywood news made it seem. And you must admit you haven't quite been yourself lately," said Dani with a note of apology.

"I know," Whitney admitted, "but I'm the same person you've always known. Can you do me a favor and set anyone straight if they mention it? Especially Nick."

"Okay. Will do. Sorry you're going through this mess. But it's good to get everything out into the open. That way, it can be put to rest."

"Yes," said Whitney. "That's what I'm trying to do."

A little later, Barbara came out of her office and said, "There's been a change. Your meeting with the fan group has been put off until tomorrow. So, rest easy for the remainder of the day. Todd will be in tomorrow, so you'll be able to meet him."

"Okay," said Whitney unable to hide her relief. As

determined as she was to go ahead with the meeting, she was glad for a reprieve. She wanted to have a better sense of what she intended to say.

The next day, Whitney met with Barbara in her office to go over job opportunities. She didn't want to give up acting jobs forever, but the more she listened to possible parts the more she realized that as she'd told Barbara earlier, she wasn't ready. She thought of Jamie and the other kids who'd worked in the play and knew she had something meaningful to contribute to Lilac Lake and beyond.

And Zane's foundation was coming along, but that too needed work in order to be completely established. A lawyer, one GG had used in the past, had agreed to work with her on it. It would be another way to put the past behind her so she could have a meaningful future.

Todd arrived for work, and Whitney was able to chat with him for a while. She decided she liked the rather quiet man. Apparently, his roommate, his significant other, had been as upset about a friend sneaking Todd's phone for long enough to get Whitney's new cell phone number.

"Do you know why Cynthi Desmond wanted it?" Whitney asked.

"Her girlfriend is the one who wanted it. Not her," Todd explained. He was of medium height, obviously worked out to have a fit body like his, and with brown hair and blue eyes, he was cute rather than handsome. "I told her not to fuck with me or my job. I'm happy working for Barbara. She's willing to teach me a lot."

"I hope you don't have all of Barbara's clients and their information on your phone. Discretion is a very important part of your job."

"No, no, I don't," Todd protested. "I just needed to send a

text to you regarding an opportunity, and as I was on my way out of the office, I thought I could take care of it on the go."

"I see," said Whitney. She knew Barbara had threatened to fire him if anything like that happened again.

"Will you be at the meeting this afternoon?" Whitney asked him.

"Oh, yes. I'm taking notes for you. Names, comments, etc. even as we record the meeting. That way we'll have a true accounting of what's being said and by whom."

"Okay, good. Nice to meet you Todd," Whitney said, shaking his hand and getting a firm grip from him.

After she left the office, she went back to her room. She wanted to do some investigation of her own. The name Cynthi Desmond rang a bell. But who was the girlfriend? Todd couldn't remember the name.

Sitting in front of her computer, Whitney looked up Cynthi Desmond. The minute she saw Cynthi's photo, she recalled the young woman who did makeup on the set for the television show. Zane had often teased her about being his girlfriend, but then he teased a lot of the women that way. It was harmless fun, nothing sexual. Whitney had always thought his teasing demonstrated his insecurity.

Whitney left her room and went out to sit by the pool. The sound of a fountain, combined with the sunny morning helped to make her relax. Lying back on a chaise lounge, she thought of Nick's text to her. Somehow, she'd have to make him understand the true purpose of her trip to California. But first things, first. She had to confront Zane's misguided fans. He'd almost become a poster boy for drugs.

Barbara had set up the meeting to take place in the sales training room at a friend's real estate office, so the confrontation would involve as few people as possible and yet make it meaningful.

Whitney dressed conservatively in a black linen dress. She wanted Zane's fans to know she, too, grieved for him. She and Barbara were the first to arrive. Whitney was quiet as they waited for the others to show up. She wanted to be as unemotional as she could while portraying herself as someone who cared about the feelings behind this group of radical fans. She hoped they would allow her to speak.

When about thirty group members showed up, Whitney was surprised by their varied ages and appearances. A couple of the young women were dressed in black jeans and T-shirts that had Zane's photo on them. One older woman looked as if she could be Zane's mother with her chestnut brown hair and similar features. But one of the tattoos covering her arms said, "Life's a bitch!" Others were more ordinary in appearance but looked as grim.

They were about to begin the meeting when a man strolled into the room.

It took Whitney a moment to realize it was Nick in civilian clothing. But anyone could see the gun at his waist when his blazer moved aside as he walked toward the front of the room.

Tears sprang to her eyes. "What are you doing here?" she whispered to him as he came up to her.

"We'll talk later," he said tersely. He held out his hand. "Hi, Barbara, I'm Nick Woodruff. Thank you for asking me to come."

Hearing his reason for being here, Whitney felt deflated but vowed not to show any weakness in front of the people waiting for her to speak.

Nick stood aside and leaned against the wall beside her, facing the crowd with a look of determination.

Barbara stepped up to the microphone placed on a table at the back of the room. "Thank you all for coming. As Zane

Blanchard's agent and friend, I felt it was important to clear the air and speak of the troubles Zane faced. Some of you have come to believe his unhappiness with his relationship with Whitney Gilford was to blame for his drug use and eventual death. Both Whitney and I are here to tell you otherwise."

She stopped talking and motioned for Whitney to come to the microphone.

Whitney took a deep breath and moved forward hoping she'd choose the right words.

"Hello. I'm not here to talk to you about Zane with any disrespect to him or you. I know how much you loved Zane Blanchard and why you feel the need to blame someone for his untimely death. Like you, I loved the man whom I thought I knew. What I didn't realize was that he had demons inside him he couldn't battle, and the man I thought I knew didn't exist. Yes, we broke up, but it was a mutual decision. Not something he didn't want. He wanted to be free from the responsibility of disappointing others and himself. I worry that by promoting him as a sort of hero, a man who was wronged, you're making him a hero when he was someone who used drugs, who refused help over and over again and hated himself for that. The foundation he asked me to set up for him will help young people with mental issues. If you want to remember Zane Blanchard at his best, use your voices to help promote his foundation and others like it."

A young woman stood. "But he told me he loved me, that he'd be with me except he was scared you'd find out."

Whitney let out a breath and lowered her head. "That was Zane, all right. Making promises he couldn't keep. Not because of me, but because that's who he was."

"But he was so talented. When you broke up, he was so upset he couldn't remember his lines. That's what was reported in the Hollywood news," said another woman.

Whitney gave her a steady stare. "Do you really believe that?"

"Yes," the woman said stubbornly. She glared at Whitney. "You're trying to make Zane look weak. What did he ever do to you to make you turn on him?"

"Nothing," said Whitney. "It wasn't a case of turning on anyone. It was a matter of making a life choice on how each of us wanted to live."

Barbara stepped forward. "Look, I know how lovable Zane could be, why you want to promote him as a Hollywood bad boy who was irresistible because of the things he said to you, how he could make you feel when he paid attention to you. He would hate that you're trying to blame Whitney for his own mistakes. Believe me, I talked to him plenty of times about this. Let's do something life-affirming in his name instead."

"You've a social media presence. Use that for good," said Whitney.

"But for all you say you loved him, now you're dating Troy Atkins," said the woman with the tattoos.

"The fact is I'm *not* dating Troy Atkins," said Whitney in a firm voice. "He just stopped at my table to say hello. We worked together on a film once." She glanced at Nick and turned back to the audience.

"Why did you run away after Zane's death?" a man asked. "A sign of guilt."

"More a case of grief," interjected Barbara. "People sometimes forget the actors you see on screen are real people with real emotions. You want them to be the people you dream up, but they aren't. Any more questions?" Barbara asked the group. "If not, we're concluding this meeting. For those of you who want to volunteer to help Zane's foundation, I've left a sign-up sheet on the table here. My assistant will take down your information. Thank you for coming here. Let's turn this into a positive thing we can all be proud of. Make this something that Zane would be proud of too."

While some people went up to the desk to sign up, others milled about. Whitney left the group and went to find Nick.

He was standing outside the office. He'd taken off his blazer and even without his uniform looked formidable. The shoulder that had been wounded was healed and his arm hung freely. Seeing him standing there, Whitney drew a deep breath. She'd thought she'd need time to decide, but he'd changed everything with his appearance.

She walked over to him. "It's so wonderful of you to come. I feel like a damsel in distress whose knight has galloped up to her on his white horse."

His bright blue eyes studied her for a moment. "It shouldn't surprise you. I once told you I'd always protect you. And I will."

"Barbara asked you to come?"

He shrugged. "No. After talking to your sisters and finding out what was really going on, I called her. It was more me telling her I was coming to help you whether you wanted me to or not. We both agreed it was a good idea."

She leaned forward and kissed his cheek. "Thank you. We need to talk."

"Yes, I know." He led her over to a stand of trees on the side lawn where they could stand in shade.

"I'm sorry about that text. I was a bit of an ass, but I understand better why you've made the trip here. I thought …"

She covered his mouth with her manicured fingers. "No need to tell me. I should've taken the time to explain things to you. But I was still pretty mixed up."

"And now?" he asked.

"Now I know who I am and where I should be." She wanted

to say more but suddenly couldn't. Her throat was clogged with tears.

"And does this new Whitney know who she should be with?" he asked. His gaze bore into her.

Still unable to speak, she nodded.

"Come here," he said softly and drew her into his arms.

When his lips met hers, all thoughts except one escaped. "I love you," she said when they finally pulled apart. "It scares me to death to know the danger you're in, but I want to be there for you, to trust that you'll do your best to be safe."

"We still have a lot of things to work out, but I want to start with that," said Nick.

"Me, too," said Whitney, meaning it with her whole heart. As people began to come out of the building, she said. "Excuse me, I need to talk to a couple of people."

Whitney hurried over to the two women wearing T-shirts with Zane's photo on the front. "Hey, Cynthi," Whitney said. "I need to talk to you."

Cynthi held up a hand. "I'm so sorry I intruded. It was wrong of me, I know."

The woman beside her said, "She took down your number for me. I was going to have my brother call you again, threaten you. I know it was all wrong. But like the other woman, Zane and I met up at the studio a couple of times and he made me believe he truly loved me. I should've known better." She was short and a little heavy, but she had a lovely face with golden eyes that drew attention.

"I understand why he might've said that to you, and I'm sorry you were hurt by it," said Whitney. "I hope you know now that his behavior was out of anyone's control. Even his."

"It's very nice of you to set up a foundation in his name," said the woman. "I'm Sarena Smithson. I worked in the costume department."

"If you're interested in helping with the foundation, I could use a creative mind like yours," said Whitney. "But no more threatening calls."

Sarena blushed with embarrassment. "Let me think about it. I've already added my name to the list."

"Thanks," said Whitney. "I'm happy to hear that."

As they went on their way, Whitney turned back to Nick. "Where are you staying?"

"At Barbara's house. She said she had plenty of room," said Nick.

"Of course," said Whitney holding in a laugh. Barbara was as bad as her sisters about making sure she made some good choices about men in her life.

CHAPTER THIRTY-ONE
WHITNEY

Barbara joined Whitney and Nick. "The meeting went well, don't you think?"

"Yes. Better than I thought it would. But again, social media made the group seem more dangerous than they are. Zane could be very charming, but he was also an accomplished liar after the drugs took hold," said Whitney.

"Changing the focus of the group was smart," Barbara said to her. "Even though the meeting was tame, it took courage to come here to talk to the group. It could've gone a very different way. That's why I'm glad you called, Nick."

Nick smiled. "A promise is a promise. There was no way I wanted Whitney to face what could've been a hostile crowd."

"I see. Well, let's go back to the house and relax. We all deserve it," said Barbara. She turned as Todd approached.

"I've got all the information you wanted," he said, handing Barbara a zippered leather folder.

"Thank you. Take the rest of the day off. I'll see you in the office tomorrow morning."

Todd smiled at Whitney. "Thanks for being so understanding about Cynthi and her friend. She texted me that they both are sincere about helping you."

"Good," said Whitney. "I need all the help I can get to make Zane's tragic death help others."

Barbara signaled to a limo in the parking lot and the black car rolled up to the front of the building.

"Hop in," she said. "We might as well be comfortable on the

way to my house. Champagne, anyone?"

Whitney grinned. "I'll have some. I can't tell you what it means to have this worry off my mind."

"And technically I'm on vacation, so why not?" said Nick.

Barbara lifted the bottle of bubbly wine out of the ice bucket placed in the back seat holder and with a deftness that surprised Whitney uncorked the bottle with a soft pop.

"Very nicely done," said Whitney.

"Did I ever tell you my father was a bartender?" Barbara said.

Whitney shook her head. "No, but he taught you well."

"Yes, indeed," said Barbara filling three tulip glasses with the wine. "Here's to Zane's foundation," she said, lifting her glass.

Whitney and Nick raised their glasses. "Hear. Hear."

"This is such a crazy business, but one I love," said Barbara. She studied Nick. "If you ever want work doing commercials, let me know. That face of yours could launch a lot of products."

Nick laughed and shook his head. "Not my kind of thing. But thanks for the offer." He and Whitney exchanged looks of amusement.

Whitney could tell Nick was impressed when the limo pulled up in front of Barbara's massive, lovely home. In Lilac Lake there were some beautiful houses, especially in the new subdivision Brad and Aaron were developing. But they seemed humble in comparison, nestled against a wooded background.

Barbara showed Nick to his suite next to Whitney and said, "The two of you can pretend I'm not here. I'll be stuck in my office for a while and then I'm going out and won't return until very late. One of those parties I must attend. My housekeeper has made a meal for you. All you'll have to do is help yourself. In the meantime, enjoy the pool." She gave them a roguish grin. "After I'm gone, skinny dipping is allowed."

Whitney gave her a quick hug. "Thank you, Barbara. You've been so understanding and helpful with all this business with Zane's fans."

"You're a very lovely woman," said Barbara. "It's my privilege to represent you. You might want to step back for a while, but I'll make sure opportunities come your way." She winked at Nick. "But I understand you want to take some time with this handsome guy."

She left them in Nick's suite.

Nick shook his head and smiled at Whitney. "I can see why Barbara is so successful. She doesn't miss a thing about what's going on with you and, I'm sure, her other clients as well."

"I'm pleased she's giving me time and space," said Whitney. "So, tell me about this phone call you made to her."

A sheepish grin crossed Nick's face. "You know I was pretty ticked off about the pictures in the news with that other guy, Hollywood dressed, and all. But I got calls from both Dani and Taylor telling me not to believe it, that you were out there to meet with Zane's fans. After the text I sent to you, I couldn't stand by and let you confront a hostile group without me. I promised to protect you. So, I called Barbara."

Whitney wrapped her arms around him and laid her head against his broad chest. "That's so sweet of you." She touched his shoulder and gently fingered the flesh wound. "But what if it had turned violent and you got hurt or killed? I'd never forgive myself."

Nick lifted her chin, forcing her to look at him. "It's my job to protect others, Whitney. It's what I choose to do. If I get hurt, it's no one else's fault, simply part of my work. Understand?"

She swallowed hard and nodded.

"Let's take advantage of being in this beautiful place and go for a swim in the pool. And later, skinny dipping sounds like fun."

She laughed at him wiggling his eyebrows. "I think so too. I've missed you."

After a delicious meal of a cold salad plate the housekeeper had put together, including cooked shrimp, pieces of lobster, and French bread served with a crisp, cool pinot grigio, Whitney was ready to take a walk with Nick, as he'd suggested.

They stepped outside the gate to the house.

"This is nice. We can do the pool later," Nick said. "I want to walk off the dinner. I'm not used to lounging around and doing very little."

"I understand. I want to walk too. It's a gorgeous neighborhood. Mindy would love it."

Nick laughed. "When Dani drove me to the airport both dogs were in the back of her car. They curled up together and went to sleep."

"Mindy will miss Pirate when Brad and Dani move into their house," she said, taking hold of the hand Nick offered her.

"When will that be?" Nick asked.

"As soon as possible. Certainly, by Thanksgiving because they want their wedding there," Whitney said.

"And Taylor's wedding?"

"She and Cooper are planning a wedding next summer. So that pretty much leaves me with the cottage, which is fine with me. I love what we've done to it."

"It's really beautiful the way you've fixed it up," said Nick. "Nice and peaceful."

Whitney laughed and held up a hand. "Not yet. But we're

working on getting answers about the ghost, a young woman named Carol, supposedly. Crystal's friend, Summer, is helping us find a way to encourage her to leave."

"Ah, yes. I remember Summer. She's quite talented, if you believe in those things."

"Well, I may have had my doubts, but I'm convinced now that supernatural things can happen."

"Good enough," said Nick agreeably.

They continued walking through the gated neighborhood admiring one house after another.

"How do you feel about your cottage now?" Nick asked when they returned to Barbara's house.

"These houses are gorgeous, but I still love the cottage. It has family history behind it and that's what makes it precious. GG has filled Lilac Lake with pleasant memories for all of us."

Nick beamed at her. "That's the answer I was hoping for. It's getting dark. How about that swim Barbara was talking about?"

Desire swept through her as his lips met hers. She gave herself to the feelings he created inside her. This was what she wanted. Somehow, they'd work things out.

Whitney met Nick by the pool. He was already in the water and waiting for her. She opened the towel and let it fall to the surface.

She saw the way Nick's eyes lit at the sight of her and smiled. She knew every woman wanted her man to look at her as if she was the most beautiful woman in the world.

She climbed down the steps to meet him and laughed when he swept her up in his strong arms, drawing her to him. It was obvious he was as anxious for this time as she.

He kissed her and then took off swimming.

She quickly followed.

After doing a few laps together, they sat on the steps at the shallow end of the pool. Nick tugged her onto his lap, facing him. She was thrilled by his response to her and nestled closer, soon moving with him in a kind of dance as old as time.

When they'd calmed, Nick said, "I love you, Whitney. I think it's time for you to meet my mother."

Whitney remembered what a big deal it was for Dani to meet Brad's family. "That's an important step. Are you sure?"

"If you're not ready to make a commitment to our relationship, tell me and I'll postpone it." His gaze bore into her.

"I think it's time," Whitney said. "I love you too."

Nick's smile lit his face. He cupped her face in his hands and kissed her tenderly on each cheek, the tip of her nose and finally on her lips where he deepened the kiss.

They climbed out of the pool and wrapped towels around themselves.

"Your place or mine?" said Nick.

Whitney grinned. "Why don't we try them both?"

CHAPTER THIRTY-TWO
WHITNEY

Whitney smiled to see Dani and Taylor waiting for them at the Portsmouth International Airport at Pease. Their commuter plane from Boston saved Dani some time and was more convenient. Whitney could hardly wait to thank both Dani and Taylor for stepping in and convincing Nick she wasn't going to go back to Hollywood permanently.

She glanced at Nick walking beside her. Their time in L.A. had been very special. She'd always remember how they'd agreed to move forward with their relationship knowing they loved one another.

Dani greeted them each with a hug and stood back to study them. "I take it things went well in L.A.?"

"It sure looks like it did," said Taylor, adding her hugs to them.

Whitney and Nick looked at one another and smiled.

"Good," said Dani. "That's what I thought when I got the text you were flying home together. They're finishing painting the cottage. It looks beautiful. The landscaping is going in and being supervised by Taylor."

"Sounds good," said Whitney. "When is everyone moving in?"

"Not until we find out more about Carol," said Dani. "I've been doing some research and have discovered that Carolyn, Mrs. Maynard's daughter, did leave town at the end of summer in 2001 and was in an auto accident in late December 2002 on her way back to visit her mother."

"What happened to her between that time?" Whitney asked.

"That's something we have to find out," said Taylor.

"I hope you can help with that, Whitney. Brad and I are working overtime while the good weather is with us and daylight holds," said Dani.

"I understand. Okay, I'll work on it," said Whitney.

Back at the rental house, Whitney spent some time in her room. Mindy stayed right at her feet. As she put her suitcase away, she looked at the one in which she'd placed the wedding dress and baby clothes she and her sisters had found in the cottage's garage.

She pulled it out and opened it up.

The satin-fabric wedding dress lay on top. Whitney pulled it out, walked over to the full-length mirror, and held it up in front of her. There was something so simple and elegant about the dress that Whitney knew if the time came for her wedding, she'd want one exactly like it.

On a whim, she stripped off her clothes and slipped it on. It needed pressing but the dress fit perfectly and was even more beautiful when being worn. She looked for a label and realized the dress must have been handsewn. She took a closer look. The stitching and the finishing work on the seams were very professional. Whitney swirled around, loving the way the skirt flared a bit at the bottom.

"What are you doing?" asked Taylor coming into her room.

Embarrassed, Whitney said, "I love this dress and couldn't resist trying it on. It's such a classic style."

"It's gorgeous on you," said Taylor. She glanced at the open suitcase. "Oh my god! Is that the dress we found?"

"This is the one," said Whitney shimming out of it. She hadn't bothered to button the back.

"Well, it's perfect for you. Are you thinking about a wedding? Was your visit to L.A. that good?" said Taylor teasing her.

"It was truly wonderful. I owe you a hug," said Whitney, giving her sister a squeeze. "Nick told me you talked to him about what I was trying to do."

"Yes. Honestly, social media made it seem as if you were dating Troy Atkins when almost everyone knows he's gay. But Nick was serious about wanting to protect you regardless. I really liked that. But then, I know what a great guy Nick is."

"Yeah, he's pretty special," said Whitney unable to stop smiling at the memory of their time together. "He wants me to meet with his mother."

"That's a good sign. I hear she isn't that social."

"Apparently so," said Whitney frowning. "I know Nick's father was a nasty man. Who knows how that's affected her?"

Taylor held up a blue, handknit baby sweater. "Cooper and I talk about having kids someday. This is adorable, isn't it?"

"Yes, very cute. Someone made that with love," said Whitney, taking hold of the beautiful yarn. And I love the color."

"The landscaping is being done on the cottage. I want you to go with me and see if you're pleased with what's been planned. I'm no gardener."

Whitney laughed. "Neither am I, but I'll come take a look. First, I need to hang up this dress."

A few minutes later, Whitney left with Mindy and Taylor, excited to see the progress on the house.

Taylor drove up the driveway to the cottage and pulled to a stop facing the building. It sat sparkling in the sunlight, its warm gray color compatible with the silver color of the lake and the granite surfaces of nearby rocks.

"Oh, the color is perfect," said Whitney. "I love it."

"The white trim really sets off the gray nicely," said Taylor with approval. "Now, walk with me around the grounds. Of course, we're planting lilac bushes, but there's so much more to think about."

"I assume you're striving to make it look as natural as possible."

"Oh, yes," said Taylor. "David Graham prides himself on that."

"Graham's Landscaping Company has been doing work in the area for years," said Whitney. "That's good."

As she and Taylor walked around the property, Taylor pointed out the bushes, flowers and trees that had been brought in. Even now, more were being planted.

"Great job," said Whitney. "When are you going to move in? Most of the furnishings are in place. There's no need for us not to do so."

"Let's take care of the ghost first," said Taylor. "Then I'll be ready."

"We're running out of time, so we'd better get to it. Have you discovered anything new about Carol?"

Taylor shook her head. "No, only what Dani said. My guess is that she's connected to the wedding dress and baby clothes, but until we know the complete story, we won't be able to encourage her to leave."

"Yes, I agree with that. I'm going to follow up with the name R.A. Thomas because I'm guessing he's tied to the birth and death certificates for Isaac Thomas."

"I think so, too," said Taylor. She stood back and studied the cottage. "One thing I know for sure is that GG gave us a beautiful gift and I intend to honor her and it."

"Amen," said Whitney. "Another reason to get at the bottom of this ghost thing."

###

The next afternoon, Whitney decided to go to the county offices to check for information on families with the last name of Thomas. She found a Chester Thomas listed as owner of property outside of town but no other mentions of a Thomas family.

She looked up Chester Thomas' phone number, and then wondered how to begin. She decided to go with doing family research.

After several rings, Chester answered the phone. Whitney could tell from the timbre of his voice that he was old and then she realized his hearing wasn't that good. When she was finally able to ask her question, Chester said there was no one in the family with the initials R. A. and no Lyn Thomas as shown on the certificates. Further, he was the last of his family, his wife having died years ago.

Discouraged, Whitney thanked him and ended the call. She was distracted when a call came in from the lawyer who was helping her with the foundation. He'd drawn up bylaws and a set of other rules and regulations and needed her to come to Boston tomorrow to discuss them.

Once they'd agreed on those, Whitney would meet with a financial manager to discuss how best to proceed with the lawyer's input from a financial and tax aspect.

Pleased things were moving forward with the foundation, Whitney asked Taylor to take care of Mindy. "I should be back sometime in the evening. If not, I'll give you a call."

"No problem. I'm here working on revisions," said Taylor.

"How about my taking you to Jake's as an early thank you. Nick is on call so I'm free tonight."

"Thanks. It'll be good for me to crawl out of my cave and be with real people," said Taylor. "Besides, I want to thank Crystal for helping us to meet with Summer. I also want to set up something with Summer before we're scheduled to move into the cottage. We don't have much time left."

Whitney told Taylor about the phone call she had with Chester Thomas.

Taylor shook her head. "Trying to put the pieces of this puzzle together is like trying to find a rare shell on a beach. But we'll get there."

"I like your spirit," said Whitney. "Let's go out and relax. It'll be an early day for me tomorrow, so I don't want to be up too late."

As they walked into Jake's, Whitney felt a sense of homecoming. She'd grown to like meeting up with friends old and new in this small town. As she looked around the room, she realized she knew more people than she'd thought. Some she knew by sight, others by name, and still others with a sense of history. She wondered what it would be like to live here day in and day out. As the wife of the police chief, she'd have a certain status. But would that make her happy? She knew then how important her work with the foundation would be.

Crystal saw them and called them over.

Whitney walked to her and gave her a big hug. Growing up, they'd been best friends. She hoped that would continue even with the odd circumstances of Whitney marrying Crystal's ex. Nick hadn't asked her to marry him yet, but Whitney was sure he would, in time. She already knew her answer would be yes.

"How are things going?" Whitney asked Crystal.

A smile spread across Crystal's face. "Great. A new doctor is moving into the area. I already told him I'd help him get settled."

Whitney laughed. "You go, girl."

Crystal turned serious. "You know I sometimes get these

odd feelings? There's something about this man and me."

"Really? That's wonderful. Keep me informed," said Whitney.

"I will," said Crystal. "I'm glad you and Nick worked things out.""

"Thanks," said Whitney.

"You two were meant to be together, you know," said Crystal, sounding like her friend, Summer.

Whitney decided she liked that a lot.

CHAPTER THIRTY-THREE
WHITNEY

The next day, by the time Whitney was ready to leave Boston, her head was spinning with facts and figures. The foundation was set up to aid kids in trouble, kids who needed a helping hand to mental health, which was what she'd hoped for all along. Zane's drug habit had come from a family history of abuse and neglect. She was no longer the naïve woman who thought her happy family life was what every child had. She knew now that no family exists without issues of some kind. Even her own family life had been marred to a certain extent because her birth father had died in an automobile accident due to a DUI. Thank God, he'd never killed anyone because of it.

As she pulled into the driveway at the house, Whitney sighed with relief. She got out of the car, lifted her briefcase, and waited for Mindy to reach her. Standing at the open doorway, Taylor called out, "She heard your car and started barking."

Whitney set down her briefcase and lifted the dachshund in her arms, laughing when Mindy's pink tongue swiped her cheek. She loved this dog so much.

"Come inside. I've made a light supper for you," said Taylor.

"How thoughtful. Thank you," said Whitney heading inside. "I didn't want to stop along the way home."

"It's nothing fancy. I think it's adorable that Dani and Brad are cooking together, but I'm not ready for anything like that.

Besides, in New York, it's so easy to pick up something for dinner or go out."

Whitney heard her name being called and turned to see Dani running toward them. "Hey! What's going on? You didn't need to stay in my condo?"

"No," said Whitney. "Come on in and I'll tell you about my trip to Boston and the phone call I had yesterday. I told Taylor about it, but haven't had the chance to talk with you."

Inside, Whitney set down her briefcase. "Let me get into more comfortable clothes and I'll tell you all about it."

"I'll pour us each a glass of wine," said Taylor.

Whitney set aside her business attire and put on a pair of shorts and a T-shirt and went downstairs to join her sisters.

Taylor placed a green salad in front of her, topped with sliced chicken. "Thought this would taste good."

"It's perfect," said Whitney. "Thanks."

"Where's the blue cheese?" Dani asked, inspecting the salad. "Brad and I like blue cheese on top of ours."

Taylor cleared her throat. "Dani ..."

"What? Oh, I'm sorry, it's that I'm so interested in cooking now." Dani winked at Taylor. "This looks delicious."

Taylor rolled her eyes.

"What's this about a phone call?" Dani asked Whitney. "Any new information on the ghost?"

Whitney shook her head. "No, but I did eliminate one possibility." She told them about the call with Chester Thomas.

Taylor shook her head. "This is a small town. Someone has to know something about this story. Someone who knows everybody." Taylor's eyes widened. She turned to Dani.

Dani's mouth dropped and she and Taylor shouted, "Melanie Perkins!" at the same time.

"Melanie Perkins? Who's she?" asked Whitney.

"The nosiest, best realtor in town," said Dani laughing. "I don't know why I didn't think of her before. She might be able to remember something about Mrs. Maynard's daughter that we don't know."

"I'm calling now to see if we can set up an appointment with her."

Taylor punched in some numbers on her phone, waited, and then left a message for Melanie. "Hopefully, we'll hear back first thing tomorrow."

"Good," said Whitney. "In a small town like Lilac Lake, the chances of finding information like this are better than they would be in a large city."

"I have a feeling that things are starting to come together," said Whitney. "I'll be glad when this whole ghost thing is over."

The next morning Whitney joined her sisters in Melanie Perkins' office.

Whitney tried not to stare at the middle-aged woman's dyed red hair and the slash of dark eyebrows above her sparkling eyes. She bet Melanie didn't miss a thing going on around her.

"So, Melanie," Dani explained, "what do you remember about Carolyn Maynard and any person you can think of with the last name of Thomas?"

"Have you talked to Chester Thomas?" Melanie asked. "He's the only Thomas left in town."

"I did speak to him," Whitney said. "He told me his wife had died, and he was the last one in the family."

"Yes," said Melanie. "I remember now that they didn't have children. She couldn't, you see."

"What about Carolyn? She wasn't in the high school yearbook, and we suspect she was homeschooled," said Dani.

"Yes, I believe you're right. She was a pretty girl but very quiet. Her father was very strict with her and thought both she and her mother should maintain a certain decorum because he was a minister in town. Honestly, the man was an ass. I was glad for Addie when he died. She became a much happier person, helping others."

"What about the daughter?"

"They called her Carol, you know, not Carolyn."

Dani raised her fist. "Bingo! I thought there was a connection. What else, Melanie?"

"There was some kind of fight with her mother, and Carol left town. To my knowledge, Carol never returned before she was killed in an automobile accident. At that time there was speculation that Carol was on her way home to make amends to her mother. I'd like to think so. They were close at one time, and everyone loved Addie."

"Carol was killed not far from Lilac Lake. I'd also like to believe she was coming home that night in December," said Dani.

"And then her mother died before they could meet," said Taylor. "It's all so tragic."

"I know there are stories about Addie being a ghost," said Melanie shaking her head. "But it didn't seem logical to me."

"We know now the ghost is Carol and not her mother," said Whitney.

Melanie's dark eyebrows rose. "Really? How do you know that?"

Whitney hesitated and glanced at Dani. "Okay, what I'm about to tell you is private. We held a séance at the cottage. This is what we were told."

"Oh, my! Of course, a secret. I get it," said Melanie, and Whitney had the feeling Melanie was already rehearsing what she'd tell her friends. In secret, of course.

"Did you know of Carol dating anyone?" asked Taylor.

Melanie shook her head and made a sound of disgust. "I can't imagine it. Even after her father died, both women felt a need to behave impeccably. Why, Addie could've remarried and had a better life, but she was not going to do anything to mar her husband's reputation. I tried to introduce her to an older friend of mine, but she refused to go out with him."

"I bet you do a lot of matchmaking in town," said Whitney.

Melanie grinned. "It sort of comes with the job, and I must say it sometimes does some good. Why the other day, I talked to a doctor who's thinking of moving here. I hope it works out. I can think of more than one young lady in town who'd be very happy about it."

Whitney exchanged amused glances with her sisters. She could think of a few too.

Melanie frowned and held up a finger. "Hold on. I remember something about a young visitor to town. Can't remember his first name but I think his last name was Thomas."

"Were his initials R. A.?" asked Dani.

"No, I don't think so. No Robert or any such R name. I'll call you if I think of it."

"We're talking as early as twenty years ago," said Whitney.

"Yes, I was just starting out in real estate. The Collisters were one of my first customers. They and others always had visitors. Don't worry. I'll think about it, and it will come to me."

"Thanks for your time, Melanie," said Taylor getting to her feet as Melanie's assistant came to the door. "We know you had an appointment."

"Anytime, ladies. And remember, when you're ready, I want a tour of that cottage. I hear it's become a fabulous property."

"Will do," said Dani.

Whitney followed her sisters out of the office convinced they were close to finding their story. It was only a matter of time. But now, she had to think ahead to the meeting Nick had scheduled with his mother. She and Nick had decided on an afternoon visit in lieu of dinner."

Standing outside his mother's home, Nick turned to Whitney. "Are you ready? Mom's anxious to see you."

Whitney faced the well-kept house and drew a deep breath. It had been almost fifteen years since she'd met Kathy Woodruff, but she'd never forgotten the woman who raised Nick. She knew that just as Nick had vowed to protect her, he'd always done that for his mother. His father, a violent man, had ended up in jail and had died young.

They walked up to the front door.

Nick knocked politely and opened the door.

A woman Whitney vaguely recognized stood there. She knew Kathy was not much older than her own mother, but she looked at least twenty years older than her age. Her shoulders bent as if she still carried the blows her husband had landed on her. But her eyes, like those of Nick's, stared out at her with a bright blue that couldn't deny intelligence and curiosity.

"Hi, Mom. Whitney and I are here to see you as promised," said Nick, bending down to kiss his mother on the cheek.

"Come in. I've been waiting for you. I've got a pitcher of cold iced tea in the refrigerator. And I bought some cookies from the Lilac Inn Café, from Crystal."

Nick and Whitney exchanged looks of amusement. Was that a gauntlet thrown down as a test?

"Good. Crystal's cookies are the best," said Nick. "May we come in?"

"Oh, of course. Please forgive my manners. I can't believe

that Whitney Gilford, the television star, is here. After all the things that have happened ..." she let her voice drift away.

"Well, she's here now," said Nick. He led Whitney inside to the living room. The house, though small, was well laid out, full of attractive furniture, and was spotless.

"It's cool enough to sit outside on the patio," said Kathy. "Shall we sit there?"

Whitney nodded. Though she knew Kathy had come from a tough background and an even tougher marriage, she was impressed by Nick's mother's manner. Refined, pleasant, but not too warm.

"While Nick gets us some refreshments," said Kathy. "I want to have a few minutes alone with you, Whitney."

"Of course," Whitney said. "I'm happy to be here. I know it's an honor."

Kathy smiled at her and though the wrinkles on her face deepened, her eyes lit with pleasure. She indicated for Whitney to follow her outside.

This was it, the interview she'd dreaded. Whitney glanced at Nick, and he winked at her for encouragement.

On the patio, Kathy indicated that Whitney should sit in a rocking chair opposite hers, where a book lay open.

Whitney lowered herself into the chair feeling as if she was a school child facing a principal. She understood the close bond between Nick and his mother and that made her feel even more nervous.

"So, Whitney, Nick tells me your relationship is serious." She smiled. "I remember you so well when you were here that summer following high school. You and your sisters were like bright stars in the sky with your beauty and energy and family goodness."

"We enjoyed coming to Lilac Lake for the summer. GG made sure we had fun with the other kids," said Whitney. "We still get together with some of them."

Kathy stared out at the lawn. "That summer Nick was the happiest I'd ever seen him. I realized then that he was no longer a boy but a man in love. And it did my heart good." Kathy faced her. "And then you left, and I could do nothing to protect him from the pain. He told me it was the right thing to do, to give you all the encouragement he could so you'd take the offer from an acting program. And look at you. A star!"

"Not exactly," said Whitney, feeling so uncomfortable she wanted to get up out of the chair and run for her life.

"Now, Nick tells me you and he are in a serious relationship. Is that true?" Kathy asked.

Whitney nodded. "We love one another and want to see where that takes us."

"I'll say this once and then no more. If you break Nick's heart again, I'll never forgive you. Hear?"

"Oh, but ..." Whitney began.

Kathy cut her off. "Nick is an exceptional person. I might be dead if he hadn't interfered in a very bad situation with his father. I owe him to be honest with you. He married Crystal, but both of us knew she could never be you. She's a nice person, totally admirable. She and I are still friends. But that isn't going to happen with us if you don't promise me here and now that you won't destroy my son."

Whitney felt as if Kathy had slapped her across the face, but she straightened in her chair. "I'm not going to say I'll be a perfect wife, whatever your definition of that might be. But I will love Nick completely and pray for him every day he goes out on the job. I'm still struggling with that aspect of his life, but when he comes home wounded or otherwise, I'll be there for him." She shook her head. "I honestly don't know what else you expect me to say."

"What you've said is good," said Kathy. "I owe him so much

I had to be sure this was right. I know you have an adoring public, the chance to live a glamorous life, make a lot of money. Why would you choose Lilac Lake and my son?" Kathy's blue eyes, so like her son's, studied her.

Whitney didn't hesitate. "I love your son and want to spend my life with him. We both know there will be challenges with both his job and mine. But we've promised each other to work with it."

Kathy smiled and clasped her hands together. "That makes me so happy. I hope you'll forgive me for this interrogation, but I had to be sure. Like he's told me, you're everything any man could want—bright, beautiful, and talented all in one. I hope we can truly be friends."

"I hope so too," said Whitney. "Especially after knowing you're still friends with Crystal. She's a wonderful person. She and I are friends, and I love her."

"I know. Crystal came to see me when she realized you and Nick were moving forward. She loves you too."

Whitney smiled and reached over and clasped Kathy's hand. "I want to make you my friend too."

Kathy smiled at her. "Loving Nick as much as you do will make that very easy."

Nick stepped out onto the patio. "Did I miss anything?"

Whitney and Kathy exchanged looks. "No," they said in unison and then chuckled softly.

By the end of the visit, Whitney felt as if she and Nick's mother could have a solid relationship. They'd talked about Nick's childhood to some extent and about how hard he'd worked in college for his degree in Criminal Justice and then his work at the police academy.

"He always wanted to do well," said Kathy smiling at Nick.

Seeing the love between them, Whitney's heart melted. They'd been through a lot together and their bond was strong.

She'd do everything she could to fit in smoothly.

As they got ready to leave, Nick said, "I've got a two-day business trip to New York. A special training course I need to attend. When I return, I'll take my two favorite ladies out to dinner."

"Lovely," said Kathy. She smiled at Whitney. "We'll be ready, won't we, Whitney?"

Whitney grinned. "Anytime."

Outside, Nick stood by the car door as Whitney slid into the passenger seat of his truck. He paused and stared at her, then lowered his lips to hers. When they pulled apart, he said, "You're my star. And I don't mean the one in Hollywood. You bring all that starshine to earth and make the people around you happy. I can't thank you enough for your kindness."

"Your mother is lovely, Nick. I hope I can be worthy of her friendship."

"You already are," he said softly. "She loves you. And in case you haven't noticed, I do too."

Their smiling lips met, and Whitney felt all the tension leave her.

CHAPTER THIRTY-FOUR
DANI

Dani headed to the work site at the Meadows. But halfway there she stopped, turned around and headed to the Collister's farm. Something Melanie had said about them being one of her first clients bothered her. That and the talk of many visitors.

When she arrived at the farmhouse, she was pleasantly surprised to find Mary Lou sitting on the porch. It being a weekday, it was slower at the vegetable stand, but still, Mary Lou never seemed to take the time to sit.

Dani got out of her car and walked up to the porch. "Hi Mary Lou. Can we talk?"

Mary Lou smiled. "Sure, honey. Come on up. I'm taking a break."

Dani took a seat in the rocking chair beside Mary Lou. "My sisters and I are trying to figure out the story behind the ghost theory at the cottage, and I need to ask you a couple of questions."

"Ask me about a ghost?" Mary Lou's lips spread into a smile. Then, seeing Dani's seriousness, she grew somber. "I'm sorry. What do you want to know?"

"You told me about a nephew of yours visiting you after you first bought the farm. You called him Alex. Was his last name Thomas?"

"Yes, why?"

"What is his full name?" Dani asked without answering her.

His full name was Richard Alexander Thomas. The Richard was for my father. The Alexander because it was my sister's favorite name." A look of sadness crossed Mary Lou's face.

"Did Alex ever date someone that summer he was here?" asked Dani, certain she was on to something.

Mary Lou shook her head. "Not to my knowledge. Of course, I was busy with four children, and he was a good kid who had his private time off in the evenings. But I never heard him talk about a girlfriend that summer or see him with one. Why?"

"If my theory is right, I believe he was dating Carol Maynard." Dani took a deep breath. "We found an envelope with the name R.A. Thomas on it. I think she was writing a letter to him. And then she left town. I believe she went to him in New York. Can you ask your sister if she knows anything about this?"

Mary Lou shook her head. "I wish I could, but my sister died of cancer a few years ago. Another tragedy. She was only a couple of years older than I."

"Can you think of anything Alex said to you that would help me discover what happened."

"I talked to him only once before he was ... killed. I asked him how things were going with his new job. He said he loved it, loved living in the city, and that good things were happening to him. That's all. No mention of Carolyn or any other woman."

"Okay," said Dani. "You've been a big help. Sometime I'll fill you in on the entire story. Now I have to get to my sisters." She stood and kissed Mary Lou on the cheek. "Thanks for talking with me."

"Anytime, honey. Simply ask," said Mary Lou. She rose and gave Dani a strong hug. "Nice to see you."

After giving Mary Lou a little wave, Dani hurried down the

steps, got into her car, and called her sisters.

Bursting with triumph, Dani entered the house and called for her sisters. They hurried into the living room to greet her.

"What's going on?" asked Whitney.

"I've got it. I know more of the story behind the ghost," said Dani so pleased with herself she could hardly get the words out.

"Come into the kitchen, sit down, and tell us calmly," said Taylor. "You're all but dancing."

Dani followed her sisters into the kitchen and sat at the table facing them. "I've figured out who R.A. Thomas is. Remember the story I told you about Brad's cousin who came to Lilac Lake to help his parents and then died in the September 11th attacks? They called his cousin Alex, but his full name was Richard Alexander Thomas. Ring a bell?"

"Oh, R. A. Thomas. So, you're implying that he and Carol dated?"

"Mary Lou couldn't confirm it, but neither could she deny it," said Dani.

"Okay, now we can figure out the rest," said Taylor. "It's all tied to the box we found in the garage and the certificates."

"Agreed," said Dani. "It all makes sense now."

"Let's call Summer," said Whitney. "Time for us to meet with Carol again."

CHAPTER THIRTY-FIVE
WHITNEY

As before, Summer waited until dusk to meet with them at the cottage. Again, she formed a large circle with lit candles and asked them to sit inside it. Whitney lowered herself onto the kitchen floor as full of nervous excitement as the others. Taylor had formed a complete scenario of events and they wanted to talk to "Carol" about it.

Summer sat in the middle of them, closed her eyes, and lifted her arms. "We wish you no harm, Carol. We want to help you. These women know who you are and what happened to you. They want you to know you can leave now. Alex and your mother are waiting for you. Your baby too."

Summer's shoulders slumped and her head rested on her chest. Once in a while, she murmured something. Then she straightened. With her eyes still closed, Summer spoke softly.

"Carol asks that you remember her. She is happy you've found true love, and the house is full of that love. Her job is done now. She wants me to tell the one of you who loves her wedding dress that she would be honored if you'd wear it for a wedding of your own. She wants that same person to use the baby clothes too. She accidentally left them behind."

Her sisters' gazes turned to Whitney. She didn't realize tears had spilled from her eyes and were now trailing down her cheeks. But for someone to share such a gift was touching, even if that someone was a spirit or ... a ghost.

Summer chanted something under her breath, the unknown words making a musical sound until they suddenly stopped.

A cool wind swept the room making the flames in the candles flicker, and then they went out, leaving the group in the growing darkness.

Summer opened her eyes and stared sightlessly around the room. Then blinking rapidly, she shook her shoulders. "I believe our mission has been accomplished. Carol is no longer with us."

Dani held out her hand and Whitney took it. Taylor clasped her other hand. It had taken a while to figure out the story of a young woman, pregnant and in love, trying to reach the father of her child only to find he'd died in the Twin Towers and then the trauma of their baby being unable to survive months later.

"Such a sad story," said Dani. They all believed Carol was trying to make amends with her mother when she died.

"But there's hope too," said Taylor, the romantic. "I think Carol's with her mother, Alex, and their baby now. At least I want to believe that. And, Whitney, when the time comes for your wedding, you'll have a special dress for it."

"Yes, that will complete the circle of Carolyn's story," said Whitney solemnly. "And as GG always says ..."

"Life is full of circles," they all said together.

"Group hug," Dani announced.

As they stood together, bound by their sisterhood, Whitney knew how lucky she was.

Later, in the privacy of her room, Whitney took out the wedding dress hanging in her closet and held it up to her. As she'd thought before, it was exactly what she'd always imagined for a wedding of her own. Now, the dress seemed to shimmer even more in the light from the lamp next to the mirror. Knowing where the dress came from and the story behind it, Whitney hugged the dress to her, determined to give it a happy ending.

She hung the dress up and went to the window and stared out at the stars sparkling in the night sky They'd always been a comfort to her, a sign that life went on as it was meant to be. A new thought came to her, and she frowned.

After doing an errand in town, Whitney returned to the house. A short while later, she stared in awe at the two lines that told her she was pregnant. The soreness in her breasts, the bloated feeling in her stomach, the yen she'd had for GG's lemonade had all been trying to tell her this. Had the ghost known it too?

Whitney sank onto her bed and let out a long breath. She, Whitney Gilford, was about to become a mother and Nick, a father. She clasped her hands to her breast, not knowing whether to laugh or cry. She knew exactly when it had happened. At Barbara's house, making love under the stars.

When Nick called her that night, Whitney was tempted to spill the news, but this was something she needed to tell him in person. And she wouldn't tell her sisters until she'd had that chance with Nick.

The next day at breakfast, she and her sisters discussed moving their personal items into the cottage.

"I've been thinking, Whitney, with me spending most of my time in New York and Dani living with Brad that you, not I, should get the master bedroom suite," said Taylor.

"Oh, good thinking. I totally agree," said Dani.

Ordinarily, Whitney might have protested such a generous move. But that would be very helpful. The suite was large enough to set up a bassinet in the corner until she was ready to do something about a baby's room. "Thanks. That would be perfect."

"I'll get Brad and Aaron to move the furniture around," said

Dani. "In fact, I'll call them now before they get too busy at the inn. They're doing some work on the interior of the guestroom wings and will be close by."

Feeling nauseous, Whitney tossed the remainder of her coffee in the sink hoping her sisters wouldn't notice. She was happy she had a lot to keep her busy until Nick came home that evening. She hoped the news wouldn't make Nick feel trapped into marrying her. True, they'd agreed to see where their relationship would take them. But he hadn't asked her to marry him. And her mother? She'd be in a dither thinking of all three of her daughters getting married so soon.

After moving several loads of her clothing and other items to the cottage, Whitney took a break. Sitting on the rock that had meant so much to all of them growing up and now, she wondered how to form the words to tell Nick he was about to become a father. She knew he'd wanted children with Crystal, but he was almost ten years older now. Would he still feel the same way?

Taylor joined her. "Beautiful day. We lucked out on the weather, though I hope we get rain soon to help all the landscaping."

"You did a great job, Taylor," said Whitney. "Seems like everything is settled for you."

Taylor gave her a quick hug. "Don't worry. Things will happen for you too."

Whitney almost said something then but held back. She'd be with Nick in a few hours.

That afternoon, Whitney waited at the nearby airport. Nick was taking the commuter flight from Boston to Pease. It had only been a couple of days, but she'd missed him like crazy. At least he'd been in a training session and not on the streets of New York.

When she saw him walking toward her, she couldn't help the tears that misted her view. The smile on his face told her so much. She rushed forward to greet him.

"Hey, there," he murmured as she clung to him. "Is everything all right?"

"Yes, I'm just happy to see you." She lifted her face and melted in his blue-eyed gaze. His lips met hers and she kissed him in a new, gentler way.

"I thought we'd have a picnic, the two of us, at the cottage. My sisters and I have all moved into it. Now, it's our Lilac Lake home."

"I really like what you have done to the house. It's perfect," he said, wrapping an arm around her shoulders. "I'm glad we'll have some time alone. There's something I need to discuss with you about this trip."

"Oh, god! You're not moving to New York, are you?" she asked, voicing one of her biggest fears about his job.

"Nothing like that, but it's important. In the meantime, I'm tired of traveling and think we ought to have a swim at the lake before the picnic. Sound good?"

"Yes," said Whitney trying to push away the memory of what had happened the last time they did that when Bud had almost killed him.

"I'll drop you off at your apartment," said Whitney. "Then come join me there. Taylor is heading to New York, and Dani and Brad are spending some time in Boston doing furniture shopping. Now that the cottage is completed, Dani wants to make sure everything will be ready for their house in time for their wedding."

"Exciting times," said Nick glancing at her and away.

Nick placed his carry-on suitcase into Whitney's car and then slid into the passenger seat. "Ah, it already feels good to be home. The mountains and lakes of New Hampshire are so refreshing after my being away."

"I feel that way, too," said Whitney smiling. She remained as quiet as Nick on the drive to Lilac Lake.

She dropped Nick off at his apartment wondering how the evening would end. There were so many things to think of.

On her way to the cottage, she stopped at the café to pick up her order.

Crystal saw her. "Looks like you're going to have a nice romantic evening with Nick. I slipped in a bottle of wine. You forgot to order some."

"Oh, thanks," said Whitney, giving nothing away.

Alone at the cottage, Whitney walked from one room to another. Thinking of a baby in the house, Whitney saw the space with new insight and approved its baby-friendly feel. Upstairs in the master bedroom, there was room for an infant. After a few months, she'd have to convince Dani and Taylor to give up one room for the baby and share the other as a guest room when needed. For Dani, that wouldn't be an issue. Taylor might feel otherwise. Maybe later, things would change, and rooms would be switched around again. The important thing was she could fulfill GG's wish by living there until it was time to be in a bigger house, like Dani's and Brad's. As GG said, life was full of circles.

Whitney changed into her bikini and studied her figure in the mirror. It was hard to believe a baby was already growing inside her. She closed her eyes and whispered a prayer that Nick would be delighted with the news because she already loved this child created with love.

Downstairs, she grabbed a towel and her phone and headed outside. Nick would find her there.

She lowered herself onto the rock and sat staring at the water. She'd left Mindy inside the house and was glad she had when a mother duck paddled by. Her babies, bigger now, followed her in a line of six. It struck Whitney then that her life now mattered in a whole different way. One she would respect.

At the sound of her name being called, Whitney turned and waved to Nick.

Smiling, he approached her. A towel was wrapped around his shoulders, and he carried a small canvas bag that she knew would hold his phone. Even though he wasn't back to duty, he always wanted to be prepared.

He set down the bag and the towel and sat beside her. "Hey, beautiful!" He leaned forward and kissed her, filling her with a desire that came so easily to her when she was with him.

When they pulled apart, Whitney drew a deep breath and said, "Nick, there's something I need to tell you."

He raised a finger to her lips. "Me first. I lied to you. I wasn't in New York the whole time."

"You weren't?"

"No, I had some business I needed to take care of." He reached into the canvas bag and brought out a small black velvet box and opened it up.

"Whitney Gilford, will you marry me? I've loved you since we were kids, but I love you more than ever as full-grown adults. I can't give you a fancy house, big cars, and a lot of material things. But I can and do give you my heart now and always. And as I've already promised, I will protect you and keep you safe. I want you for my wife and, hopefully, the mother of my children one day. Will you? Will you marry me?"

In the open box, a round diamond was flanked by two smaller stones.

Noticing the way Nick's eyes had filled, Whitney couldn't stop tears of her own.

She threw her arms around him. "Yes, Nick, I'll marry you.

I love you." After he slid the ring on her finger, she pulled away and gazed into his face. "You know the part about being mother to your children?"

"Yes," he said, looking serious.

"Do you remember making love under the stars at Barbara's house?" She grinned and caressed her stomach.

He stared at her and then as the meaning of her words registered on his face, a look of wonder crossed his face. "Do you mean it?"

Whitney took hold of his hands. "I know it's not something we planned."

"It's great news," he cried, hugging her. "It couldn't be better timing because I hope for lots of children in the future. Five or six."

"First things first," she said, chuckling softly, a little overwhelmed by the thought of so many children.

He wrapped his arms around her and kissed her with a new tenderness. "Mrs. Whitney Woodruff, mother of my child. I like the sound of it."

"Me, too," she said, nestling against him. She suddenly pulled away. "Wait! What business did you want to tell me about?"

"I went to visit your parents. I needed to ask your father for your hand in marriage. I know that's considered old-fashioned today, but I felt it was necessary. I grew up with a man who disrespected both my mother and me. I wanted to begin our life together with a sense of respect between your father and me."

"That's so honest," said Whitney. "I'm touched."

Nick beamed at her. "Your mother and father both approve. In fact, they're coming to Lilac Lake soon. Do they know about the baby?"

Whitney shook her head. "You're the first person I've told.

I felt it was only fair. But we'd better not wait too long to tell everyone because I don't want to wait to get married. Maybe we can have a ceremony the weekend of my parents' visit. Something small and quiet. Family only. What do you think?"

"When your mother asked about wedding plans, your father told me all a groom needs to do is show up. I intend to make sure you have the wedding you want, and I show up."

She laughed. "We've got a lot to settle before then. How would you feel about living at the cottage?"

He gave her a thoughtful look. "We could live there for a while but maybe not permanently. You're sharing the cottage with your sisters. Right?"

"Yes, but they too must get their lives settled before we can figure out exactly how that's going to work. In the meantime, you and I will guarantee that someone is living there long enough to satisfy GG's arrangement."

"Oaky, I can live with that," said Nick. He glanced around. "It's a great place to raise kids. Guess the ghost is no longer a problem, eh?"

"There's a lot I need to tell you about her story. Especially about her wedding dress."

They cuddled and talked about plans until the skies began to turn gray.

After calling her parents, GG, and his mother, Nick stood. "I'm hungry. Let's eat and then we can look through the house. See what we think." He extended his hand and pulled Whitney to her feet. "Almost Mrs. Woodruff, I love you."

"I love you too," she said, pleased to think they'd soon make it official.

As they walked back to the cottage, Whitney's cell phone rang. *Dani.*

"Mom called me with the news. I'm so excited for you, Whitney. You and Nick both. When's the wedding? You're not planning one for Christmas, are you?"

"No, because of the baby, we're planning it the weekend of mom and dad's visit. Family only."

"Baby? Mom didn't tell me about a baby. Maybe because I screamed and hung up. But you're having a baby?" She was silent. "How did Carol know that?"

"I don't know. I've wondered the same thing myself. But I'll do as she asked and get married in her dress. I love it, and it seems only right to put it to use with a happy ending."

"That's so adorable. And it does seem right that you as the oldest will be married first. Gotta run. Brad's waiting for me. Give my love to Nick and kisses to you."

Laughing, Whitney ended the call. Typical of Dani to make sure all was logical and right. She was wondering what Taylor would say about the news when Taylor called.

"Mom called me with the news. Congratulations, Whitney. I'm so happy for you. It's such a beautiful love story. One I'd be happy to write myself. Friends to lovers. Good that you're now using the master bedroom at the cottage."

"Yes, it will even have room for the baby," said Whitney, waiting for a shriek from Taylor. She didn't have to wait long.

"Baby? You're having a baby? Oh my god! Carol knew about it. The dress and the baby clothes. That's so scary."

"No, it's very special and that's how I see it. I want to think of our experiences in the house as an energy source of love and leave it at that. She wanted the house filled with love, and that's how it'll be. Just as we promised GG we would live there, it'll be the three of us making sure love lives with us."

"Oh, Whitney, you gave me goosepimples thinking of that. Love you. Give my best to Nick. It'll be so nice to have him in the family."

Whitney ended the call and turned to Nick. "My sisters are so happy you'll be part of the family."

"I heard the part about making sure the house is full of love. That's going to be easy."

He lowered his lips to hers, and in her mind, Whitney saw the light from the stars above them shimmer around them.

EPILOGUE
WHITNEY

On this early fall day, Whitney watched from her bedroom window as her family gathered on the front lawn of the cottage. Battery-operated candles were placed in a circle lending enough light in the darkening dusk for people to see but giving the impression of stars fallen to the ground.

Her father would walk her into the circle of her family—her mother, GG, her sisters and their fiancés, Nick's mother, and, of course, Nick. He was looking handsome as always in dark slacks and a white shirt. Everyone had honored her wishes for a simple ceremony, plain attire, and soft music.

Melanie Perkins had found them a harp player and then had announced that she was qualified as a Notary Public to conduct the ceremony for them if they should choose. She now stood next to Nick while the musician sent harmonic notes aloft in the air from her place on the porch.

Sighing with satisfaction, Whitney turned and faced her father.

"Ready?" her father asked, his eyes already shiny with tears of joy.

Whitney glanced into the mirror and trailed her hand down the satiny feel of the simple white dress she wore. A garland of orchids ringed her head. The diamond studs in her ears coordinated with the solitaire diamond hanging from her neck, a gift from GG.

Her father took her arm, and they went down the stairs and out to the front porch. Pausing a moment, Whitney gazed at the people she loved. This is where she belonged and with whom.

Her heart beating with anticipation, Whitney and her father made their way downstairs, onto the porch, and out onto the lawn to join the others in the circle of light. The sound of the harp music made it seem to Whitney as if angels were singing. But then, to her, this was a holy event, a coming together of souls.

Nick held out his hand as she approached him, and she took it, her lips quivering when she saw him struggling not to cry.

"You're so beautiful," he murmured before kissing her.

Melanie, quiet and subdued in a robe of black, whispered, "You're supposed to wait to kiss the bride. Ready to begin?"

Whitney smiled and nodded. This felt so right.

As words were spoken and the lights shimmered around her, Whitney felt as if she were in a dream.

Nick took both her hands in his.

"I love you, Whitney. I always have and I always will. I want to spend the rest of my life with you, raise our children together, show them what true love is. I want to be that person who fills you with happiness, knowing how much I treasure you. I trust you to be here for me so I can do my job to keep you safe and warm and happy just as I'll be here for you and your work. You are my star, the shining love of my life."

When it was her turn to speak, Whitney said simply. "I love you, Nick. What we share is so much deeper because of our earlier love—the love of children who were meant to be together. I promise to be beside you through good times and bad, to have faith in you in your work, to help you heal from past wounds, to become the best mother I can be for our children. This I promise with my heart because your love is my greatest joy."

"Lovely," said Melanie. "Let's all share love and best wishes with the bride and groom. Nick, you may now kiss your bride."

Amid applause, Nick swept her up in his arms. As his lips met hers, Whitney knew this would be the first night they'd make love under the stars as a married couple, and always, even with her eyes closed, she'd feel their love shimmering like the stars above.

# # # # #

Thank you for reading *Love Under the Stars*. If you enjoyed this book, please help other readers discover it by leaving a review on your favorite site. It's such a nice thing to do.

Here are the links for the other books in The Lilac Lake Inn Series:

Love By Design:
https://books2read.com/u/mg1YB7
Love Between the Lines:
https://books2read.com/u/3JoE9e

We are doing a spin-off of five books that take place in Lilac Lake. The first one is *Love's Cure* – A Lilac Lake Book due out in 2024. Others will follow.

Enjoy an excerpt from my book, *Love's Cure:*

CHAPTER ONE

On this summer day, Crystal Owen stood in the middle of the Lilac Lake Café in the center of Lilac Lake, a small town in the Lakes District of New Hampshire. At thirty-two, she was the proud owner of a thriving business on Main Street. She brushed back a curly lock of purple hair and let out a sigh of satisfaction. Her success hadn't come easily, but then she'd had a hard life growing up and sometimes felt as if she was hanging onto this dream with bruised fingers.

And now it was time to do something for herself.

Alone, Crystal sat on a bar stool and sipped her cup of coffee. She wanted to settle down in a way she'd been unable to do in the past. She'd married and divorced Nick Woodruff under the best of circumstances. She and Nick would always be friends. They'd married for all the wrong reasons—loneliness and the ease of living in the same town. Besides, Crystal had always known Nick loved Whitney Gilford enough to let her go to Hollywood and become a movie star.

Crystal set down her coffee cup and shook her head. Life sure could get complicated. In the community, she was known as "the poor Owen girl" who'd grown up with an alcoholic, drug-addicted mother and a younger sister to care for. Few people knew that if it hadn't been for Genie Wittner, her best friends' grandmother, "GG," she would never have had the funds to buy he tired old Café several years ago. She'd long since paid the loan back to Mrs. Wittner but she'd never forget her generosity.

After spending summers with GG, Whitney Gilford, her best friend, was now living in Lilac Lake and had married Crystal's ex-husband, Nick Woodruff. Whitney's two sisters, Dani and Taylor, also lived in Lilac Lake. Dani was married to Brad Collister, and Taylor, the youngest of the sisters, was married to Cooper Walker, an editor at a publishing house in New York City. Taylor spent as much time as she could at the cottage the three sisters owned jointly. Someone tapped on the door.

Crystal turned and smiled when she saw Whitney. Any awkwardness about being married to Nick had long since been worked out, made easy because Nick was one of the nicest guys around. He'd always had been that way.

"Hey, girlfriend," said Crystal opening the door. "What are you doing up at the crack of dawn?"

Whitney gave her a quick hug. "Nick got an early call about a possible robbery at the Beckman Lumber Yard, and I thought this would be a good time to take an early morning walk with Mindy and the baby."

Crystal observed the black-and-tan dachshund, Mindy,

and grinned. "Those short legs can't carry you too far, huh?" She bent over and peeked into the baby carriage, smiling at the sleeping little boy named Timothy. "He's adorable," whispered Crystal, feeling a momentary pang of jealousy. Lately, she'd been thinking about children of her own.

Mindy wiggled with excitement when Crystal rubbed her ears. "C'mon, you know where I keep treats for the dogs who visit our patio."

The dog trotted behind Crystal, and Whitney followed, pushing the carriage.

"I've got time for a quick cup of coffee. The sweet rolls are rising, the cookies and pies are cooling off, and I'm pretty much ready for the day." Crystal sighed. "This early morning work can drag you down. I'm glad the Café closes at 4 P.M."

Whitney chuckled softly. "You're so positive all the time. I don't know how you do it."

"Practice, practice, practice," said Crystal.

Whitney sobered. "I admire you, Crystal. What are you doing for fun? Are you doing any summer theater work?"

"Not now. Maybe later. The Ogunquit Theater in Maine keeps me informed about small parts that become available from time to time." She poured Whitney a cup of coffee, sat down on a bar stool again, and faced her. "I'm ready to settle down in a way I wasn't able to do before. My mother is gone, my sister is happy teaching in Florida, and with the Café doing well, I'm freer since I can remember."

"By settling down, do you mean finding the right man for you?" Whitney asked, gazing deeply into her eyes.

"Maybe. I'm thinking of taking some vacation time, getting away for a while, giving myself a break, and letting life happen. See new places, new faces."

"Who would you get to run the Café?" Whitney asked.

"I'm not sure. I'd have to wait until early spring, after ski season has ended, when the Café is slowest."

"Good for you," said Whitney. "I'd be glad to help you in any way I can, but it's difficult with the baby."

"Thanks. I'm very happy for you and Nick," she said sincerely, though a fresh pang of regret rolled through her. She hadn't wanted children earlier with Nick, but now she was ready.

Crystal rose. "I've been overthinking things. I've got a Café to run. That should be enough for me right now."

Whitney stood and wrapped an arm around her. "It's never wrong to think of finding love and having a family. You're going to make a wonderful partner for the right man. Someone who deserves you."

"Thanks," said Crystal. "You truly are my best friend. You'll never know how much I looked forward to having you and your sisters visit your grandmother and the Lilac Lake Inn each summer."

"It certainly made our summers special while we were growing up. You and the other local kids meant the world to us. You still do." Tears shone in Whitney's eyes, and she fanned the air in front of her face. "Maybe it's my hormones making me teary, but I mean every word. I've always loved my time here."

Crystal faced Whitney. "We loved having you be part of our summers. Those few weeks were magical. Maybe that's what I'm looking for. Something magical. Am I being foolish?"

"No," said Whitney firmly. "We all need a little magic in our lives, something to heal us from the wounds of the world."

Crystal gave Whitney a wry smile. "Are you saying I need love to be my cure?"

Whitney laughed. "I guess you could say that."

A customer knocked on the door.

Crystal became all business and went to open the door. It

was time to get back to real life.

That night, Crystal sat with Dani and Brad Collister in Jake's, a favorite spot for locals in Lilac Lake. After working in the Café all day, it was a great place for her to unwind and grab a light dinner.

Melissa Hendrickson, who was a chef at her parents' restaurant, Fins, showed up with a man Crystal hadn't seen before.

"Hey, everybody, I want you to meet, Emmett Chambers. He's visiting from New York and is thinking of going into medical practice here. He came to my parents' restaurant last night. You all know how my mother talks to everyone when she's acting as hostess, and she convinced him to get out and meet some of the people in town."

As Brad stood to shake hands with him, Crystal studied the newcomer. Of average height, he had straight brown hair and unusual eyes, a mix of blue and green. He was dressed in jeans, a green golf shirt, and moccasins. He was attractive, but the look he gave them was reserved, making him seem a little stiff.

Crystal returned his smile and listened as everyone asked him questions about the kind of medical practice he was interested in.

Emmett spoke about attending Cornell, specifically The Weill Medical School in New York, and the agreement he'd made with the school to practice in a rural area for a full year after his residency before opening a practice elsewhere.

"That's why I'm here," he said. "Lilac Lake and the surrounding area was one of the places they'd listed."

There was something about him that didn't ring true. He made it seem as if he was a hard-working guy who'd made it on his own. But his manner suggested otherwise. Gazing around the table, she noticed that she seemed to be the only one who felt that way. Were her disappointments in life making her cynical? She drew a deep breath and told herself to relax and enjoy a new face in the crowd.

"I'm glad you chose Lilac Lake," said Melissa. "Dr. Johnson has been here for years, but he's ready to retire. Portsmouth Regional Hospital is closest to us, and, of course, there are the Dartmouth-Hitchcock Medical Centers here in New Hampshire, and Boston and all the facilities there are not that far away, except for emergencies."

"My sister had her baby in Portsmouth," said Dani. "But as someone who lived and worked in Boston, I would choose to travel to Boston for something more serious."

"I like the idea of Family Medicine," said Emmett. "That's why I chose to enter that field. I want to get to know my patients and their families."

"Well, then, you've come to the right place," said Dani. "Lilac Lake is a true small town where everybody pretty much knows everyone else."

"Where are you staying?" Crystal asked.

"At the Lilac Lake Inn," Emmett said. "It's beautiful."

That nagging feeling of not knowing who Emmett really was traveled through Crystal. As she studied him, his turquoise eyes settled on her. She felt her face burn and drew in a breath as a rush of desire caused her pulse to race. She looked away, wondering why he was bringing out so many different emotions inside her.

"If you chose to work here for a year, where would you live?" asked Melissa. "I've just built a house in The Meadows, a new development of Brad's."

"That's a possibility," said Emmett. "Dr. Johnson wants me to buy his house."

Crystal stood. "Guess I'd better go. You all know how early

I must rise."

Her friends said goodnight to her, and she turned and walked away.

In her apartment over the Café, Crystal tried to get comfortable in bed. But her earlier thoughts about wanting to settle down became mixed up with her strong, uncertain reaction to Emmett Chambers.

She stared up at the ceiling and drew deep breaths as she tried to settle herself. Her life was nicely organized. She had many friends who truly cared for her. She'd never been anxious to have a deep relationship with anyone until Nick convinced her that it was safe, that unlike her mother, friends could be loyal, kind, and loving.

Now, honesty was something she demanded of anyone close to her. That's why it bothered her that she had the feeling Emmett wasn't being totally open with them.

# # # # #

About the Author

A *USA Today* **Best-Selling Author**, Judith Keim, , is a hybrid author who both has a publisher and self-publishes, Ms. Keim writes heart-warming novels about women who face unexpected challenges, meet them with strength, and find love and happiness along the way. Her best-selling books are based, in part, on many of the places she's lived or visited, and on the interesting people she's met, creating believable characters and realistic settings her many loyal readers love. Ms. Keim loves to hear from her readers and appreciates their enthusiasm for her stories.

Ms. Keim enjoyed her childhood and young-adult years in Elmira, New York, and now makes her home in Boise, Idaho, with her husband and their two domineering dachshunds, Winston and Wally, and other members of her family.

While growing up, she was drawn to the idea of writing stories from a young age. Books were always present, being read, ready to go back to the library, or about to be discovered. All in her family shared information from the books in general conversation, giving them a wealth of knowledge and vivid imaginations.

"I hope you've enjoyed this book. If you have, please help other readers discover it by leaving a review on Amazon, Goodreads, Bookbub, or the site of your choice. And please check out my other books and series:"

The Hartwell Women Series
The Beach House Hotel Series
Fat Fridays Group
The Salty Key Inn Series
The Chandler Hill Inn Series
Seashell Cottage Books
The Desert Sage Inn Series
Soul Sisters at Cedar Mountain Lodge Series
The Sanderling Cove Inn Series
The Lilac Lake Inn Series
Lilac Lake Books

"ALL THE BOOKS ARE NOW AVAILABLE IN AUDIO on iTunes! So fun to have these characters come alive!"

Ms. Keim can be reached at **www.judithkeim.com**

And to like her author page on Facebook and keep up with the news, go to: **http://bit.ly/2pZWDgA**

To receive notices about new books, follow her on Book Bub:

https://www.bookbub.com/authors/judith-keim

And here's a link to where you can sign up for her periodic newsletter! **http://bit.ly/2OQsb7s**

She is also on Twitter @judithkeim, LinkedIn, and Goodreads. Come say hello!

Acknowledgments

And, as always, I am eternally grateful to my team of editors, Peter Keim and Lynn Mapp, my book cover designer, Lou Harper, and my narrator for Audible and iTunes, Angela Dawe. They are the people who take what I've written and help turn it into the book I proudly present to you, my readers! I also wish to thank my coffee group of writers who listen and encourage me to keep on going. Thank you, Peggy Staggs, Lynn Mapp, Cate Cobb, Nikki Jean Triska, Joanne Pence, Melanie Olsen, and Megan Bryce. And to you, my fabulous readers, I thank you for your continued support and encouragement. Without you, this book would not exist. You are the wind beneath my wings.